SHRED OF DECENCY

JODY KAYE

Special Edition Paperback
First Print: January 2024
www.JodyKaye.com

Splinter of Hope
Shred of Decency
Sliver of Truth
Holding Onto Hope
Home Wrecker
Deep Gap
Bleeding Heart
Shattered Soul

When pain and loneliness become unbearable, the most unlikely person stops my world from caving in...

For all the women healing from what they prefer
not to discuss.

Chapter One

Aidy

"You should report this, sweetheart." The nurse practitioner's voice is soothing, and in harsh contrast to the echo of the speculum clattering onto the metal tray. She rolls it out of the way, placing a reassuring hand on my shoulder as I sit up.

I don't want anyone touching me. Shrugging her off, I reach for my clothes heaped on a nearby chair. I pull my panties and slouchy sweatpants up to cover myself before a physician excuses themselves from the room during a normal exam.

"What is there to report?" I ask with a quiver in my low voice, hardly audible as the vents in the small room kick on.

My internal thermometer is off. I'm bone-chilled and my skin is prickly hot. Tunnels of darkness and spots have threatened my vision for hours. The walls have been closing in, even when I walked outside across campus to the health center.

I push up my sweatshirt sleeves and am as quick to drag them back down, covering my wrists. Having my skin exposed to the nurse was enough. I don't want anyone to see any part of me and will risk becoming overheated and passing out to keep covered.

After slipping on my shoes, I focus on my bent knees. She crumples the blue paper that covered the tray and the trash can clangs open and shut. Coming into the clinic was a mistake. I was trying to prove to myself I was being stupid. That if I didn't remember what happened then it couldn't possibly be the truth.

The nurse steps in front of me. She holds out an appointment card. I take it because my parents raised me to mind my manners and, in this situation, I don't know how else to act.

"Aidy, you may not have bruises on the outside, but it doesn't mean there aren't any on the inside. Your confusion is obvious." She looks at me with so much sympathy. It's as if she can see red gushing out of the gaping wound in my heart. "Sweetheart, there are people who can help you. I'd be glad to stay with you the whole time if you need someone. If it means anything, I don't think you changed your mind."

Gee, what made that obvious? I think to myself. I have zero inclination to be sarcastic when she's trying her best not to rattle me any more than I already am.

I'd confided I wasn't on birth control when we were reviewing my medical history. There was no reason for a healthy nineteen-year-old to be when they weren't sexually active. My periods were enviable; a few light days on the twenty-eighth of each month. Can I be any luckier? Even February has that number on the calendar. Because of this, I've never had an internal exam until a few minutes ago. I hadn't been sure what to expect, but the way the speculum hung from my lower area reinforced the discomfort I'd already been feeling.

"It's best to report a rape right away."

The shame and self-loathing connected to the word is

too much for me. I haven't been able to meet her eyes the whole time. How did I allow myself to become a woman who had to deal with these emotions?

"I can see how troubled you are accepting this, Aidy. I want you to understand I'm here no matter what you decide." She wraps her hand around my fingers, now holding the appointment card. "Come back this week no matter what your choice is. I'd like to see for myself you're okay. Can you do that for me? It would make me feel better, and I'd be glad to answer any questions you think of between now and then."

I finally look up. The kindness in her face reminds me of my mom's. She wants to help me, but this isn't a skinned elbow from landing on the grass when I skidded, missing while trying to catch a fly ball. I want to forget whatever game this is because my name wasn't supposed to be on the roster. I'd gladly rewind to the point where I booked this appointment. I'd almost rather have lived the rest of my life in limbo than know this happened to me.

I stuff the card into my hoodie pocket next to the wallet holding my Pinewood College ID. Clutching them as if a thief will steal them the way my virginity has been stolen, I run-walk back to my dorm.

I'm filled with anxiety and unanswerable questions. How could he have done this to me? How could I have been so naive? Was it even him? And if it wasn't, then *who*?

I take the stairs up to the fourth floor because I'm petrified to be with anyone in an enclosed space. Halfway up, I start to cry because maybe waiting for a group of people to get on the elevator was safer. I fall to my ass on the concrete step, choking down sobs. The rocky texture of the formed stone grinds into my bottom, making my butt hurt. I may not have bruises, but it hasn't stopped everything from aching. When I regain the strength to walk again, I make it to my door.

With my head ducked low, I fumble with the lock. It opens and the door swings wide. In a swift motion, I have it shut and flip the bolt.

The wet towel I'd used to shower with has fallen on the floor and there is the faint outline of the puddle my shampoo caddy had sat in while it dried. The sight of my long twin bed attracts my attention. Its perfect hospital corners mock me. I couldn't stand the rumpled sheets, thinking about what's been done to me without my consent. I'd tidied up as best as possible in between trips to the bathroom to clean myself off, waiting for my lower GI to settle, and pressing cool compresses between my legs. I sat in my roommate's Papasan chair for twenty-four hours before the burning sensation from the angry hives on my inner thighs became too much to handle and I called the health center.

I approach my desk and take a puff from the inhaler for my asthma. The nurse said with my latex allergy it was best to keep using it the way I have been. I thought it was a simple anxiety attack that had made it difficult to breathe. The allergy is another way she saw through to what he's done to me. I am, *was* a smart girl. I would have told him we couldn't use those types of condoms.

I take the throw pillow off the chair and lie down on the area rug with my back away from the bed. My slouchy sweats are the only thing covering me. The appointment card pokes into my stomach.

My mind reels over all the questions the nurse asked that I was unable to answer, repeating the ones I could as if they can save me still. *How many partners have you had?* None. *Did you know you were allergic to latex?* Yes. *Do you remember anything?*

I remember getting ready and being excited to wear the new Rincon dress I'd found on a clearance rack because the weather going into fall has been so beautiful. The curved, athletic hem scooped above my knee, which I loved since I have longer legs and a shorter torso, and simple summer dresses are my jam since you can put them on and run out the door when you're late.

It's the beginning of my sophomore year. Students have just moved back to campus. My new roommate went home for the weekend. When we agreed to bunk together, I was aware she picked up as many hours as she could at her job. I don't go places alone at night, and my other girlfriends—many of whom scattered amongst other dorms and Greek houses this year— hadn't approached me with a plan. So, when Brandon invited me to a welcome back kegger on Friday night, I agreed.

I'd met him while standing in line at the college store for what seemed like an eternity. We'd struck up a conversation which led to lunch together in the cafeteria a few times over the past week.

When we got to the party, I saw a friend I hadn't seen yet this semester. While she and I were catching up, he asked if I'd like a drink and took off to get our beverages. I didn't think anything of the grin on his face as he walked back with those two red plastic cups. He'd bought me a fountain drink not eight hours earlier. I'd let him put the plastic tops onto our cups and the straw in mine while I'd reached for some napkins to wipe up a spill.

Bass pounded from the speakers in the house and the music got incredibly loud, so we went outside to talk. The sounds became more muted and my recollections foggy. I have no clue how I got back to my room or if Brandon was the one who brought me here. I woke up on Saturday feeling like a truck hit me. My dress was rumpled past my midsection. The tie at the waist bound at my armpits. My bra was trapped underneath, unclasped in the back. The straps hung loose at my shoulders. I later found the underwear I'd worn in a knot where the sheet tucks into the mattress. The ache between my legs didn't register at first. My head throbbed too hard. Then all I thought, as searing pain stabbed inside me, burning my thighs, was how this couldn't have happened? I would've known.

I waited twenty years for that moment. It was supposed to be...Unforgettable.

There's no erasing the past few hours from my memory and back in my dorm, lying on my side, the seconds tick by like minutes. Time stands still, mocking me. I stare at the dust bunny clinging to the mini-fridge under my roommate, Hailey's, bed watching it get pushed around by the whirr of the motor as it clicks on and off. As if attached by a tiny invisible chain, the puff of dirt never lets go of its captor.

The sunlight has faded to a deep navy shadowing the room when a key tumbles in the lock. Hailey flips on the light, throwing her clean laundry bag and the backpack she took home with her on her mattress. Like mine, her parents live in the area and her weekend job at a cinema is near their house.

"What are you doing on the floor?" she asks in a laughing tone, suggesting I've partied too much while she was away.

"I don't feel well. I think I came down with something." I'm surprised at how easy the lie rolls off my tongue.

"Make sure you go to health services tomorrow if it gets any worse," Hailey says, scooting a trash basket closer in case I'll need it in an emergency.

"I've already been."

I've had blood taken. Urine. Pictures. The nurse gave me the morning-after pill to be "on the safe side". Safe seems like a comical word. Safe is pouring your own drink. Safe is not having sex with someone who is blacked out so that they don't have to safely use medication to prevent an unwanted pregnancy. Should I be grateful whoever it was used a condom to be safe when it protected them?

"You want a blanket?" She tugs at my bedding.

"No!" I sit up too fast and have to lay right back down when my head spins. I cover my eyes with the crook of my elbow. The material of my sweatshirts absorbs the moisture from my eyes and hides the harsh and critical light shining down on me.

Chapter Two

Aidy

It's been days since my roommate found me in a heap on the floor. I exist in the spot now, not venturing farther than the vending machine at the end of the hall. Nothing has seemed more important than yellow bags of Peanut M&Ms. I'm not even sure why I'm staying at school. My parents will kill me if they find out my tuition is going to waste. Textbooks sit uncracked on my desk. I've missed classes before most students consider starting skipping.

What I didn't miss was my period, along with the big fat zit on my chin you'd have to be blind not to notice. Although, I hadn't expected the relief is yet another thing to send me spiraling down in a puddle of tears.

I went back to health services today after the nurse called me a bunch of times as a reminder. Her true intent—to get me to file a report—was obvious, and her persuasive techniques were a failure. The pity etched across her forehead was enough of a deterrent. I don't want anyone else looking at me that way. Who will believe me, anyway? I don't know if it was Brandon and have struggled with his absence. *Am I putting distance between us? Did he decide we weren't compatible? If it was him, had Brandon gotten what he wanted? Am I worthless now?*

The nurse convinced me I should go on the pill. I've brought the prescription to a local pharmacy. However, I don't know why I'm taking it besides the fact that a medical professional told me to. *Does what happened mean I'm sexually active if I'm not planning to have sex and never was?*

Why are there so many unanswered questions floating around in my head? I'm so confused, and it's easier to take her advice than fight with my morals.

My parents took me to church. It's how my birth mother met them. But my choice to abstain didn't have much to do with God. More, I hadn't wanted to make the same error and have any of the three of them upset with my lapse in judgment. Me, of all people, understood the consequences. I am the outcome.

All I ever wanted was to make them proud. Be the best person I could be. I'm not sure why I've bothered.

"Do you have any questions about your prescription for the pharmacist?" The assistant slides a white bag with red lettering toward me.

I shake my head. I haven't had a lot to say recently, and my voice is squeaky and scratchy when I open my mouth. Hailey thinks I have the plague. She keeps spraying disinfectant in our dorm room that makes me gag. It'll take a lot more than a stream of Lysol on my pillow to banish what happened in my bed.

I nibble a finger, walking toward the far aisles on the perimeter of the store. *What happens if they find out?* I'll have to step up and explain missing classes at some juncture or they'll know.

It would be easier if I'd been more rebellious, less honest. Owned my flaws the way some of my friends do and tried imperfection on for size. It hadn't occurred to me those qualities might come in handy until it was too late.

I stand looking at my drawn face in one of those skinny makeup mirrors. My red hair is a matted mess, pulled back against the nape of my neck with a hair tie. There are black circles under my blue eyes and my lips are chapped, not only from crying but from dehydration.

What did he see in me that made him do it? Nothing. I look like hell and hunger has me feeling the same way. My bones and muscles hurt from sacking out on the carpet and not moving for days. Maybe I was attractive once. I hate my hair, my skin, my stupid zit, and the dull frost in my gaze.

I turn away from the mirror as if hiding my reflection will stop everyone else in the pharmacy from seeing what a wreck I am. I feel exposed, which is funny since I have on three-day-old sweats, tube socks up to my knees, and untied running shoes with the laces tucked inside. The sun beats down in September in North Carolina. I'm a sweaty, ugly sight to behold. I don't want to be me anymore. There was no reason to better myself. No excuse for straight-As. No logic behind waiting for the love of my life to sweep me off my feet. Not when all of it can fall apart at the drop of a hat.

I run my fingers over the silky hair dye swatches in the next row. A small shift catches my eye and a skitter of apprehension rankles over my spine. A girl about my age lifts a cheap pair of earbuds from a bin. She places them into her pocket. I glance around the store. Nobody has seen her except me. I should say something. Instead, I pick up a box of purple hair color, watching her with my peripheral vision as she peruses the candy selection. It's like a movie scene. I can tell by the way her hand moves to rest on her hip she's slipped another item in her pocket.

A friend calls to her and they shuffle toward the exit,

being loud and making goofy jokes, holding up items and putting them back. Then the friend buys something. They both look happy. Why are they cheerful if they need to steal?

I look at the box of hair dye. The woman on the box looks as carefree as they are. She's pretty too, with all those highlights and tones of violet.

The girl's friend finishes paying for her purchase. I walk toward the exit, wondering what the hell I have left to lose. And, if there is more, why should I care?

My shoulders hitch to my ears when the three of us get to the door and the store alarm goes off. The cashier runs around the counter. My eyes widen at the girls and he looks at my prescription bag.

"You're fine." He scowls, pointing at the friends. "You two, empty your pockets on the counter now."

My breath gets stuck in my lungs, but I turn to go with the box hidden under my sweats.

"Hi, is this Aidy?" a pleasant voice asks when I pick up my phone. It's the nurse from the clinic.

I'd been so wrapped up figuring out what the hell my lecture today had covered answering was automatic.

"Ye-Yes." I clear my throat and she reminds me of who she is. Like I'd forget.

"I want to start by saying my call is not to pressure you. I wanted to check and make sure you were okay."

"I'm fine." I lie the same way I tell my roommate I'm all better from whatever bug I'd caught.

"Good to hear, sweetheart. If you need someone to talk to—"

"I won't." I cut her off.

"It's okay, Aidy. I don't mean now, maybe in the future? I'm here. There's also the campus counseling center and, if you'd rather go someplace else, I have a list of private and group support resources." A lot of what she's saying was information provided each time I'd seen her. "You aren't alone. You're not the only woman this happens to."

Her last sentence is too much and I hang up on her as she's babbling on about a great survivor network in Brighton.

My biological mother, Kimber, lives in Brighton with her husband and their new baby. Kimber was eighteen when she gave birth to me. She chose a wonderful couple to become my parents. For most of my childhood, I reaped the benefit of an open adoption. Kimber showed up at my birthday parties and we sent letters and cards on holidays, or rather, my mom did for me.

The same mom whose texts I reply to with an exaggerated "I'm soooo busy", "I'm soooo tired" or an appropriate emoji to make her think I'm not failing all four of my classes the third week of school.

I've always been able to go to my mom with anything. Right now, I don't want to see or talk to her. Kimber's on my mind.

We became close after I turned eighteen. However, I've never asked Kimber who my father was. Until recently, it hadn't seemed right for me to pry into her personal business. I do know she was younger than I am now, and made her choices alone during a time in her life wrought with emotion. I've always feared my life began because of someone more sinister and, not knowing the truth, meant there was still the possibility I was conceived by two people who loved one another. Now, more than ever, I'm left wondering if Kimber experienced what I did. I couldn't bear for it to be the reason a child of mine existed. And, for as cherished as my mom and dad made me feel, I'm not sure I'd be able to give away someone who grew inside of me to anyone.

Kimber is so much stronger than I am. There's no way something like this happened to her.

I go back to highlighting a textbook and realized the entire page is yellow. I've been dragging the marker from one paragraph to the next without reading.

"Great," I mutter, tired of the constant distractions my thoughts cause.

I rub my eyes and reach up to my desk to snag a rubber band to pull my hair into a ponytail. A few purple flyaways get tucked behind my ear.

"Concentrate." School has always been easy. I've never been so far behind. Or so tired. I refuse to touch my bed.

As if I've conjured her, my cell dings on the hard floor beside me.

Kimber: Hey Dumplin'! Can you call me when

you're out of class?

I scroll my contacts and call her right back.

"That was fast!" I catch bass thumping in the background. The music ebbs away, but Kimber's enthusiastic voice carries on. "It's not a huge emergency, but Trig's out of town and our don't-want-to-disturb-Dumplin's-studies-sitter is busy."

I beam. "You have a back-up sitter?"

"Of course, we do. I don't want to bug you when you're supposed to be off having a good time."

"It's never a bother."

Owen grows like a weed in between my visits. Her having him excited me. I was an only child and, while Ghillie and Don Fairley aren't ancient, they are older than most of my friend's parents. It's also not as if my mom and dad were ever having more kids. Owen is the only sibling I'm getting.

"I know you'll never say no even when you should and it's why I keep someone else's number handy."

True. After Owen was born, I sort of went baby-crazy and volunteered to watch him every chance I got.

"Anyhow," Kimber continues, "I have plans with Sloan I'm trying to salvage for tomorrow. If you can't do it, don't worry."

Chapter Three

Morgan

I shut the back door to the utility van, taking my time to walk up the path to Trig and Kimber's front door. Their house is at the back of a neighborhood surrounded by a fuck-ton of other gigantic houses. Each has a fenced backyard, patch of grass out front to mow, and signature southern low slung porch. About every third one is the same cookie cutter-style. The only difference is the paint color or materials used. This one is a periwinkle blue with white trim.

Nothing about the suburbs of Raleigh is like the rural part of North Carolina I grew up in. I can't believe this is the place I'm calling home. My last zip code was chain-link fences with barbed wire, not the white picket kind.

Tamping down the urge to knock, I let myself in the front door. I've lived here a few months, worked for Trig doing security system installs as long, and still feel like an intruder. They have a new baby, so I'm not sure why they're putting me up and letting me cramp their style. Although, I'm sure my record is the reason a place wasn't offered to me at the refurbished cotton mill where my sister, Celine, lives.

I toe off my shoes and place my fast food dinner bag on the stairs by the front door before heading through the living room, following the voices to let Kimber know I'm back. I don't ever want her shocked she isn't alone in the house. If she's agreed to me squatting here out of the kindness of her heart, then the least I owe her is common courtesy.

"Morgan, you're home!" Kimber is behind a long island chatting with two women. One of them is Sloan. She's seated on a barstool opposite Kimber and gives me a bright "Hey you!" in a similar enthusiastic tone.

Sloan does live in the old factory building the way Kimber used to. She, Celine, and Kimber were floormates until Kimber married Trig and Sloan moved her stuff to Carver's apartment on the second floor. Or maybe Carver moved Sloan's stuff. Who knows? It's Carver's building, and he makes the rules for all of us.

My sister set me up with Carver when I had no prospects. I owe him for what I have now, which isn't much, but after losing everything I once had, there is nowhere to go but up. I know whatever happens around here works off of trust and I plan to keep Trig and Carver's, Kimber's too.

A girl a bit younger than me is bouncing Owen, Kimber and Trig's son, on her hip cooing to the baby. She's got long purple hair that Owen is fisting, dragging handfuls to his mouth. The innocence of it makes her let out a tinkling laugh.

"Have you met my daughter, Aidy, yet?" Kimber asks.

I'm shocked when the girl raises her gaze to me with a polite hello. I didn't know Kimber had a daughter. Sure, I'd seen a picture on the mantle of Kimber's family. However, there was an older couple in it too. The woman standing before me had the same red hair as Kimber's in the snapshot. I'd figured they were sisters. Kimber doesn't look old enough to have a kid my age. She and Trig have been together for give or take five years. I doubt Aidy and Owen have the same father. Maybe that's why it's never come up before.

"Morgan Wescott." I make it a point of telling people my full name. It's a weird habit I picked up over the past few years and am not sure I'll ever fall out of. Doing it at least means nobody can ever insinuate I wasn't upfront about who I am.

I hold out my hand. Aidy maneuvers the baby, so she's still got a grip on him, shaking upside down and with the wrong hand. We all chuckle nervously at the absurdity.

Aidy ducks her head, embarrassed and clinging to Owen. I feel awful, especially when she offers, "There's pizza by the toaster if you're hungry."

"I got dinner for you, Dumplin'. Your freshman fifteen has turned into the sophomore shed sixty." Kimber has to be exaggerating. Aidy could use a little meat on her bones, but there's no way she's lost that much weight.

"I don't mind." Aidy moves her purple locks to cover her porcelain white skin, seeming lost when Kimber takes the baby from her.

"Thanks. I snagged something on the way back." My takeout is getting cold on the steps as we speak. I'm not sure why I'm still standing here. I'm intrigued by the purple curl hitting Aidy's bare arm, and the way her creamy skin contrasts her charcoal black t-shirt.

"There is plenty." Kimber winks in my direction. She offers me food a lot and I tend to say no. I think she's trying to make both me and Aidy comfortable. "Sloan and I are going out tonight. Aidy is staying overnight to babysit Owen since Carver and Trig are busy." Her eyes roll. I know what busy means so I don't press for details. It's not like Trig will tell Kimber what he's up to anyhow. Her eyes dart to Aidy. Some things are better left unsaid.

"I'm on the schedule and walking Cece home tonight." I'm casual telling them my plans so Aidy doesn't think she's stuck babysitting me too.

I pick up a few extra bucks at Sweet Caroline's, where Kimber is the manager, making sure the dancers are safe. I'd do it without getting paid because my sister works there. I'd prefer Celine did something other than use her body to rake in the cash for her college tuition, but in this life, you take what you can get. Cece swears she's only stripping and there's some convoluted rule about living at the mill and not turning tricks there. I hope it's enough to stop her from hooking altogether.

There's no reason for me to stick around. I excuse myself and grab my takeout bag off the steps on the way to the attic. The footprint of the room matches the entire second floor, but otherwise, my space isn't much. A queen size bed was here and made when I moved in, and I pushed it flush to the wall. The random coat hangers in the closet are the type you'd get your dry cleaning returned on. My underwear and socks are in boxes in there on the floor. I have no dresser. My clothes are hung or folded on the shelf. The sparseness aside, I don't feel confined. That's why I haven't bothered to go to the thrift shop to find more furniture. Plus, I don't want to ask Trig to help me lug it up two flights of stairs when I don't know how long I'll be living in his house.

I lie back on the bed, eating my dinner, and staring at the ceiling thinking about Aidy before taking a nap. The alarm for my second shift of the day goes off a few hours later and she's still on my mind. I haven't paid attention to women over the past few years. The only ones I'm around now are married, the security company's clients, or strippers at Sweet Caroline's. Some of those girls are hot, and Cece's been upfront about which of the dancers to avoid. Otherwise, no one is going to want to invest in a relationship with someone who has no future.

I should wait on showering to see what I'm in for at the club tonight. If I'm lugging boxes, I'll work up a sweat. Hell, If I have to haul someone out who can't keep their hands to themselves, I will too. Yet, I wash up in the small bathroom because there won't be much time between getting home and getting up again.

Jeans, tee, wallet, keys. I'm dressed and ready to go. My shoes are still downstairs by the door. Fool that I am, I stop to make sure there's nothing in my teeth before taking the stairs.

Aidy's on the sofa with her eyes closed. She's changed into baggy sweatpants and an oversized Pinewood College hoodie. I try not to disturb her, but Owen's laundry and baby toys are on the wing chairs. There's no place else to sit but on the couch.

"I know you're there." She yawns, cracking an eye.

"I won't tell your mom or stepdad you were asleep on the job." I lean to tie my shoes.

"I wasn't asleep. Only resting to get him to settle." She pats the baby's back. "Trig's not my stepdad." She lets out a sardonic laugh. "I've actually never thought of him that way. He's been Kimber's husband since I met him last year, right before Owen was born."

"You never met your mom's husband until after they got married?"

Stranger things have happened.

"Kimber's my birth mother."

"Huh," I say like that explains it all.

"Huh, what?" She becomes defensive, mistaking my comment for judgment.

I reach to take Owen from her. I watch the little guy a lot, so it's a natural action. She's not hot to give him up, even when he scrunches his baby form into a ball and snuggles into my chest.

"Do you consider him your brother?"

"I do. What a silly question." Focused on her lap, she tucks a long strand of hair behind her ear, revealing a single lobe piercing. The diamonds shimmer. No doubt they're real and expensive.

I shrug. "Just making sure I have it right."

For the first time, Aidy looks directly at me. She's prettier than I'd even thought with high cheekbones and a full lower lip. I search the bridge of her nose for freckles, but it's either too dark in the lamplight or they aren't there. She's got deep circles under her eyes that don't detract from her beauty. It's the blue of her eyes which gets to me. Dead on her feet, Kimber's sparkle. It's as if she's grateful for what she's got and in the darkest moment can see hope shining around the corner. Aidy's eyes look as if someone has snuffed the life out of them.

My brain shouldn't go there, but I remember those dead eyes staring back at me. My stomach bottoms out and my knees weaken. Without warning, the burrito I had for dinner makes me feel like I'm about to shit myself. I try to play it off by putting Owen down in his playpen thingy and covering him with a blanket.

"Kimber doesn't like it when Trig sleeps with Owen on his chest. Hard not to though, isn't it? He's calming. When he's not screaming his head off." I try joking to lighten the mood. "Catch forty winks. You could use it. Up late studying already?" She's gotta be a student if she's wearing the college insignia.

"No all-nighters yet. I don't sleep well," she's quick to add, "in those beds. I have more room to stretch out at my parents'." She won't meet my gaze again.

"Yeah," I agree, running my hand through my brown hair. "Dorm beds are the worst."

They aren't. Although, Aidy doesn't need to know the ones in prison cells rank lower. I slept sitting up with my back wedged into a corner until my release. I wonder where she's sleeping? I wonder if I'm wrong. If

I'm not, then why doesn't anyone else notice the way Aidy shrinks away when I talk to her? Is she shy? Does she do this around Trig too? Logically, I get that I'm reading into Aidy's behavior. However, it's not stopping my pulse from pounding.

"I, ah, I have go—" I point to the door as if she doesn't have a clue where it is or that it leads to the driveway. Where a vehicle is parked. For me to leave in. I'm a fucking idiot trying to act like these four walls aren't closing in on me. "You should sleep. While you're here. The guest room has a big bed." I continue to stumble, getting out, "I'll set the alarm."

I punch the keypad by the door without saying goodbye. The door hits me on the way out. I choke on the night air until I get behind the wheel. It takes more than a minute to get my bearings and, like a struggling drunkard, six tries to get the key in the ignition. If Cece weren't counting on me tonight, I'd blow off my shift and drive to the beach to clear my head. Backing the truck out of the driveway, I've never wanted to see anyone again more in my entire life and I've never been so scared to.

Chapter Four

Morgan

I sling the bucket of ice I've been carrying on my shoulder down and tip it into the cooler, refilling the ice bin. The bartenders—all females who either have shorts too tiny to cover their asses or their tits on display—scurry about, filling glasses and mixing drinks for the people waiting at the bar. I get an unexpected "thanks" from one of them as I move out of the way.

Everyone is in a mood tonight, which seems to happen when Kimber is off. Someone on the waitstaff or a bar back calls in sick to avoid dealing with Jake, the owner's, continual foul mood. The dancers get in one another's faces. Some drunk asshole starts something a bouncer has to finish out back.

In the beginning, I'd racked my brain over why Kimber bothered to work here. It's obvious based on where she and Trig live she doesn't need the cash and she's got a new baby at home. Doesn't seem as if the headache is worthwhile. However, the place is a well-oiled machine when Kimber is here, and you feel more like you're hanging out rather than doing a job.

I like it here on those nights. They have more of a party vibe, something I missed out on during the past few years of my twenties when I took responsibility for my actions. Though, the other thing I've noticed is how much illegal shit happens without finger-pointing or repercussions. We're expected to look the other way for the petty stuff unless it gets out of hand, brings heat on Jake or has the potential to close Sweet Caroline's down.

Ignoring a drug deal in the parking lot doesn't bother me as much as it should. I'm no angel. I'd seen them, participated even while I was in high school and college, and had gotten used to the same hand-offs in prison. Nobody on the inside is going to narc unless they want a beat down. And no other inmate in their right mind is standing up for you if your conscience trips up your survival instincts.

That makes the people here different. They have each other's backs. Even Kimber defends Jake, for as much as he lets her. The guy takes sadistic pleasure in his persona.

Nodding at Holly, a barmaid, I go back to holding up a wall by the front entrance, scanning the crowd for any trouble. I'm hoping for a distraction since Cece goes on stage soon.

I might've swallowed my own vomit the first time I witnessed my sister strip. My second chance came at her request. However, the only thing stopping me from hauling Celine's ass out of here after the performance was the glimmer in her eyes shone brighter than the sequins on her costume when she showed me her grades. Straight fucking As and one step closer to her dream of getting into a physicians' assistant program. All I could do was hug her and tell her how proud I was of her achievement. Anything else makes me an ungrateful douchebag.

Dusty, the maintenance guy at Sweet Caroline's and

at the mill, squeezes through the packed crowd. If I ventured a guess, Dusty's about thirty. He's a beast of a guy, carrying a bucket like the one I'd used to fill the ice bin. Wet rags and an auger hang out the top. He should have used the back entrance. I haven't decided if he gets cut a decent amount of slack because he can fix nearly anything, or if his stammer means he's slower on the uptake. Dusty's a good guy, nonetheless.

He stops next to me and puts the bucket down, crossing his arms over his chest and taking in the last minutes of the current striptease.

"What happened this time?" I'm not surprised he's here this late.

"Catfight. One of the girls flushed pasties down the dr-ressing room toilet," he stutters. "Fucking body glue got 'em stuck in the drain. The backup was shitty." Dusty looks down the hall toward Jake's office, disgusted. "This crap doesn't happen when Kimber's in charge."

"She can't work seven days a week." My lip lifts at the corner.

It's Kimber's regular day off and she's on a date with Trig. It's been ten days since I met Aidy at their house. Neither brought up her name since the morning she left. About the time I got Aidy off my mind, figuring it was better not to ask questions, Trig mentioned she was babysitting for Owen again tonight.

I've got to be up early to do an install with Trig down near the golf clubs in Pinehurst, so I'm hoping for a glimpse of Aidy before she leaves. I don't want to be alone with her. Maybe we'll all have coffee together. Her mother prays to the Arabica gods, does Aidy? I keep telling myself the need to see Aidy is to prove she's not going through anything bad. I shouldn't make it my business if she is. In all likelihood, she's a sweet girl who got her heart stomped on and I'm superimposing my fears on her to create a connection. I might have had a chance with a woman like her once, but the tides changed.

"That's a big ass smile for a guy whose sister's taking her clothes off in front of a crowd." Dusty mocks me.

I hadn't noticed the music changed. Cece is up there in all her glory. I'm ready to gouge my eyes out. Dusty's not. From the way he watches her, it's hard to believe he caught my goofy expression while I was thinking about Aidy.

I scrub my face and glance at the dial on my wrist. "Listen, I came in two hours early so I could cut out the same and get some shut-eye. Trig's got us wiring a house tomorrow that's a haul to get to."

"Botha you?" Dusty stops gawking at my sister.

"Big place. He wants it done ASAP."

He makes a noncommittal sound, which doesn't carry over the music pounding out of the speakers. Some dancers have said Dusty isn't all there, but from what I've gathered, he's trustworthy. Trig and I haven't done an install together since Trig hired and trained me. If Dusty didn't already know we worked separately for a reason, it's unlikely he'd put two and two together. Jake and Carver wouldn't keep him on as a handyman or let him anywhere near their businesses if they thought otherwise. I'm curious what else Dusty does for the older guys that I'm not aware of.

"Do you mind walking Cece across the street so I can go now?"

Dusty cod-fishes for a second before agreeing. "You want me to stand here until her set is done?"

"Yeah, man, you can handle it right?"

Cece doesn't have to stay until Sweet Caroline's closes. It may take her a bit to change. The parking lot leaves a lot to be desired, but there's still traffic at this time of night and the street and mill are well lit. My sister's in good hands.

"Sure." He puffs up.

"Thanks," I tell Dusty I owe him and slip out the door.

I make it back to Trig and Kimber's past midnight. The windows are pitch black in contrast to the porch light that's still on. I let myself in, cautious to silence the beeps from the house alarm so it doesn't wake anyone. Stopping in at the sink for a glass of water, I hear a click and notice a faint yellow glow under the door to the guest room off the kitchen where Aidy stays. Her bedroom backs up to the rear of the house. I feel like shit disturbing her and creep up to the attic, doing my best impression of a cat burglar.

I take off my shirt and jeans, slipping between the sheets in my boxers. On my back, I put my hands underneath my head, counting cartoony sheep that remind me of the ones hanging from Owen's mobile. Sleep has been easier to come by since being released. But tonight my mind won't shut off anticipating seeing Aidy. Hoping she's different in the light of day. Not as tense. More carefree. I lie, telling myself it's not like I'm looking to start a relationship with her. Although, the sense of *what if* lingers the way it had years ago when I met a cute coed in class. I should have enough respect for Kimber than to drag her daughter down to my level.

The point in coming home early was to sleep. Instead, I roll to one side then the other, flopping in bed, and punching my pillow every few minutes. The alarm goes off, and it's not until I'm done shoving the heels of my wrists into my eye sockets that I remember why I wanted to hit the shower at this hour.

On the way to the kitchen, I hear Owen fussing and everyone's voices. I've learned to make a hell of a lot more noise coming down the stairs than I had going up them last night. There are plenty of conversations I'm not supposed to hear. The past few years have taught me how to interrupt without offending anyone.

The first person to greet me is Aidy, probably because

hers was the face I'd latched onto. Her soft "hi" has me stammering to find something to say back. "Good morning" would've worked, but I repeat the same word back in as low a tone.

"Coffee, Morgan?" Kimber is already pouring into a cup for me.

"Yes, thank you, ma'am."

"Trig's loading the truck. He'll be back in for his breakfast. Can I get you anything?" Kimber pulls a dozen eggs and a pound of bacon wrapped in white paper from the butcher's market out of the fridge.

"I'll make toast. You don't have to go to any trouble."

"It's not a bother. I'm cooking for the three of us anyway. Aidy's offered to feed Owen for me while I do."

I turn toward where Aidy is sitting at the kitchen table. She's facing Owen and they both have their tongues out. Aidy's making funny faces. The baby laughs and then tries to copy her. Green drips down his chin. If Owen wasn't so happy, the tinted drool would be disgusting.

"What's on the menu, little man?" I crouch down by the high chair.

"Sweet Peas." She holds up the full spoon and flashes me the jar label.

"For breakfast?"

"They're leftover. I didn't want them to go bad." Kimber answers from the stove.

"I guess if there's such a thing as breakfast for dinner, then dinner could be breakfast."

"Like cold pizza," Aidy remarks. She'd left at least half the box for me to indulge in the last time she was here.

Aidy spoons the next bite into Owen's mouth. I rub his fuzzy, red head and he tries to chase the peas with his whole hand.

"Not quite ready for congealed pepperoni, are ya, dude?" I lean into him. "Believe me, it's the breakfast of champions." Before I can move back the baby smacks my cheek with his slimy fingers. "Thanks," I say, sarcastically.

Aidy's not laughing out loud, but I see her body shake. She feeds Owen another bite. He gets an odd look on his face. His nose scrunches up and he sneezes the whole mouthful right at her.

"Oh my God!" Aidy's laugh bubbles up and echoes. It's the prettiest sound. Pretty like her. The glee loops on repeat between my ears. Kimber realizes what's happened and when her voice joins in, it's like a chorus.

I go to the sink and wet a towel, handing it to Aidy so she can wipe her face. She uses it to get some green off my cheek. Then, recognizing the intimacy of what she's done, swallows hard and returns her attention to her brother.

We hardly know one another. Her action reminds me it's something I'd like to change.

"It's okay. Yucky peas aren't my favorite either." She wipes the tray.

"Peas are awesome. Except if they're canned." Mushy, canned peas that had lost their taste because they were about ten years past their expiration were a staple of my diet not too long ago. You yearn for food with a hint of flavor after a while. Fast food, health food, any food not the color and consistency of wallpaper paste. "All other peas; green, black-eyed, sugar snap, I'll eat those in a hot minute."

"You'll be eating breakfast in a hot minute. But knowing you like black-eyed peas the way Trig—"

"Who likes black-eyed peas?" Trig is coming in from the garage.

"Morgan does." Kimber tilts a spatula at me.

"With collards and turkey sausage?" Trig smacks his hands together and I can almost taste the jalapeños. "You are a southern boy after my heart!" He points at his wife with a challenge.

"Fine, I'll make it. But I'm not eating any. I barfed that out of *my* nose when I was pregnant." Kimber shudders. "It used to be my favorite dish."

"I thought I was your favorite dish?" He wraps her up in his arms from behind and they rock back and forth with smiles on their faces. "You like black-eyed peas, Aidy? We'll have you over for supper that night."

"Only the kind that makes music."

Aidy

I hadn't realized I made a joke until Morgan let out a throaty, baritone chuckle. A little warm spot grows in my chest. Perhaps I can say more when he's around and not embarrass myself. It's not as if I have anything against Morgan. In all honesty, the rapport he keeps up with Owen makes me like him more. That's the dangerous part.

Morgan is a few years older than me. It's obvious from the way his t-shirt clings to his chest and his long legs fill out his jeans, he's got the body of an underwear model. I can almost imagine the added depth of his dark hair and tanned skin in a sepia tone magazine photo. He'd lean against a white wall in the casual clothes he's wearing. Maybe with cigarettes rolled in his sleeve and the rebel without a cause vibe. Except, I doubt he's a smoker and on both occasions we've met, Morgan has been well-mannered. It may be more like a cause without a rebel. Who knows?

I'm having a hard enough time understanding the tricks my mind is playing on me. Only a fool wouldn't notice how attractive Morgan is. I get all the hot-guy notions in my head that have happened since I was old enough to realize boys didn't have cooties. Anticipating him talking to me has my stomach in knots. Then he says something and I'm flustered. What's happened to me comes back full force. I'm afraid of what he thinks of me already. Terrified of the change in his opinion if he knew. Realizing the confidence I used to have—or downright girlish stupidity that I had any shot with a guy like him—is gone. Therefore, it doesn't matter if Morgan gives me a second glance. He's nice to me because he has to be. It's an extension of the kindness he shows to Owen out of respect for Kimber and Trig.

Morgan has to mean something to them or he wouldn't be staying here. I've racked my brain for a logical conclusion. The only thing I've come up with is Morgan is Trig's the way I'm Kimber's. He'd have mentioned that when he was poking around about Trig being my stepdad, wouldn't he? I wish someone had the decency to set me straight. If we share a brother, it's gross worrying about being alone with Morgan. He hadn't struck me as the type to take advantage. However, I never put it past anyone to have a string of nameless hookups when plenty of my girlfriends have done the same. My parents sheltered me, but I'd like to think I'm not dense.

Owen pops his pacifier in his mouth, done with the peas. I put a few toys on the tray to keep him occupied and then get the plates out of a cabinet and place them at each seat. Kimber brings over the entire pan of scrambled eggs and a platter of bacon covered in paper towels to soak up the grease the way my mom does. We all sit down. Everyone looks at me and I become a shrinking violet.

"You're our guest, Aidy. Go ahead and serve yourself first." Trig sips from his mug.

I haven't eaten much lately and feel their eyes boring

in on me as I scoop enough eggs to be considerate. The bacon is easier. How can you not want your fair share of that deliciousness? Thoughts like this make life seem normal. Although, the way I dwell on the contrast of abnormal and normal isn't.

"… Pinewood State?"

I stop nibbling the bacon and look across the table at Morgan. He's asked me something. God, I am dense. I'm a flipping idiot who has lost the ability to act human around a handsome man.

"Yes, I go there."

Morgan's brow raises, I haven't answered the question right. Thank goodness I'm saved by my baby brother throwing a toy on the kitchen floor. I duck under the table to retrieve it.

"It's a hike between Brighton and there."

"I'm not traveling up here during commute, so it's manageable. My parents live south of Raleigh… A little closer to campus."

Morgan checks his watch. "You going to have enough time to make it to class today?"

"Lucky me, she's got the morning free," Kimber supplies. "I might even get a shower before Sloan comes over. She's got to go to an appointment then Carver is dropping her by. Do you have time for lunch, or do you have to get back to campus?" she asks me, getting excited. "Oh, you know what, Aidy? You're about the same age as Jasper's girlfriend. She goes to State too. Maybe we can all do brunch next time?"

"Who is Jasper?" I ask, warily.

"Sloan's younger brother. His girlfriend could use a friend who she has more in common with."

"There are plenty of girls who go to the same school and are close to her age who live at the mill." Morgan smirks.

Trig clears his throat, ending the side conversation when he asks Morgan to pass the bacon.

"You could talk me into going to lunch today," I reply to Kimber's earlier question. Easily, considering the way I'm struggling with my classes.

Morgan turns his attention back to me. "Used to love loading my schedule so I could sleep until noon."

"You went to college? Where?"

His teeth roll against his lips. "Long time ago. It was fun while it lasted."

The table falls silent. I can hear everyone chewing and find it peculiar Morgan doesn't spill any information I could use to get to know him when he's the one who'd started chatting me up.

"We gotta get moving." Trig pats Morgan's shoulder. They take their dishes to the sink. Morgan thanks Kimber and Trig kisses her goodbye. The loving way he does it reminds me of how my parents are together.

I haven't seen much of my mom or dad, which is unusual. Freshman year, I tended to go home every other weekend. Most of the time it was unintentional. Our house is close enough to whatever I was doing on the weekend, making it easy to stop in and grab an apple, borrow or return something.

My mind trickles over wanting to forget I am a student altogether. I've always excelled at school, but those first weeks my concentration failed and now I'm stumbling trying to keep up.

The professors start the lectures and I want to curl up like a hedgehog does and cry. I get overwhelmed and my mind wanders so I miss even more. Dropping out this semester seems defeatist, and what excuse do I give my mom and dad? They'll be crushed at the lie I'd tell to protect them. I'll be heartbroken destroying their trust. And what do I do until the next semester starts? Will I even want to go back in January?

I'm glad my only class today is later because going to lunch won't be an acceptable excuse to skip. There is plenty of time to do both, and while I should focus on studying, I can't get past the "why" of it. Why am I bothering to better myself? What difference did all those good grades mean? Straight As or my SAT score didn't help me out when it mattered. I'm not even sure they are the life experience I needed anymore. All of this adds to the guilt I carry.

"You okay, Dumplin'?" Kimber catches me staring off into space. "You look like you haven't slept a wink.

On the contrary, after settling Owen down for the evening, I sat in the guest room bed reading. I woke— surprised at how deeply I'd fallen asleep—when I thought I'd heard something in the middle of the night and clicked on the light. I don't think it was anything, but my subconscious started spinning tales of intruders and I became unsettled the way I get in my dorm room.

"I'm fine. I just need a shower." I can feel the heat at the tips of my ears. It's a telltale sign I'm sick or lying. I'm glad Kimber doesn't get all of my idiosyncrasies. My mom would call me on it.

As if her intuition spans from one point of the Triangle to the next, my cell vibrates in my pocket. I hold it up, wiggling my mother's picture on the screen so Kimber can see who it is.

My bio-mom's cheeks apple. "Take your time showering once you're done talking to your mom. I'm sacking out while Owen has his morning nap. Tell Ghillie I said 'hello'."

"Aidy, Sweetheart, you're a tough cookie together ahold of!" Mom is chipper on the other side of the line.

"I've been busier this semester than last year," I explain away my avoidance without telling my mom where I am. I love Mom too much to hurt her feelings and make her concerned I'm choosing sides. She and Kimber aren't in competition for my affections. However, nothing about my biological mother's life reminds me of what's happening when I'm on campus and my nightmare ceases to exist for a moment.

As a child, my mom kept me safe from the monsters under my bed. Now, I'm trapped with the monster living in the room and between the sheets she'd taken me out to purchase when my college acceptance came in the mail. All of the amazing memories, how my mom studied with me and cheered me on, are tarnished because I trusted the wrong person. I'm ashamed of myself for letting her down and feel guilty for lying to protect my parents.

"We'll if you can spare a minute for us, it's Daddy's birthday today. He'd love a hug and if you could make it home for dinner."

How did I let that slip by? I feel awful. Mentally, I rearrange the things on my agenda. Preoccupied by cake and gifts, hopefully my parents won't notice if I'm acting off. And maybe it's a good test to see if I can control my emotions in front of them. I hope the evening with them proves as big a distraction for me. All I have to do is hold it together and make sure I don't cry when my mom or dad hug me.

"I'll be there." I can't disappoint them, not today.

I shower and get ready to go back to campus.

Sloan arrives as I'm about to tell Kimber my plans have changed. I've met Sloan a few times before. She exudes a cool confidence I aspire to. Almost as if nothing gets under her skin.

She and Kimber are also thick as thieves. I find this funny since finding out they aren't childhood besties. According to them, they're the only other person who understands what it's like being Trig or Carver's better half.

"If I don't take off now, there won't be time to get a gift for my dad and get to class." I apologize to Kimber and Sloan.

"Never be sorry about putting the people you love first." Sloan's thick accent next to her jet black hair, almond-shaped eyes, and exotic features make it hard to believe since her roots are southern. She's the kind of gorgeous that makes you understand how men, and women, could drool over a person.

"Drive Safe, Dumplin', and wish Don a Happy Birthday from me and Trig." Kimber pulls me into a tight embrace. I use her strength to push through my fears.

Aidy

Spending the evening of my dad's birthday at home helped. I'd been hard on myself that I wouldn't be able to act normal around my parents. It stopped me from seeing the forest for the trees.

Mom had urged me to spend the night, and as much as I wanted that escape, I needed the solitude of the car ride back to Pinewood last week to let my trapped emotions out. I'd have sobbed too hard that night in my childhood bed, and they'd have found out for sure.

Since my trip home, mom and I have sent more frequent texts to one another. Simply feeling closer to her and the extra bit of support has helped me catch up on one whole class. It's an elective I should have taken this upcoming spring, but because of a schedule conflict, the other course I was supposed to take instead was at max capacity. Elective doesn't mean easy by any stretch. There's a reason behind waiting. I'm certain I'm missing the building blocks for this one, but it's far more interesting than the others I'm taking. Seeing the red ink circle around a B-plus boosted my confidence, and I've been throwing most of my initiative behind maintaining the grade.

It's late when I close the textbook propped in my lap. I stretch, leaning forward. My pillow falls from where I have it propped up against the desk. I slide the book on the top and open a drawer, searching for something to chew on. My fingers touch a packet and out with a stick of gum comes the cards the nurse had given me. I'd stowed them in there because not throwing them away was the only decision I was capable of making. It was too much effort to do anything more than hide them.

My pillow goes back against the closed desk drawers. I shuffle the cards in my hands, stuffing them between folds in the blanket I have tossed over me when my roommate comes back from the bathroom down the hall.

Hailey sits down on her bed. Her knees bend and she slides to the floor, sitting with her legs crisscrossed. "I got it when you were sick, but don't you think the bed is more comfy?" She braids her wet, sandy blonde hair, looking at me with eyes wide enough to give an LOL Surprise doll a run for their money.

"I think I got used to this. It's like camping." I push my fingertips into the carpet pile to prove it's plusher than the bumpy ground under a tent.

She gives me a noncommittal shrug, snags her pillow, and props it against the chair that's pushed underneath the desk so we're seated next to one another. While Hailey's distracted, I slip the cards some place safer where she won't find them.

"I'm glad you're feeling better." She unloads the hall gossip about who is sniffling on our floor and someone who has gone home with mono. I let Haley continue talking, soothed that I've become the sounding board for her small troubles like the wilted lettuce on her burger at lunch, how her cell phone keeps using too much data and then slowing to a snail's pace, and the bad movie ending she saw last weekend at her part-time job.

I met Hailey in class last year. I'd never classify her as a narcissist. Hailey works hard and we have similar family backgrounds. Well, in as much as our parents stayed married to their first spouses and we both used to go home a lot on the weekends. Hailey still does so she can work three days a week to afford her tuition. Now, I give my mom an excuse that I'm babysitting Owen even when I'm not even headed to Brighton.

"You know the guy you went out with when school started, Brandon?" Hailey asks, picking lint off of her pajama bottoms.

The mention of his name makes me uneasy. I swallow hard and look to the doorway. In my head, Brandon is "he" or "him". More of a lurking shadow I can't place who interferes with the foggy memories which don't quite align in a proper sequence. Giving Brandon a name again makes him corporeal, human. It reminds me of the person Brandon led me to believe he was before that weekend instead of being the boogeyman keeping me from a regular night's sleep in a bed with sheets and a mattress.

Hailey doesn't wait for me to respond. "Alexa, who was in Freshman English with us, went out with him. She said Brandon was all hands. Stupid jerk. Don't they know us girls *all* talk and his reputation will get around. I mean, what guy does that? She even said, 'I'm not telling you again, take your hands off of me' and he acted like it was her who was doing something wrong… Although Alexa has sort of had a carousel of boyfriends in the past, if you know what I mean? So maybe he figured she was one of those girls who'd be okay with it. I still say he was a colossal asshole. I'm glad you dodged the bullet there. He's probably the kind who hits on your best friend when you leave the room."

"Yeah…" The words of agreement come out low. Not

once has Hailey pushed for a reason why I stopped seeing Brandon. I guess she thought me being "sick" was what put the kibosh on any longer-term relationship. I'm not about to tell her otherwise.

Hailey scrambles back up to her bed when her phone dings. She texts someone back with a smile on her face. I ask her to turn out the light a few minutes later and scoot my pillow down under my head and shoulders, laying on my side and making a nest of blankets and whatever else I've found that's squishy and warm to placate my senses.

The screen on Hailey's phone keeps lighting up. Her nails *clickety-clack* on the glass, responding to the incoming messages. It must be a guy. If it weren't so dark in the room, from the shy but happy expression, she could be blushing. I roll over, pretending to give her privacy.

The comforter for my bed hangs in my face. I touch a hanging thread. I miss happy. I want the normal pressure of college life back. The life I led six months ago when everything I was going through seemed hard, but I hadn't realized it could get harder. I want to sleep in a bed the whole night through. Not this one, but at least the way I had those few hours at Kimber's before I'd woken up thinking someone was outside the guest room.

The only place things seem normal is when I'm in Brighton with them. Maybe because it has an air of unfamiliarity. My life with my adoptive parents was distinct from the one my biological mother led.

I haven't known Kimber as a full and unique person for long. Until I was older, she was more like a mythical fairy who bore me. At the point when I started college, everything in my life was changing. Our interactions became more frequent as I made my own choices as an adult. I like being with her and Trig and Owen. I've pondered, based on the comments at the kitchen table, if Jasper's girlfriend has few friends and if she needs one the way I feel like I tend to when Hailey's not around. And—no matter how hard I try not to—my thoughts land on Morgan.

It's not just that he's attractive, or the mystery surrounding why he lives with Trig and Kimber—which wouldn't be mysterious at all if I bucked up and asked, but it seems rude. It's that he's part of their inner circle and I'm an outsider. When it comes down to it, I'm not under any illusions I'm girlfriend material for a guy like him. I'd love to have Hailey's secret smile, glowing in the dark, spreading from one side of her cheeks to the next. However, Morgan won't be the one to put it there. I guess I'm curious if I'm good enough to be friend material for any of them.

As it is whenever I try to sleep, my eyes flutter open and shut as the clock ticks on toward twilight. The phrase "good enough" lingers throughout the night. I can feel the cards under my hip where I hid them. I'd had plenty of confidence before. I didn't worry about my grades or if anyone considered whether I wasn't good enough for anything. I didn't care if I didn't fit the girlfriend mold for the rugged and built, drop-dead gorgeous guy. I could still admire him, and the men who paid attention to me weren't any you'd need to fight off with a stick. It wasn't until my world came crashing down all the second-guessing began. Am I worthy of a friend, a boyfriend, my parents, my grades, the life I had?

I'm tired of feeling like this. I'm exhausted. And I don't know how to get the rest of it all to fade away the way sleep used to give me a reprieve from my ridiculous worries.

I pull the blankets up over my head until after Hailey has left for her class. Inspecting the hotline call number for the group in Brighton the nurse recommended, I have nothing left to lose. It's not like learning the date they meet obliges me to go to the session.

My thumb slides across the digital numbers on my phone. It rings once. I panic, ready to hit the red hang-up button.

"This is Dr. Nash." A cheery female voice answers my call on the second ring.

"My name is Aidy—" I begin because my mother taught me it's the polite thing to do. Like the questions plaguing me, now I'm not so certain if I'm supposed to give my real name or if this is anonymous.

"Hi Aidy. What can I do for you?"

"I—" I don't even know where to start or what to ask. "There's a group?"

"We meet in Brighton. Is that near you?"

"No, but not far away." I'm relieved Dr. Nash knows what I'm referring to without having to explain.

"Wonderful. I'm so glad you reached out. We'd love for you to join us." Dr. Nash tells me she along with a few graduate students facilitate the program and the number of group members varies depending on the week. She also emphasizes the organizers leading the discussion "fully understand" what the group members have been through. At first, I take her reassurance at face value, but reading between the lines I realize what Dr. Nash isn't saying; the psychology graduate school moderators have all been victims. "Our goal is to give women a chance to connect in a positive environment, express their concerns, and many times find solutions based on other's experiences after trauma. What's shared we ask for participants to keep confidential."

"Do you have to talk?" How would these women react if they knew I remember nothing but what happened afterward? I can't even prove who it was and, even more than a judge and jury, I doubt they'd accept me when the stories replaying in their heads are vivid or viscous.

"Share only what you're comfortable with. No one

will stop you, but there's no expectation within the group that anyone bare their soul. Many women prefer to keep certain aspects of their experiences to themselves or between them and their therapist or crisis counselors. We're about moving forward. Sometimes it helps to know you're not traveling the path alone. That another woman has had the same feeling of overwhelm about a situation others may deem insignificant. Even taking small steps can be hard, but those little leaps of faith add up."

Dr. Nash has a quiet comfort to her voice. Her words are strong, yet tender. It's like she's in the room with me. In all likelihood, she isn't saying anything I hadn't been told at the health clinic. The difference is, I'm willing to absorb it.

"Our meeting is today. If that's not too soon for you, Aidy, please come. Feel free to come observe and see if our group is a good fit for you. Maybe go back and discuss it with your own counselor."

I won't admit I don't have a therapist but agree I might come.

Chapter Seven

Aidy

Driving to Brighton means missing my sole class for today. Academically, I'm so far behind this one instance won't affect it. I'd rather be too chicken to get out of the car once I'm there than sit in a lecture hall worrying I should have gone. My mental distractions on campus already prove more than I can handle.

I get to the address Dr. Nash gave me over the phone with a few minutes to spare. Several women are walking into the building at the same time. A few clutch the straps of their purses. My grip tightens on my wristlet. Two ladies chat as if nothing is amiss and I'm surprised when they follow the signs to the same room. Before I can take a seat, a woman in her mid-forties approaches me, introducing herself as Dr. Nash. The slightest crease in her brow releases when I tell her who I am.

"Welcome. We've all been the new person in this room," she reminds me without mentioning our call.

"Thank you," I respond, taking a spot a few down from the others so I'm not listening in on their quiet conversations and close enough I'm not a pariah. I'm antsy waiting. Removing a hairband from my wrist, I tie my purple locks up into a messy ponytail. It's better than wringing my hands, and there's a sign stating cell phone use is prohibited.

I laugh inward at the things about myself I no longer understand. I stole the first box of hair dye. I want to sink into obscurity, but I liked the color and touched up my roots. Apparently, I'm also still a person who will silence their cell phone before the message flashes across a movie screen.

There's a momentary lightness to my mood. Then someone brushes beside me and the metal chair scrapes on the floor. I see a swath of long black hair as the woman takes the seat beside me. Sloan lets out a long breath as I catch her profile. She doesn't turn to face me. Instead, Sloan pats my knee and I close my eyes, fighting back tears.

Embarrassment has my heart wildly beating until I realize why Kimber's friend is here. This is rape, incest, and sexual abuse survivor group. The way Sloan behaves outside of this room, I wouldn't have had an inkling she'd ever belong here—as if it's a club with membership privileges.

My hands are folded in my lap. Sloan holds out one of hers, palm up. When I take it, she laces her fingers through mine. The rest of the session she doesn't look or react to me. Sloan's focus stays on the young woman speaking who has concerns about going on a business trip with a male counterpart at the company she works for. The description she paints of him is that he's never given her any reason to doubt his fidelity to his wife. No one insists her fears are unfounded because he's a family man with small children. They encourage her in small ways they've found emboldened by. I get the impression based on her reactions that whatever has happened to her was recent. Like me, she's gun-shy, picking apart every nuance of her existence. A few other women give her advice, making me recognize their personal stories' involved someone they trusted.

Later in the hour, it's not the case. I'm wiping away tears, watching someone else rub spots on their arms where her bruises have faded away, but her horrible memories linger. I've hated the shadow not knowing what really happened that night with Brandon cast on me. But these women? They live each day with the vividness of those demons.

As each of the ladies gathers their things to leave, I'm drained. For weeks I've been alone in my head and I'm also struck by how being here has changed me. Anyone can throw whatever statistic they want out, but people make things real.

Sloan squeezes my fingers before she stands. I've been so wrapped up in the session I almost forgot she was here. Embarrassment flows back over me.

"So—" She huffs. "What happens in Vegas, you know?"

I nod in agreement.

"I want you to know Carver is outside in the car, though."

Sloan's comment makes me deflate.

"I've never met him."

"That doesn't mean he's unfamiliar with you. Carver, Trig, and Jake are close—Like share-the-single-brain-cell-mother-nature-gives-to-an-alpha-male close. I'm never sure who has custody of it." Sloan rolls her eyes. "Carver insists I come to group at least once a month because he loves me. And, believe it or not, I need Mister Superiority to force me to do this. He sits and waits for me because he's protective. If I fall apart after a session Carver wants to be the one to catch me and put all the pieces back together. I can't fault him for it. But Carver has his own set of rules. I can't guarantee his silence."

My lips twist and tears burn behind my eyes. "I don't want Kimber finding out," I whisper.

"Oh, sweetie. I know." Sloan holds out her arms. "Can I give you a hug?"

"Yes." My voice quivers. She holds me tight like my mom had whenever things went wrong growing up.

We agree Sloan will leave the building first and I'll watch in the window for Carver's car to pull away. She gets into a sleek Maserati. When the trident emblem on the grill passes by, I'm uncertain I've ever seen a car as posh as this one. My dad drives an upscale import, and it piques my curiousity about what kind of job Carver has.

Sloan describing Carver and Trig—and whoever the other guy was—as overbearing doesn't click. Trig's kindness gives me the impression he'd look out for me, but he doesn't put Kimber in a bubble or on a pedestal.

I shake my head. Okay, the last part is wrong. Trig adores Kimber. He might kiss her toes if she told him to.

The following week, Sloan is getting out of the driver's side of the same car as I'm entering the building. I hadn't expected her to show up where she'd mentioned she didn't come to the group often and I'm happy to see her. Neither of us has time to say more than a quick greeting before the session begins. Yet again, Sloan takes up a spot next to me and threads our fingers together.

I'm confident in my choice to miss class for the second week in a row so I could be here. Reality is, between initially not being able to get out of my own way and the urge now to listen to and find strength in more survivor stories, it's unlikely I'll ever get the grade up. However, I'd made the effort to go to the second day it met last week. That has to count for something, right?

"Is it okay if we hang here for a bit longer?" Sloan

asks Dr. Nash when group is over. "I have nothing going on. What about you, Aidy?"

I shake my head, realizing Sloan didn't show up for herself today. She did it for me.

Dr. Nash gives us a genuine smile, telling us it's not a problem at all. She closes the door to the conference room we're in, slipping away to her office around the hall. I'm grateful for the few minutes extra it gives Sloan and me to speak in private.

"How are you doing right now?" Sloan stops and holds up a hand. "I mean that honestly. How are you in this moment?"

I take the time to think over my answer, rubbing my thumbs against one another before letting a long sigh escape a slight break at the corner of my lips. "Better than last week?"

"Good," she says. "Actually, it's great. Some weeks you step forward, others you step back. Let's just admit my first week here I stepped so far back I might not have been in the same decade."

"But you came again?"

"To appease Mister I-know-what-you-need-better-than-anyone. I didn't have any energy left to fight Carver. And I admit, in this case, he might have had a decent idea of what I did need than me. I came a lot more often in the beginning. Now it's less frequent unless I'm stumbling or caught up in a bad way. Sometimes to share and sometimes to listen, remember where I was and where I am today with Mister I-told-him-to-mind-his-own-business."

"So Carver doesn't know where you are today?"

"He does. He's aware you are too. But Carver also understands I'm not spilling my guts about what anyone says at these meetings or the reasons behind why you've shown up."

"I'm sure Captain Obvious can come to his own conclusions." I roll my eyes.

Sloan giggles. "I like that you have a sense of humor, but don't give 'em a rank. It'll go to his head." She winks. "Mister Obvious is good enough." She pauses before asking me again where my head is at, giving me the impression Sloan's concern is genuine.

"I thought about talking when that other woman was speaking about her boyfriend abusing her while she slept. I'm not sure I'm ready, though."

"You don't ever have to be. Opening up is cathartic. But once you do, there's no going back. What happened to any of us won't change, but the way we address it when we're ready does. It's okay to own your privacy, Aidy. You owe no one your story.

"Personally, I think it's one thing people forget when they say survivors have to stand up and lend their voice to stop it. Everyone has a part to play, but how they chose to play it doesn't have to include shouting from the rooftop how someone victimized you. Sometimes it's as simple as supporting someone else who has been through what you have. There's not a damn thing wrong with guarding your privacy. A lot of people won't give you the amount of their last tax refund, let alone admit to the number of partners they've had. Saying one of yours didn't happen with your consent isn't compulsory.

"Some are the warriors leading the fight. Others take a softer approach; we find good men who support us. And raise more of them, who understand how to treat another human being with the decency they deserve."

"Do you have kids, Sloan?"

"None of my own, no." Brief sadness washes over her features. "I meant Kimber."

"Was she—" My mind reels, worrying about how I came into the world.

Sloan is swift to grab my hand. "Oh gosh, Aidy, that's not what I'd intended at all! And I'd never discuss anything Kimber told me in confidence the same way

I'm not telling her you've shown up here...My point is you don't owe anyone your story. And if you share what happened to you, put up a firm barrier of what you will and won't discuss. Not everyone will understand a woman's reasons for silence."

My lip twists. I'm still unsure anyone will believe me if I do open up.

"The other thing is, Aidy, when you're ready to talk, someone will be there to listen." Sloan squeezes my palm, offering her ear and making me feel less alone than I have in I can't remember how long.

Chapter Eight

Morgan

It's past midnight when my cell buzzes in my pocket. Trig's number flashes on the screen.

"Hey, kid. I need a favor."

"Name it," I say without missing a beat. There's nothing I won't do anymore and no reason to add a caveat.

My place in society's pecking order has been solidified. I used to think I'd serve my time and, once I was done, there'd be a splinter of hope I could go back to the plans I had for my life. How wrong I was. The charges brought against me changed that perspective. Fast. Then there was the ugly reality of confinement in a lawless building run by people protecting everyone on the opposite side of the barbed wire.

"I got an X-text from Aidy."

My pulse speeds up hearing her name.

"She needs a pickup from a party. I'm with Carver and can't leave. Baby is sick—not that Aidy wants Kimber involved. Someone's gotta go get her."

"Where is she?"

Trig gives me a street name I wish I wasn't familiar with. "You sure you're good with this, Morgan?"

"I'm on it." I scrub my hands through my hair, tugging the roots more than normal.

"You run into any issues, I'll take care of it. I don't want anything happening to Aidy. You get picked up, then give her your company truck keys and tell her to drive it back to my place. I don't have the patience to deal with the fucknuts at the impound lot."

"What if she's been drinking?"

"She hasn't." I hear him breathe out. "I think it's why whatever is going on isn't for her. She sounded a little rattled."

The bit of information is more than Trig gave me in the truck when I'd fumbled trying to engage him about Aidy the morning we did the install together. Trig is tight-lipped. He doesn't read into people's emotions or motivations. "Ask her yourself," were his instructions. I guess tonight I can.

I roll through the University, stopping a full five seconds at each stop sign and using the directional whenever I have to turn. The last thing I want is trouble. Pulling to the curb, I put the truck in park and send Aidy a text using the contact info Trig has given me.

A few seconds later, she's scurrying from the shadows. Intent on waiting in the cab, there's a shift inside of me. I get out and slam the door.

"What are you doing?" I boom.

"Why are you so angry?" she asks, incredulous. Her feet skid to a halt right as two sets of red and blue lights pull up, blocking my vehicle in front and in back.

I'd been about to step up onto the sidewalk. Instead plant my feet by the hood. "You shouldn't be waiting in the dark. It's not safe."

"I was inside by a window. I saw the truck when you turned the corner and didn't want you to wait for me.

Your text didn't come until I was already walking out."

"Is there a problem here?" A campus police officer approaches us.

"No." I put my hands up as Aidy says the same.

His line of vision tosses between us, but he looks at the nondescript white truck and my dead giveaway hands. "Why are you here?"

"She called for a ride." I tilt my chin in Aidy's direction.

"And you expect me to believe you're her uber? In that?" The van is white and windowless. "Got some ID?"

Fuck. I groan. This is not good. The cop watches as I give a running diatribe of what I'm doing, reaching in my back pocket, finding my wallet, pulling out my driver's license. He's about forty and with my luck has been at this gig for the past five to ten years. He may not be able to place me in the darkness, but once he sees my picture I'm screwed.

I offer my identification to him.

"Bring it over here." He's close to the grass, not budging.

"I'd rather not if it's all the same to you."

He scoffs and saunters toward me, snatching it out of my light grip. My arms hang straight at my sides.

"I called my, uh, I called for a ride." Aidy is getting anxious. "He couldn't come so he sent Morgan. I'd planned to leave with him." She babbles about how I'm taking her back to Pinewood College. The officer points a finger to silence her.

"Morgan Wescott?" The guy nods a few doors down to a residence hall no students live in anymore.

"That's me."

"You're trespassing."

"No sir, I'm not. I'm in the street." Which we both know is owned by the city. "I haven't placed a foot on campus property. The dashcam my boss installed can prove it." I'm so glad paranoia got the best of me and I turned the thing on when I was on the highway.

"This isn't your vehicle? I want to see the registration."

"I'll walk to the driver side to lean in and get it out of the glove box."

"No use the passenger side," he instructs with rigid posture.

"I'm sorry, no can do."

He's trying to goad me into breaking the terms of my parole.

"I'll get it." Aidy stomps to the truck. "I'm not sure what difference it makes. Morgan works for my stepfather," she white lies, giving the man a dirty look.

"What kind of asshole employs a prick like you?" he sneers at me like I'm dirt. "Let's you anywhere near his kids, let alone a daughter?"

I don't bite back. He's looking for any reason to slam my head against the roof of his patrol car.

"Here!" Aidy holds out the registration. "Do you want me to call him too? He's probably waiting to hear if I'm okay." She waggles her phone in the air.

"Aidy, let it go," I say. "We're not doing anything wrong. We've followed all the guy's directions. The sooner we get out of here the better."

This house has a reputation for large obnoxious parties and the police had to have been called for a noise disturbance. As soon as the cops went in, the students flowed out. We're attracting a crowd and the last thing Carver and Trig like is unwanted attention.

The officer looks around, noticing Aidy's not the only person with her cell out. There are a few drunk kids poised, ready, and waiting to hit record if something goes down so they can be the first to upload the video.

He snaps the papers back at Aidy. "You're going with him?"

"Yes." She huffs.

"If you come back on campus," he motions in my direction and then ground as if he'll put a bullet in my chest and then bury me out back, "I'll have you arrested for trespassing."

"I was never on campus to begin with." I remind him before getting in the van and slamming the door. that Aidy's waiting in the passenger seat. "Fucking fake cop," I mumble under my breath. "Why were you even here? This isn't where you go."

Aidy crosses her arms, staring out the window while I get us the hell away from the brick buildings.

"I was considering transferring here… Now, I'm not so sure."

"Don't make your choices on account of me." The response is laced with sarcasm. Although, I don't want her to be the target of my bad mood.

"I wasn't," she scoffs. "I wanted a change of scenery and a girl I knew in high school invited me to the party."

"Was she your original ride?"

Aidy's shoulders hit her ears. Her chin cocks a fraction of an inch. "She would've been if I'd been interested in her boyfriend's buddy. I didn't know it was a setup. But, whatever." Her voice hitches. She shakes her head back and forth. "You're right. I'm not bright. It was dark and not safe."

"I'm sorry. You said you waited inside." I press the brake, stopping at the next light, and look at her through the eerie glow in the darkness.

"Does it matter?" Her sad eyes pull me in.

"You did your best to protect yourself in a strange place in the dark. So, yeah, it does." I'm aware I overreacted and of why I did. "You want to go to the beach?"

"Now?" She laughs like what I've said is hysterical. "It's the middle of the night and the beach is over two hours away."

"Which means we'll get here as the sun is coming up. I've got a sweatshirt in the back you can use as a pillow if you want to sleep on the way."

"You're serious?"

"We could salvage the weekend. Have a good time. Do you have other plans tomorrow?"

"I think you mean today. And no, I don't." She glances out the windshield, worrying her lip as she makes a decision. "The light is green. Are we going to the beach or not?"

I smile and snag my phone, shooting off a text to Trig. We don't need his permission. However, this is his truck, and he asked me to pick Aidy up and get her back to her dorm.

Me: Aidy and I are driving to Wrightsville

Trig: Take care of her or my wife will shove your balls down your throat after I cut them off. Are we clear?

Fuuuuuck.

Me: Message received.

Trig: I'm kidding kid. Wouldn't have sent you to get her if I didn't trust you. Have fun.

Me: Thanks. We will.

Trig: Also, don't put it past Kimber to lop your balls off if you hurt Aidy. I'll just be the one holding you down while she does it.

He follows it up by sending me the damn LOL emoji. I'm not even sure what he expects me to text back, so I set my phone in the cup holder.

The road is dark and lonely other than the beams of big rigs hauling livestock. Outside of the Triangle, North Carolina's economy is agricultural-based. Farmers raise poultry and pigs. There are a lot of slaughterhouses off the exit ramps. It's better to ignore the chicken feathers flying into the path of the headlights and accept the hog is about to become somebody's meal.

An hour later, Aidy's following behind me into an all-night truck stop to use the ladies' room while I pay for gas and soda from the wall of refrigerators. I worked all day yesterday, but sleep is something I've gone without before. Staying awake is nothing new. The caffeine jolt is all I need to get us back on the road.

We climb back into the van. I hand Aidy the cold bottle to hold.

"Do you mind if I unscrew the cap to take the first sip?" she asks.

"Not at all." I hear the crisp carbonation escape while fishing in back for my sweatshirt.

We exchange the cola for the makeshift pillow she tucks between the seatbelt and her cheek. She's adamant she's not tired. Yet, her eyes are closed before the van pulls back onto I-40. I have second thoughts and consider turning around, heading west, dropping her at her dorm the way I was supposed to, and going back to Brighton.

Taking a sip of soda, there's a hint of berry lip balm on the plastic rim. I realize it's hers. The likelihood I'll ever taste Aidy another way overwhelms me. It also bolsters my confidence over where I'm taking her, and why it's an experience she may need. I have one hand on the wheel and one curled around the cool bottle. With each sip and mile closer we inch toward the beach, the caffeine rush has me anticipating Aidy's reaction when she wakes up.

At the causeway, the bridge is up and we wait for a taller fishing boat to get through before continuing on. Warning lights flash, coloring Aidy's skin the way the campus police cruiser lights had. The red is different. It reminds me of driving back from the grocery store on a December night and seeing holiday displays.

With the exception of a hard plastic snowman—

whose black top hat had faded in the southern sun, and that had a broken lightbulb and frayed cord for as long as I can remember—my folks didn't decorate our house when I was a kid. My dad said it wasn't worth the electric bill. My mom wasn't ever going to stand up to him. For Cece and I, the twinkling in other yards brought home the magic of the season, leaving us with a little faith Santa might be real.

There wasn't a point when we found out the truth either of us felt misled. Deep down, we always knew. Plenty of kids got more gifts and better ones than we did year-round. But we also saw people with less than us giving what they had to those who were even more unfortunate. It's the spark of what made us want to reach for more ourselves so, eventually, we'd have more to share and more to give.

I don't hate believing, or not believing in the spirit of Christmas. I hate how every good deed I'd done to better myself got wiped away by a single bad one, landing my name on the perpetual naughty list.

Aidy

"Hey, Aidy, we're here." Morgan's voice is feather-soft along my skin. It's almost as if he's touched my arm.

When I stole the sip of cola from Morgan's drink, I'd expected the buzz from the caffeine and rush from agreeing to go with him to stay on an even high. The whole way to Wrightsville my consciousness remained aware of him behind the wheel, but I succumbed to the rhythm of the road. The motion lulled me deeper, into the kind of sleep I haven't had in weeks.

I tense, wiping my mouth, hoping I haven't drooled, and blink.

The van idles in a municipal lot on Lumina which has a bathhouse and public access to the beach. I know this area. My parents took me here when I was a child and my friends and I parked along this road during the summers in high school when we went to the beach. It's a straight shot back to civilization. The big hotel and pier are to my right. All I'd have to do is walk past the beach houses to where the littler motor inns are and I could find my way home. It's interesting I'm making an exit plan when I'd felt safe enough to let down my guard with Morgan a few hours ago. And have probably been snoring in his ear.

The sun is breaking over the dunes. It's the most beautiful, vibrant orange and yellow fading to shades of periwinkle blues. A few strings of clouds are passing over us, headed inland. The tall seagrass on the sand dunes sways like a lazy porch swing. An hour from now this will be a surfer's paradise.

Morgan pulls his key from the ignition and the sound of waves crashing beyond the mounds of sand reaches my ears.

"What time is it?" I stretch, then sink back into the warm seat. Morgan's sweatshirt falls to the side. I fold it over and place it in my lap. Tucked up by my chin, it had a musky aroma. Almost like deodorant. It's ridiculous that I like the clean scent and I won't be lame and make a comment on how good it smelled. Who sniffs armpits? I don't. And I don't want to give Morgan a reason to tease me.

"Coming up on seven o'clock." My jaw goes slack and I stare at Morgan's timorous smile. He's got a dimple in his cheek. "Seemed like you needed the rest. Besides, it was pitch black out until ten minutes ago."

Morgan doesn't notice my tooth sink into my lower lip. He digs in his back pocket for his wallet and goes to pay the meter, giving me a chance to fully wake.

I sit still, silently berating myself for getting into a car with a man I hardly know to go on an hours long road trip where I freakin' fall asleep during the ride. I could be dead by the side of the highway with no one the wiser. Okay, maybe Trig since Morgan texted him. But, like, when would they find my body?

"Awesome choices. Get your shit together, Aidy," I mutter.

Glancing at the sweatshirt on my lap, I steel myself. Morgan is a good guy. Kimber and Trig trust they are safe with him living in their home. From what I've seen he's fantastic with Owen. I should take what's happening at face value and give Morgan the benefit of the doubt.

And maybe that's what is wrong with this whole situation. Going to the campus party wasn't to meet anyone. It was to prove to myself I could have a good time. One foot in front of the other. The same way the women in group have shared their baby steps toward normalcy.

Sloan showing up without Carver and our talk afterward impacted me. From what little she's told me about Carver, he treats her well. It got me to thinking someday I might have a chance for that.

The problem is, there's TNT wobbling inside of my belly. I'm determined to diffuse it before the bomb explodes into full-on excitement. Morgan is out of my league. I don't want to read into what makes an attractive guy invite me anywhere, let alone here. There is no way I'm letting a naive and bruised heart blow my life up in my face again so soon. Not when I'm trying to get my bearings.

I flip down the mirror, ensuring I don't resemble a crusty old sailor and embarrass either of us. Then I follow Morgan to the kiosk where he's feeding a ten-dollar bill into the machine. It spits a one out.

"Think three hours will do?" he muses.

I nod. In actuality it seems like a lot more than we need, but there's no sense in spending fifteen minutes on the beach after a two-hour drive.

"If not, we can come back and feed the meter," I suggest, hoping it appeases the local forecasters that I have confidence in the weather, Morgan, and... well, me.

As we pass the van heading toward the beach, he sticks the white slip on the dash and the single into the cup holder. Morgan also removes his empty soda bottle.

It goes into a recycling receptacle near the bathroom. The van alarm chirps behind us and he stuffs the key into his pocket. We walk up the ramp and then down the winding wooden path over the piles of windswept sand separating the beach from the parking lot.

Stopping near the end of the ramp, we take our shoes off to make it easier to walk in the doughy sand. The beach is deserted. The sun is above the horizon and the waves dance, rippling up to the shore. As we get closer to the shore, I'm struck with the impression that I could walk straight out over the waves and keep going. If I looked back in this direction, I'd be carefree.

"This is beautiful." I'm not sure I've been here this early before. I dig my toes into the firmer, wet sand that's cool from the waves that have flowed over it. Yet it's warmer beneath, holding onto the heat, the complete opposite of the way I'd made a hole to cover my feet with sand when I was a little girl and the scorching summer sun shone high in the sky.

Morgan's staring into the distance. I've never considered him uptight, but his posture is completely relaxed. Even his jaw hangs softly, the way everyone's is supposed to while practicing yoga. I'm not sure he recognized I was still standing next to him until I'd spoken.

"Yeah. I, uh,—I wasn't able to get out here for a while and it's the first place I came when I got back. Now, I'm here every chance I get."

His gaze never wanders to me and I look out over the ocean, trying to focus on what he sees. Gulls squawk over our heads. The waves break in a rhythm, the sound crashing into my ears and drawing my senses back outward, anticipating the next white peak. A man strides with a longboard between us and the water. His footfalls are audible over the wet grains despite the cacophony of noises.

I find my senses opening. I taste the salty air filling

my nose. The humidity encases my skin. My shoulders fall with palms open wide. There's a click-crack of my spine as the tension I've been holding loosens. And, to my utter amazement, excitement overtakes me when a pod of dolphins breaches the surface, each arching their bodies into the air at various heights. It slows my pulse to the point I have to stop and wonder if I'm still breathing.

For the first time since it happened, I'm at peace, and I revel in the tranquility wrapping itself around me.

Morgan and I are alone within each other's company. We don't speak again until the pink of daybreak is gone, and the sun is fully awake and he suggests strolling toward the pier to find breakfast.

Spying a coffee shop sign ahead, we plot a steady course in that direction. Morgan gives me a wide berth. There's room for both of us to spin in dizzying circles and never collide. Our current environment doesn't have us packed in like sardines.

Along the way we stop to watch pelicans dive-bomb, scooping fish into their oversized beaks. We laugh, broad smiles straining our cheeks, and make kamikaze sounds. My stomach grumbles and Morgan chuckles under his breath.

"Come on, whatever you want to eat is on me."

I hold up an emergency twenty I keep stashed in the teeny tiny pocket of my denim capris.

"What is that?" Morgan's lip twitches.

"Lunch money if we're staying?" The cash is folded into a flat square. Only the green print is visible, not the denomination. I unfurl it and Morgan takes the bill with a little "huh."

"Mind if I hold on to this?"

"Nope." I shrug, unwilling to read into his reasons.

He thanks me while ironing out the creases with his short fingernails and we keep going toward the shop. Inside we order two regular coffees and I tack a gooey cinnamon roll onto the tab.

"Sweet tooth?" Morgan inquires as the woman behind the counter puts my sugar-laden treat into a white waxed bag.

"Hungry tooth," I reply.

"Make it two." He holds up his fingers and the barista adds one more. He slides the bag over the top of the glass case closer to me so I can pick it up and leaves a generous tip when she makes change. We go back outside into the sunshine.

It takes a minute for my eyes to adjust. I hold my hand up to shade my face, making a visor with the bag. The bakery waft gets the best of me and I decide there is no one to impress and dig in.

"Sorry, but I can't wait much longer." I pull one bun out, positive by the way Morgan reacts that there is a hashtag hangry sign appearing over my head like a lightbulb would in a comic. I've got the bag and my coffee in one hand and use the other to shove the first gooey bite into my face.

"Come sit. You can't do it like that." He encourages me to walk faster toward the sand.

"Like what?" I lick at the roll, the chunk I'm trying to bite missing my mouth and making Morgan lose it.

"Cinnamon rolls have to be eaten around and around. In a swirl."

"Is this like Oreos have to be opened up and the cream frosting licked out before you can eat the chocolate wafers?"

"See, you get my point." He settles onto the beach.

I cross my legs and glide down next to him, hoping the chunk covered in thick opaque icing with a crunch to it won't fall. In the same haphazard manner Morgan and I shook hands when we first met, I'm bumbling, trying to get his breakfast in front of him and make an indent in the sand for my coffee. "I've underestimated how empty my stomach is and might fight a seagull if I drop this."

Morgan snorts, fiddling with something over his lap. "Then eat mine too."

"And gain ten pounds."

Morgan looks me up and down. "I don't think you have a problem there, Aidy. Plus, Kimber said you weighed more last year."

I blink a few times. "Everyone puts on weight their freshman year. Did you?" I poke, wanting to know more about him. Morgan's picked up details from a conversation weeks ago, putting me at a disadvantage.

"Nope. I played sports back then."

"Do you now?"

"Sometimes Jasper, Skye, and I will have a pickup game at the mill. Mostly we work out together."

I take it Jasper and Skye are his friends, but "What's the mill?"

Confusion mars his features. "It's ah—It's this big refurbished cotton factory across the street from Sweet Caroline's."

"The strip joint in Brighton?"

"One and the same. Jasper and Skye live there along with my sister."

Oh! Morgan has a sister. Now I'm getting somewhere.

"So it's like apartments."

Morgan busts my confidence. "Carver and Trig run their business from it. But there are rooms on the upper floors. Carver's got an enormous pad he shares with Sloan. Your mom—Kimber and Trig lived there for a long time. Why don't you know this?"

I bite my lip, inspecting the stump of the cinnamon roll. "I only got to know Kimber once I was old enough to make my own choices. She's not my mom. More like a really amazing friend who happened to give birth to me and lets me have a relationship with my brother. There's a lot of stuff I'm not sure I'll ever know at all."

Like who my father was.

Morgan

From the frown overtaking Aidy's face, I've stuck my foot in it. I forget her relationship with the family I live with is non-traditional. Aidy's got parents. The kind who will stick up for her and gave her the all-American life I'd wanted not only to lead but to pass onto my kids.

I sip my coffee and grind it back into the sand so it's half-buried. It reminds me of where I am and by that I don't mean the beach. When I was Aidy's age, I didn't think much further about my future than any other nineteen-year-old. I had a rough plan to do better than my parents. Have a wife. Raise a few kids. Be a respectable member of society.

Everything changed overnight. The closest I'll get to the dream girl and fantasy life is probably where I stand today; half-buried by my past and offering Aidy a token of friendship and a safe space to let go of her troubles for a few hours.

She's eaten the swirl of pastry around until all that's left is the core between her sticky fingertips. Suddenly green in the gills, Aidy looks at the remains of her cinnamon roll like it might hurt her to finish it.

"Full?"

"Yeah," she mutters, searching for somewhere to drop the last bite.

"Wrap it in a napkin." I suggest. "I'm saving mine for later."

My assumptions have washed away the comfort of our previous silence. I kick myself for not being in tune with Aidy's feelings. I want to blame it on the lack of women in my life. Dating becomes less of a priority when you're a social pariah, worrying about how many free days you have left on the outside. On the inside? Your future becomes so precarious. It's all about making it to tomorrow. You don't give two shits about anyone's feelings. Admitting I'm out of practice is an understatement.

Aidy whips the final mouthful toward a flock of gulls that have gathered, waiting on her to feed them. They swoop like vultures.

"Sorry," she apologizes, the contentment I'd seen in her posture slipping. "I didn't mean to waste it." She squints, creating minute crow's feet at the corners of her eyes. The icy expression criticizes her actions.

"No worries. You're paying for lunch. I'll scatter a few fries and we'll call it even. If it helps, I'm sorry too. Here, you'll need this later." I hold out a tiny paper crane made from her twenty.

"How? When did you do this?" There's a lilt in her voice.

"While we were sitting here. Over the past few years, I've had a lot of time on my hands and stacks of used paper going to waste, so I started folding." I'm intentional giving Aidy an in so she's able to ask what I know she's dying to know. It's the biggest albatross in the room, or rather on the beach.

"Origami. It's so pretty." She edges closer to the

question on her tongue, but then I see her swallow it down. "I'm sorry too, if I'm acting weird. Can I tell you something?"

I nod.

"I've never asked who my birth father was. Knowing Kimber wanted the best for me is easier to accept than finding out that he didn't want me. It's safer."

I acknowledge what she's said, but won't judge Aidy's reasoning. My parents were there when I was growing up and still didn't want me. I also appreciate that she's confided in me.

We both stare back out over the ocean. Now, I'm more scared of what happens if the truth stays locked up. I don't want to hang around Aidy without her aware of who I am. It's obvious she's hurt having been left in the dark about details of other people's lives.

I wonder for a few minutes if she'll cross the bridge when she finally does.

"Morgan, why did the campus cop call you out for trespassing last night. Why aren't you supposed to be there?"

I look straight at her delicate features, into her blue eyes. "If I'm caught on campus, then I get sent back to jail."

Boom. It's out. My credibility with this woman evaporates, along with the fleeting chance I might have had with her. I pick up the bag and pull Aidy to standing.

"Why were you in prison?" She brushes sand off of her bottom.

"You know what parties are like during pledge season?" I'm not running, expecting Aidy to keep up or give chase. I've gotta move to get the rest out.

Aidy nods, letting me take her empty cup and toss it in the trash along with mine.

"My roommate didn't make it through hazing." I scrub my face. My pulse quickens.

Slow it down, dude. All you're telling her is the same story everyone else gets. How you got there. Not what happened once you were there.

"I didn't expect you were the fraternity type."

"I'm not. I had a basketball scholarship. All four years… Well, one and a half of them anyhow. Got kicked off the squad and had to quit school."

She shakes her head as her opinion of me shifts. "You lost me, Morgan."

Yup, I'm damn sure I did, and way before we met.

"We weren't supposed to be drinking. Most of us were underage. Even if no one talks about collegiate sports hazing, it happens. Athletes doing anything wrong are a university's dirty little secret because, if it comes out, that affects the bottom line. Without big-name starters, who is going to the games? We get away with more. Back then anyhow. I can't speak for what it's like today."

"You forced your roommate to drink?"

"No. I didn't stop Rob, though and I could have. It was my second year, I'd already been through it. Most of the shit the guys did wasn't to break you down. More to see if you'd stand up. I knew my limits. Took no crap and the upperclassmen left me alone. I garnered their respect. Rob was a freshman. A big to-do in high school sports. They pushed him around a lot, but it wasn't bad. I'm not making excuses, I mean in terms of what I'd seen happen to other new players on the squad. Anyhow, Rob wanted to impress them. He wanted to be a part of it. College. Drinking. We were all young and stupid, thinking we were on top of the world. Half of the clothes on our backs were free from national advertisers. People bought us stuff. Not even expensive things; coffee, lunch, all random crap. None of us saw it as abnormal. It was the reward for years of effort. My roommate was another piece of the pie, and on the court we made a great team, which is almost impossible if you hate one another. Nobody set out to do anyone dirty. We liked him. It was a brotherhood of sorts. A bigger regret for me is if Rob hadn't died, then there's a chance he'd be a part of my life to this day."

Looking back on the day before Rob's death, I still honestly believe it. In my mind's eye, I could see us leaving each other those bullshit comments on social media or texting the way I do now with Skye and Jasper. That's not the same, though, is it? I only met everyone at the factory because Cece convinced them to take pity on me. They haven't been my friends long.

"Anyhow," I wave my hand. "I guess it doesn't matter because I don't speak with anyone from my past. My other teammates who took responsibility went to jail too. It was better we lost touch."

"But why did you go to jail?"

"I was there the night before when everyone was drinking. A bunch of us left to go to a party at the house I picked you up from and got hammered. When I got back to my room, Rob was lying in bed so I didn't think much of it. I passed out drunk too. The next morning, I woke up—"

God, the memory of the smell lingers at the back of my throat.

"Dude, the fuck? Did you piss yourself?" I sit up and hang my legs over the side of the mattress. The heat is on and my bare feet are hot the way they are when I have a fever. Another acrid smell fights for attention. It's worse than a stopped-up toilet.

He's a lump in the bed a few feet away. I stand and walk over, scrubbing sleep from my eyes and praying someone has pain killers that will knock out the pounding in my skull. I'm dehydrated and thirsty as hell, but the stench has me ready to double over gagging.

"Man, get up and hit the freakin' shower."

I'm about to offer for us to get the hell out of here and go to the dining hall once we can walk a straight line. I'm still feeling the effects of the rum, vodka, beer? I don't even remember what was in my cup at the party.

I pull the covers back and almost upchuck. Rob's lifeless eyes stare at me. His face is contorted, like something you'd see in a horror flick. His hard jaw hangs open. Vomit trails down his cheek and neck.

My knees give out, slamming into the floor. Somehow I've managed to turn before I fall forward on top of him. I crawl on all fours to the door and open it. The fresher scent of the hall chokes me as I gasp for cleaner breaths to fill my lungs. I'm not sure when I started crying, but I'm also screaming for help. One of the guys grabs my shoulders, picking me up while I try to use the stair banister to find my footing.

"I see it all in slow motion every time I think about it," I say to Aidy. Tears trickle down her cheeks and I use my knuckle to wipe one away. I hope she's crying for Rob and not for me. "I even see the guy who picks me up jump back as I throw up all over the carpet." Puke spattered on the hem of his flannel pajama pants. "It's still vivid years later."

"You said you left. Your roommate was drinking with someone else."

"Yeah, but I was fuzzy on the exact time I came back to my room and Rob had been dead for long enough the coroner couldn't pinpoint the exact moment when it happened. There was enough overlap that he may have been alive when I walked in. But I was too trashed to know any better. And I'd been there when he'd started drinking. Being able to intervene might have made the difference."

"You could be innocent. What if he was gone before —"

"No, Sweet Pea. Don't go there. Don't rack your brain the way I do. It's not worth it. Rob was my friend and we all…I played a part in his death and take responsibility for my actions. I could have asked him to go to the party instead of leaving him with those teammates. I could have checked on him when I got back to our room. I could have taken him out for coffee and a flippin' cinnamon bun. I didn't. We all made choices and had to live with the consequences."

"How can you be so calm about it?"

"I was angry at first. Felt like Rob's parents were going after me. But then it didn't matter. I got kicked out of school, lost my scholarships, had fucking legal bills, and my parents washed their hands of me. You couldn't kick me any lower than I already was. The only person who got hurt taking the plea deal they offered was Cece. If I dragged it out, my sister would have court-side tickets to watch a drawn-out trial, reinforcing she was alone—or would be for a lot longer if I got a harsher sentence. Rob's family wasn't going to move on or heal. So I did my time, thought about my crime, and made my peace with how one fucked up choice knocked over the dominoes. If he doesn't get a do-over, neither should I."

Morgan

I don't for a moment believe Aidy thinks any less of me than I ever have, but her perception has changed. She's quiet for a long while, pondering my confession. I take it as a good sign that she's not on a hot tack, begging to head back to Brighton. I don't think her concerns overrule her readiness to leave the tranquility of the beach.

We make idle chit chat interspersed with a few random questions from Aidy about my time in jail, which I don't mind answering. Eventually, we make it back to the part of the beach close to the lot where I parked the van. We wind up sitting in comfortable silence watching the waves crash onto the shore for a while longer.

When she's done, she's done. Aidy stands up, brushing the sand off of her bottom again and says, "Enough of that." She wants to go back to having fun.

I feel like it's what I promised her. A few lighthearted hours someplace seemingly farther away than it is. It doesn't matter if you live on the ocean. Setting foot on the beach is a momentary escape from reality.

My life is so different than what I'd expected, even when I was let out earlier this year. I come here a lot to reflect on my blessings and let the negativity go. I need the open space as a reminder that I'm no longer confined. Which I also find humor in since my prospects nowadays don't include a glimmer of playing professional basketball, let alone a white-collar job. It's difficult to find an employer who will take a chance on an ex-con and harder to establish a career path. I'm stuck in the confines, struggling to learn how to make it through the next four decades as a productive citizen with less than half of the prospects I had four years ago.

Maybe if I'd had a silver spoon in my mouth the "slap on the wrist" sentence outraging many for my part in Rob's death would have stopped stinging when I peeled off the orange jumpsuit.

Family connections have helped some of my teammates move on. But I came from a small town and my parents are embarrassed to be associated with me. My A-game on the court was all I had going. Now, I'm back to living the life perhaps I'd been predestined for since it's the same path of least resistance the rest of my family and their surrounding community trod down.

Cece is the only exception to the rule. She saw me work my ass off to get, *earn,* better and did the same. I thought I'd be pulling my sister up instead of dragging her down.

Aidy reaches her hand out to me. I grasp the olive branch and we leave our shoes lying on the beach to wade into the water.

It's October and while the rest of the world is embracing pumpkin spice and breaking out their sweaters, we're still experiencing what other regions call Indian Summer. Daytime temps haven't dipped below seventy, and the same can be said at night. The waters off of the Eastern Carolina Coast won't come close to giving beachgoers frostbite. Some days in the winter, it's warmer than the air.

We both pace in the shallows and, after an accidental nudge as the undertow has the sand shifting between our toes, a kick-fight ensues with us splashing one another. Aidy laughs the way she does when she's with Owen.

I'm grinning like a fool because—despite it just being the subject of conversation—for a few hours I've left my baggage behind.

Telling Aidy and not having her harsh criticism is a weight lifted off my shoulders and I embrace the small freedom, enjoying her company.

The gradual receding tide moves us out further to where the waves lick the backs of our knees. A wave overtakes us. And once our pants are wet, we give up and begin body surfing, swimming out and letting the current carry us back to shore. I'm laughing as loud as Aidy is now and catch her eye as she wipes a stray purple lock from her face.

The ice-filled cloud that had me so concerned when we first met is gone. I glad I must have been wrong and was projecting my problems on her.

An hour later, we're meandering past the lavatories, soaked through and hoping the steamy pavement assists the drip-dry so we get on the road without ruining the upholstery.

The van belongs to the security company. Trig lets me drive it like it's my personal vehicle. This isn't my first choice of cars, but beggars can't be choosers. Even my fucking gas goes on a company credit card. Any time I've paid cash, he's gotten on me for the receipt so he can match the mileage to the expenses. It took him giving me three dirty looks for trying to be a good guy before it sunk in. Trig isn't okay with me forking over part of my paycheck. I know his method isn't on the up and up, but I'm also not in a position to argue. In stark contrast, the only way I could get a driver's license was by paying for my gas and insurance. My freakin' father wouldn't show his face in court for my hearing. So, forgetting about him helping with my mountain of legal bills took no effort.

"Where can we go like this? I'm still drenched." Aidy's got a point. We look less like beach bums and more like we've endured a hurricane.

"There's a surf shop a few miles down the road next to a restaurant." I lift my brow in question. Aidy hops in the van.

When we get up to the store, she pokes her finger at the no shirt, no shoes sign. The only thing presentable about us is our sandy footwear. Aidy snags a vintage state flag t-shirt and holds up a retro baseball tee for me.

"You should get that one," I say. Aidy mentioned in passing she played softball.

In the end, she puts the flag style back and we both get the same style shirt with different logos. Aidy also selects a pair of board shorts, rubbing her fingers against the wicking fabric. "We should have thought about this beforehand," she says, pressing a pair in my direction.

"I don't think they were open when we decided to go for a swim." I place the shorts back on the display. "My jeans are fine."

"You've been swimming in the ocean in those. They're nasty wet and the salt!"

"I'll live."

Aidy has her wallet out to pay for everything. I don't want to add to the bill and she's not letting me go Dutch.

The store manager allows her to cut the tags off and Aidy disappears behind a curtain in the changing area. I whip my damp shirt over my head and replace it with the new one. When she's changed, we head next door to the restaurant looking like tourists.

Aidy spends the better part of the time before our meals arrive humorously bickering with me over why I should have let her get me a pair of shorts.

"No twinsies," I respond firmly, and insist on picking up the lunch tab. Too many people are giving me a hand out right now. Accepting people's generosity is difficult for a kid who grew up like me. I want to give back, repay them, and do my part whenever it's appropriate.

"I have my origami crane still. Oh," she gasps, disappointed and holding it up. "It's a little crushed from my back pocket. But still good to spend."

"Nah." I take the twenty, adjusting the folds so it's crisp. "Save it."

"How do you know Trig and Kimber?" Aidy changes the subject, munching on the onion ring topping her burger.

"Through my sister. When I was sent up-river, as she likes to call it, it was only for a few months. However, the university kicked me out of school long before and the lawyer's fees had mounted. My scholarships didn't cover all of my tuition, and without being enrolled at the university any longer, the bills were coming due. She knew I had nowhere to go once I'd served my sentence and went to Carver for a favor...Not that she should have. Carver does her a solid giving her somewhere to live...Anyhow, Carver had no use for me and, even though there's plenty of rooms there, he's picky about who stays at his place. Trig happened to need an extra set of hands, like an apprentice. So he trained me and offered me the third floor."

"Why's Carver picky?"

"Would you want a felon staying in the same building as your business?" I pose the question to throw her off. When there are no installs, I work in a tech room at the mill and I'm certain plenty of illegal shit goes down there.

Aidy's nose wrinkles. "I didn't think of it that way. You're you. I was more worried you were Trig's kid than I am concerned you went to jail."

"I look nothing like Trig." I place the top bun on my grilled chicken sandwich and take a bite. Melty pimento cheese oozes out. I smile, wiping the grease from my lips. This is living. Something as simple as tasting life brings me pure joy. "You, however. Even with the purple hair camouflage, there's no doubt who you're related to."

Aidy twists her wet locks. "I needed a change. Everyone says red-heads are fiery."

"You're not?"

"I may have inherited the wrong color gene by accident. I'm more, steady?"

"Fires smolder too, Sweet Pea. There's a lot underneath the surface that goes unseen."

She winces, and I catch an ice crackle back at the corner of her eye. "What's with the food nicknames? Kimber calls me Dumplin'. You've got the veggie thing going."

"As I mentioned, embers burn too." I smirk at her. "The pea thing is because you laughed when Owen sneezed them on you. It's sweet how happy he makes you. Heck, being around him makes me happy." *The same way as being with you does.* "He's full of possibility and doesn't have a care in the world. Wouldn't it be great if it was like that for everyone?"

"Yeah, it would." She agrees with a sardonic huff. "But then you grow up and nothing is what you were told it was supposed to be."

"How did you grow up, if you don't mind me asking?"

"Only child, maybe a little spoiled. Hopefully not too coddled that it turned me into a brat. I think I tried everything once before picking up a bat and taking my first swing. My dad was thrilled. He'd played ball in high school and my mom went to all of his games. So softball became my sport, and we traveled. Oh gosh, with all those tournaments and weekends away, sometimes I longed for my own bed, you know?" Those last words are wistful. More like a recent memory than a distant one.

"You still play?" I clear my throat and swallow.

"No. By my senior year, I'd run myself ragged and I was done competing. I wanted to focus on college and didn't need scholarships for my family to afford school." Aidy's been animated while she speaks, and she catches the error of what's slipped past her lips before I do.

"I'm sorry. I shouldn't have brought that up. Playing basketball had to have meant so much to you and—"

"Aidy." I reach across the table for her hand to reassure her. "Believe me, people have said far worse to me than speaking their truths. I get it. I guess I understand even more now why Kimber gave you up for adoption."

Aidy had gotten everything Kimber wanted for her. She was raised the way I thought I'd be raising my kids someday.

We finish up and I lean back in my seat, cracking my spine. The meal sits in my stomach like Thanksgiving dinner and I yawn.

"You must be exhausted."

"Nothing a power nap won't cure. Do you mind if we go back to the beach for an hour so I can sleep this off?" I rub my gut.

Aidy's gaze follows my circling palm. I like her eyes on me and the wondering she does about what muscles are hidden under my shirt before she straightens and looks away.

"It's not a problem." Pink tinges her cheeks.

I feed the meter for the second time in the municipal lot. This time we stay in the van with the windows down and the back doors wide open to the sidewalk. There's enough breeze to cool the interior. We rest in the shade in the back, stretching out on the carpet since I have no cargo, and away from the sun glaring through the windshield.

I'm on my back and Aidy's tucked her knees to her chest. She uses my sweatshirt as a pillow again. I watch her fight to keep her eyes open the way she had on the drive last night. It's surprising when she falls asleep on the hard floor before I do, but I may have stayed awake to make sure she was okay. I wake hours later as her body shudders beside me and I roll on my side to face her.

Tears pool in the crook between the slope of her nose and her eye. One rolls down, moistening her cheeks and landing on my sweatshirt. Her breathing is labored, and she's crying in her sleep. In the darkest recesses of my own fears, I know this isn't normal.

I use the pad of my thumb to trace around Aidy's closed eyelids. "What happened to you, Sweet Pea?" I whisper.

Chapter Twelve

Aidy

"Hey, kid, what's new?" Trig asks as I come in the front door a few weeks later. He doesn't seem shocked at my presence or me knowing the correct digits to input on the keypad outside to let myself in. Heck, his doorbell cam probably alerted him as I pulled up to the house.

"Not too much." I drop my stuff in the guest room off the kitchen and make gimme fingers so he'll hand over my baby brother.

"Aiy!" Owen tries to say my name, squeezing his chubby arms around my neck.

"Ooh! I missed your snuggles!"

Trig chortles, rubbing the baby's back. I've spent way too much time here as of late. If it's been a whole three days since I've seen Owen, it's saying a lot.

"He's got new tricks."

"Tricks?" I nuzzle Owen's nose. "What are you a puppy?"

"Woo." My brother leaves off the "F" and it's so stinking cute I have to squeeze him once more before handing over to his dad.

Trig's boots tromp over to the other side of the room and he places Owen's feet on the floor. "Kneel down," he instructs me. Owen bounces on his knees, mimicking Trigs' bent posture. "Not you, ya goof!" Owen giggles and they wrestle a bit before Trig plants Owen back on his feet. "Go on, show Miss Aidy all the trouble she's in for now. Your sister is waiting."

My heart pitter-pats as Trig acknowledges our connection.

Owen bounces a few more times looking in my direction before Trig taps him on his diapered bottom and then he's crossing the tile like walking is second nature to him. He gets to the final two steps and flings himself into my arms, confident I'll catch him and my chest is full-on pounding.

"I'm so proud of you!" I squeal. I give him loud kisses up his baby-fat rolled neck and Owen slobbers on my cheek. Trig tries to get him to toddle back, but Owen flops down in my lap, content to cuddle.

While I keep Owen occupied playing on the floor, Trig goes back to prepping dinner. From the spread of cutting boards, knives, and ingredients on the counter, it had to have been something he was doing before I showed up.

"I'm in tonight. You're under no obligation to stay and watch him." Trig concentrates on chopping vegetables.

"My roommate is never around, so if it's all the same to you—"

Trig's brow furrows. "Morgan left some cash for you to order out."

I notice two origami frogs stacked piggy-back on the table. Last time. Morgan folded the bills into a fox. I bite my lip, trying not to blush. Are these little tokens more than they seem? It doesn't matter how much time Morgan and I spend in one another's company, it's moronic thinking there's any hidden meaning behind them. However, I wasn't asleep as much as embarrassed to open my eyes when we'd napped in the truck at the beach. I heard the sincerity in Morgan's voice and fought the shiver his light touch sent flowing down my spine.

Trig interrupts my thoughts. "I figured you both might want some healthier grub than what I've seen from the takeout bags in the trash can."

"Does it bother you I'm here?" I want to add *so often*, but I don't. Between babysitting and Morgan and I hanging out, I'm staying overnight in Brighton almost more than anyplace else. I've been inclined to go home to see my mom and dad on a few occasions. But I'm most comfortable here, and I sleep like the dead, making up for the nights on the dorm room floor.

"Not in the least. I'd be cautious of your parent's feelings, though, Aidy. I'm not saying it to upset the apple cart. Kimber has a lot of respect for Ghillie and Don. The last thing I want is for them to feel threatened by her when they don't understand the situation."

"Situation?" I bring Owen to his playpen.

"Don't play dumb with me." His voice is serious, but Trig's eyes dance with mirth. "I appreciate you're taking this slow."

"Do you mean me and Morgan? He doesn't like me!"

"Do you like him?"

"What? No. I don't kn— No," I deny, flatly. "We're, you know."

"Yup, I know." Trig sing-songs with a smirk.

I'd tell him he didn't know a damn thing if this wasn't his house. And he isn't cooking us dinner. And my mom hadn't raised me better. But I also get Trig's point about Kimber. He's protective of his wife and my parents don't have the foggiest I'm not in Brighton because I'm trying to reconcile some fairytale relationship with the mother I wanted more. My family has two equal branches. Don and Ghillie are on one side and Kimber, Trig and Owen are on the other. I love them both. It's a far stretch to say I love Kimber and Trig the same way as Don and Ghillie because my mom and dad are exactly that. It's unlikely I'll understand how you could love anyone more until I fall in love and have children of my own. There's only one moment in my life I'd redo, but it's impossible.

I pull out a chair and sit with a frog grasped in each hand. Morgan's sweet and gentle with me. No one can ever prove beyond a reasonable doubt his friend was still alive. Morgan took responsibility anyway. Meanwhile, I can only presume to know who the man who took advantage of me was. If I'd agreed to report it, there's no guarantee the police charged the correct person.

My emotions battle within, slipping out. "It doesn't seem right Morgan went to jail. It wasn't his fault."

"Who gets to judge, you? Sweetheart, the so-called rules are inconsistent and depend on where you fall in society. If Morgan was from an influential family, maybe things would have turned out different for him. But he had no one standing up for him, so it was easy for the DA to railroad him into taking a plea deal instead of going to trial. The university needed for those players to take the heat. The community used those convictions as proof they held those boys accountable, and it allowed Morgan's roommate's family to settle their case against the college without lugging it through the courts." His comments are dispassionate facts.

"It still doesn't seem fair; it ruined his chances. What if he was the next NBA all-star?" That might not have been Morgan's endgame, but "He doesn't even get to finish his degree."

Trig wipes his hands on a towel and places a palm on my shoulder. "For Morgan's sake, keep your opinions on this to yourself, Aidy," Trig advises. "He paid a high price and doesn't deserve for you to think any of his choices were wrong. Morgan's list of regrets is already a mile long."

Trig drags up a chair and hunches over so we're face to face. "Morgan's a good apprentice. He's trying to put his past behind him and move forward with the cards life dealt him. Same as I'm asking you to shield Kimber, I'd like it if you didn't dredge up Morgan's past. Unless he's telling his truth, the less who knows about it, the better off he is. We're all in this together."

For as calm as Trig's words are, the last sentence seems like a warning. Yet, I can't place why. I understand his concerns. Sloan maintains my story is my own, and she has no right to spill the beans to anyone. Outside of the group our connection is very different. I've seen her here since. She acts normal. No one would ever realize Sloan's the person I text when I get overwhelmed.

Morgan comes in a few minutes later. He's casual putting his hand on my upper back. Half of me feels like I could sprout wings underneath his palm. The other part wants to shrivel and hide. The emotions warring inside of me are too much to handle. When Morgan goes to shower, I run and hide in the guest bedroom, shooting off a message to Sloan.

> *Me: SOS*
>
> *Sloan: Are you alone? I can call.*
>
> *Me: Yes! But let me call instead.*

I hit her contact information. It only rings once before Sloan's skipping the pleasantries answering, "Are you okay?"

"I'm so lost. There's... Uh, There's this guy I'm supposed to hang out with tonight." I realize I'm panicked and my words are coming in a rush.

"Is he bothering you? I can come pick you up. Let me know where."

"No. It's the opposite. He's not doing anything wrong. I—I sort of like him," I admit. "But that's not... He won't..."

"Slow down and take a breath." She pauses, setting my mind at ease when she says, "You're safe."

My cheeks puff out and wind blows past the receiver as I let the air out of my lungs.

"You like a man."

"He's... nice."

"Go on."

"Nothing is happening between us that's more than friendly. But I keep having these thoughts, *feelings*."

"It's all perfectly normal." Sloan understands my meaning by the way I emphasized the word.

"It doesn't feel that way. It's like nuclear meltdown sirens go off." The problem isn't the way Morgan's touch makes my pulse speed up. It seems like it's too soon to consider a relationship with any man. Biological function or not, from my perspective there's a point of misplaced promiscuity to my body's response.

I hear a snicker on the other side of the line. "I'm happy for you."

"About warning bells?"

"You're acknowledging what they are, Aidy. You called because you wouldn't have reacted to the situation this way before...and you're not asking me how to make one feeling or the other go away now, are you?"

"No." It's not as if I have a chance with Morgan, but I want to know how to deal with them so I don't make a fool of myself in front of him. Or anyone else.

"They'll exist in parallel for as long as it takes. How long is up to you. Everyone heals in their own way because our experiences are unique to each of us."

"I'm afraid if someone finds out they'll judge me for, I don't know, jumping in like a love-sick puppy."

It gets silent and I'm about to ask Sloan if she's still

there before she speaks again.

"I made a lot of mistakes while I was recovering. Who am I kidding? I still do. The people who judge haven't walked a mile in your shoes. What they have to say has more to do with their perception of the way they would have lived your life. What they think they'd have done in similar circumstances and the fear they have surrounding them being hurt in the same way.

"Simply because you have feelings toward the opposite sex doesn't mean you're acting on them."

"But I don't like the mix of both feelings at once," I admit to the confusion.

"Nobody does. You bide your time waiting for one to win out. And it will at the right time *for you*. I promise."

I sigh.

"Is he cute?"

"Sloan!" I close to whisper-yell.

"Your reaction tells me all I need to understand. Enjoy his company for what it's worth. Everyone can use another friend."

"You're right." I agree with her last sentiment. Morgan definitely needs friends.

"Good lord, can I introduce you to Mister Bossy-pants and have you tell him I'm right about something? Anything?"

I laugh.

"I love Carver. He's my person. I waited what seems like forever to meet someone who loves me back unconditionally. That said, he drives me up a wall." I can hear the smile in her voice. "And someday you'll have someone there to making you crazy too. Be patient with yourself."

"I will. Thank you, Sloan."

"Anytime. Now go have some fun while you're still young and not yet in love with this handsome fella."

Chapter Thirteen

Aidy

Morgan is back in the kitchen, fresh and clean, setting the table for the three of us when I get off the phone with Sloan.

I act as if nothing is amiss and help Owen into his high chair. My nerves ease, listening to Morgan chatter on about his commute. Appreciating the home-cooked dinner, Morgan and I do the dishes when our plates are clean, and Trig heads up to bed with Owen.

We're sitting on the couch. Morgan's arm lounges over the back of the seat. His fingers absently touch the strands of my ponytail where my head rests. The tips tickle my neck and I'm trying not to let on how much it affects me.

The show we're watching ends and Morgan flips through the channels trying to find something else to entertain us.

"This is a lame night. We should go do something," he suggests.

I shrug. We've eaten, and it's drizzled most of the November day, so mini golf is out. It's been cold enough to see my breath in the morning on the way to class.

When it comes down to it, I'm fine with the night in. I'm in a safe place, getting to know someone who interests me. But I also don't want Morgan becoming bored by my company and feeling obligated to spend time with me. I'm not a laugh riot to be around. This relationship will peter out when Morgan gets a real girlfriend and feels stifled having to babysit me and Owen.

His cell dings with an incoming text.

"Cece," he says, tapping a response to his sister. "She needs an emergency chaperone. I have to walk her home tonight."

He stays put while I'm thinking we need to call 911.

"Why are you just sitting there?"

Morgan shakes his head, brow furrowing like this isn't a huge deal. "She doesn't go on stage for another hour and I think she's performing for two acts. Most of the dancers are covering for another who's had bronchitis."

I blink a few times. Of course, dancers get sick. However, I hadn't given a thought to what happens if they're in no shape to take off their clothes. I'm still trying to figure out how they go on when they get their periods, but who am I going to ask? I live in a bubble.

"Hey, wanna go hang out for a while? Some of my buddies are there. You can meet them."

"At Sweet Caroline's? Are women allowed in who aren't dancers?" I let it slide that Morgan's been inside and has seen at least part of the show. Revue? I've only ever heard Sweet Caroline's whispered about like it's a seedy dive. It could be upscale. *Please make it be like a true gentleman's club you'd see in a movie.* Morgan's family works there, and my attitude is judgmental when I haven't met Cece yet.

"Sure. Women come all the time with their

boyfriends, or girlfriends." His shoulders hit his ears and Morgan slides our shoes toward our feet. "Husbands. Wives. Anyone who's curious."

I take it we're going. Biting my lip, I summon the courage to do something new. It's not safe, and it's so far from my wheelhouse that my wagon is all the way up in New England waiting on Darius Rucker to thumb a ride south. Jesus Christ, the next thing you know I'll be smoking pot.

I stop tying my shoes and laugh because I have toked and now I'm being irrational, forgetting I'm not so good a goody-two-shoes that I've had zero life experience. I'm underage and alcohol contributed to my… Not going there.

"You okay with this?" Morgan's bemused.

"Yes." I snort. "I was thinking about one of my all-time favorite songs and it struck me as funny."

We don't say much in the van driving through Brighton. I'm nervous, even though I know I'm not the one taking my clothes off. Morgan keeps swallowing. All I can think is he's anxious I'm meeting his friends. Although, I'm not sure why.

I need to shut off the dumb romance fantasy playing in technicolor between my ears and before I get carried away.

We pull in the parking lot. Neon signs flash. It's only half as bad as I expected and that may be because the rain and dark sky give it an ominous feel. Morgan parks facing toward the two-lane street. Beyond the sidewalk is a wrought iron fence. I can see through it to where a bit of a grassy area merges with the parking spaces. The front entry of a three-story restored factory is lit up with flood lights shining in every direction. I'd expect to see in, however, the windows are all tinted like a one-way mirror reflecting what's outside and keeping the occupants' activities disguised. The wet, old, red brick exterior is a deep monochrome and green window sills give it a touch of class.

"Is that the mill?" I ask, suddenly curious about who and what's inside.

"Yeah, we can come back another day when everyone's at home." He reminds me actual people live there.

Morgan pulls his key from the steering column. "There's something I gotta tell you." His words rush out.

"Uh." Door fee? I am expected to strip? My neurons fire in fifty-seven different directions.

"I work here too."

"Doing what!" My mind finds all the other possibilities I hadn't yet considered.

"Kimber hired me to barback and I bounce, work the door a few nights a week."

"Kimber, my birth mother, the person who—"

"I manage a bar, Dumplin'," she told me.

It strikes me I hadn't plied Kimber for more information, simply took her words at face value, and figured she was a glorified hostess at Applebees' or one of those nifty craft beer places with "growler" in the name which keep popping up on every corner.

A normal person would've dug. Me? I was so damn happy my birth mother wanted anything to do with me that I gave her a free pass so I could see my brother. I told myself it didn't matter Kimber had a menial job when she had a degree. My mom has a masters and she's a housewife.

"Let's go inside." I need to see this for myself for any of it to make sense.

"Hey, man." Morgan bumps knuckles with the bouncer at the door. We slide in like butter spreading on warm toast. The immense room is as dark as it is outside. There's cheesy velour fabric on the seats and leather, *pleather?* on the stools. The floors have lit pathways like the faint lights that turn on in an aircraft cabin and the music is loud.

Morgan's had his hand pressed to my lower back and he nearly stumbles over me as I take it all in. The customers, the waitresses, *the dancer on stage*. His arm wraps protectively around my middle, forcing my feet to move.

"Come on. I'll get us drinks."

"Water. Bottled water. Cap on."

"Don't worry Aidy, You won't catch anything here. I've run the dishwasher before. The glasses are sanitized," he jokes.

Over at the long bar, scantily clad female bartenders scurry back and forth with smiles on their faces. It reminds me of how nonchalant the girls who stole in the drugstore had been. A flash of red hair whips around. The woman places a scotch on the rocks on the bar, collects a wad of cash, and dumps it in a tip jar. Then she playfully spanks the barmaid next to her on the butt to get her to move so she can move past. They both start giggling, though I can't hear the sound over the thump of the bass.

Kimber wiggles her fingers, mouthing she'll be back to the others. She turns. Blue eyes meet mine as Kimber moves out from behind the bar. As she catches sight of me, the smile falters and Kimber has to plaster it back on.

"Dumplin', what are you doing here?" She holds her arms wide, bringing me into a protective hug.

I mumble something about Cece and meeting up with Morgan's friends. "It doesn't bother you I came?"

"Of course not, I'm just surprised to see you."

Not as much as I am.

"Hey, Morgan," She rubs his arm. "I was about to make next week's schedule. Mind taking a look at when I have you down for?"

He shakes his head. "Lemme get Aidy set up and I'll be right over."

Morgan guides me to a round booth at the side of the room and I sit with my back to the stage. "You'll be okay here?" It's more of a statement.

Shock and the awe over my surroundings have me unable to respond.

Morgan walks back to the bar where Kimber's got a notebook out and is penciling things in. On the way over, he taps a younger man with cropped black hair on the shoulder and tosses his thumb back in my direction, saying something I can't hear.

The guy, dressed in a dark button-down and black trousers, gets up and walks over. "So you're the infamous Aidy?" he holds out his hand to shake. "Jasper Somers. It's nice to finally meet you."

"You're Sloan's brother." His almond shaped-eyes are the identical shade as hers, and they have the same skin tone that reminds me of the surfers on the big island in Hawaii. The familiarity allows me to relax a fraction, but I start wringing my hands in plain sight because I have nothing to keep them busy.

"In the flesh." He chuckles. "Mind if I keep you company."

Seeing as Morgan's sent Jasper over here, it doesn't do me much good to say no. I glance over to where Kimber and Morgan are. They're staring at me.

"Is Kimber upset at Morgan for bringing me here?"

"If she was, you'd already be out in the parking lot. Kimber is pretty much the least judgmental person on the planet."

"Eek!" A squeal emanates from the side and I'm crowded into the booth by a brunette in a silk robe. "I knew it was you! I saw you come in from behind the curtain and I wasn't letting Morgan get away with not introducing us."

"Uh, how'd you know it was me?" And who is this person?

"The hair. I think at first I expected you to look like

Kimber—and up close you do. Anyhow, your mom was like the most amazing dancer. When I started here, she was a performer and I swear she still kicks all of our asses during warm-ups and rehearsals."

"She's not my mom." My clipped response is the complete opposite of the way Jasper has described Kimber a moment earlier. I'm ashamed as it slips from my lips because it's obvious everyone here has the utmost respect for Kimber. I want to sink into oblivion when Jasper tells Cece to tone down her enthusiasm.

"Oh, I'm sorry. I'm not on anything. I thought Morgan was keeping you all to himself forever."

My brow flares. What is that supposed to mean?

"He came to walk you home." I try to act normal. Morgan's sister is being nothing but kind to me. Her excitement seems genuine and there's humor in Celine not wanting me to think she's stoned. We both want to make a good impression on the other. "We didn't have anything going on, so we showed up early," I say as if Morgan and I are a package deal.

Cece smiles. Stage makeup accentuates her exceptional beauty. She has big brown eyes that match her long brown hair. A bunch of men continue glancing at her from behind their glasses—both the ones on the bridge of their nose and the ones filled with liquid courage they're hiding behind. She notices I've noticed.

"Ever been to Sweet Caroline's before? I've gotten used to ignoring the stares. I can't even see these guys when I'm on stage and the light is glaring in my face." She tips the crown of her head like a princess who is unafraid her tiara might fall. "You're good here. This is Jake's table and the patrons are as scared of him as anyone else is, so they won't approach you. Don't worry."

"I'm not…It's all…No, I've never been to this kind of club before," I admit.

"The more times you do, the less extraordinary it

becomes." Cece acts as if I'll be at Sweet Caroline's as frequently as she is. It's a weird sort of welcome.

Morgan

I pull a sealed bottle of water out of a fridge behind the bar and Holly hands me a new concoction Kimber's experimenting on to taste test. I drop a ten in the tip jar.

"Take your money back, douche canoe." She fishes it out.

"I'm off tonight."

Holly lifts the edge of her bralette and pulls out a five, tucking the original bill I gave her into its place. My hands are full so her manicured fingertips shove the other half of the money in my front pocket, pulling me close as she does. "Spend it on your girl."

I don't bother correcting her. If I could be so damn lucky.

By the time I get back to the table, Cece's gone, but Jasper's stayed put the way I'd asked him to. Aidy looks as if she's having a decent time. Although, I'm sure it's been unnatural for her in a strange venue with fucked up sociological rules. Not that it makes a difference, but I wonder if Aidy's realized how much further up the food chain she ranks than I do because of Kimber.

My butt slides into the booth, touching Aidy's and the water goes in front of her. I taste my drink. "Have you tried this one yet?" I ask Jasper. "It's decent. Missing something, though."

"Yeah, the booze," he barbs, taking the glass I offer.

I hold the cup up for Aidy. She shakes her head, so I place it back on the table and she opens her water bottle.

"If you will excuse me, I'm going to check on my girl." Jasper holds up his cell.

"Does she come here too?"

I choke, trying not to laugh. Carver would have a conniption if Jasper's girlfriend got past a bouncer. "Nope. She's away at school and his boss is wicked overprotective of her."

"Jasper's dating his boss's daughter."

We're speaking close so we can hear one another over the din. I tip my drink before taking another sip, acknowledging Aidy got it right.

"I'm on information overload." Palms with straight fingers hit the sides of Aidy's face, reminiscent of the guy in that shrieking painting. "Is she mad at you?"

"Kimber? Nah, it really was a schedule thing. Listen, I'm sorry I didn't know you didn't know—"

Hoots and hollering as the next dancer comes out on stage cut me off. Aidy takes advantage. "It's not your fault. I guess I let people tell me what I want to hear instead of pressing for answers."

"Sometimes there's stuff you're better off not knowing until you need to."

"How did you ever get a job here?" It's obvious what Aidy's trying to figure out is how her bio-mom wound up in a place like this. But she's attempting to ask questions, which is a huge step forward given what she's just said.

I feel like the douche canoe Holly called me,

recognizing nobody had been upfront with Aidy. I'd taken what she knew for granted.

"I walked Cece a few times when I first got out. Kimber wanted to know if I was interested in extra hours since I was hanging around waiting for my sister anyway. It gives me some extra pocket change."

My hours at Sweet Caroline's are under the table. My student loans are in default, I have a fuck ton of legal bills, and the powers that be garnish the wages in my actual paycheck. There's not a lot left at the end of the month. I'm not sure how I'd be able to afford rent.

Trig keeps telling me not to worry. He's got my back, and it's all going to even out. But my boss and his wife —also my boss—do so much for me that whenever they need a helping hand with Owen, or anything else, I jump on it.

"So, ah, Cece said this is Jake's booth. Should we be sitting here?" she asks with wide-eyed trepidation.

"He never shows if Kimber is managing."

"Why not?"

"Depending on where he is in his cycle, Jake hates women."

"That doesn't sound great for a man who owns a strip club."

"Now you get why Kimber's the manager everyone respects, especially the dancers since she's been there and won't put up with their drama."

Aidy looks at Kimber with a deeper sense of pride and that's saying something since the only time I've seen it take a hit was the initial shock when she walked into the bar. "Everyone does what she says. It's sort of amazing. I didn't grasp—"

"She treats us like family, which is good since a lot of us don't have one."

"Cece?"

"My sister could have washed her hands of me. I don't take it lightly. And Jasper's the same with Sloan."

"What's that supposed to mean?" She leans forward defensively.

"It's not my place to say, Sweet Pea. But looks can be deceiving, and not everything is perfect. Everybody's got baggage—even if it's something dumb like forgiving a sibling for breaking your favorite toy when you were a kid."

The crowd is clapping as Jasper comes back with a shit-eating grin. "Want my spot? Cece is about to go on."

"Shut up." I ball a napkin and throw it across the table.

"You don't watch?" Aidy asks, curious.

"Not if I can help it."

"Do you mind if I do?" Aidy swings herself around so she's up on her knees, peering over the back of the seat.

Jasper's appreciation for her backside is obvious.

"Stop it, fuckface." I mouth.

His finger motions back and forth between Aidy and me, wanting to know if I'm interested in her.

Kimber floats nearby the table on her way to the back office. Jasper makes an "ah" and taps his head as if I'm smart to think about my actions beforehand. It's pretty much all I do in my room; ruminate over Aidy. Too often with my hand wrapped around my dick.

"Oh my god, She's really good!" Aidy's impressed when Celine ends her performance.

"I keep trying to tell him." Jasper mocks.

"What if it were your sister up there?"

"I got no qualms. However, if Jake hired Sloan, Carver's the one Jake should worry about burning Sweet Caroline's to the ground."

"Skye still up north?" I ask as we settle into the conversation.

"Yup, and Dusty took his Bruce Banner persona home before his alter-ego appeared."

"What's he pissed about?"

"Got me." Jasper leans back, indifferent. If it weren't for the fact he treats his girlfriend like gold, I'd wonder if he cared for anyone but himself.

A while later, Cece's beckoning us down the hall to the back exit with her bag slung over her shoulder, ready to go. The music doesn't carry and Aidy asks to see the dressing room. I'm holding up a wall for the next eternity until they reappear. Cece and Aidy titter like little birds on the way to the parking lot as if I don't exist.

We reach the light pole I've intentionally parked the van underneath, and I open the passenger door for Aidy. "I hate to tear y'all apart." I jest. It's nice to see them getting along. Now that Aidy's been to Sweet Caroline's I can bring her more places with me when we get together. "Mind waiting here while I have a moment with Celine?"

Aidy gives me a cheery "Nope", saying her goodbye to Cece and promising to come back another night that we're having a tough time figuring out what we want to do. I hand over the keys so she can warm up the cab. She locks the door as soon as it closes.

Celine and I jog across the road to the sidewalks. I look over my shoulder while crossing the street.

I'd convinced myself that my company tonight bored Aidy stiff. Us sitting on the sofa, flipping through channels seems further away than a few hours ago. I'm grateful the night is ending on a different note.

I can see Aidy and, the way the property is lit past the stone entrance, our profiles are on full display.

"Thanks." Celine tugs me into a hug as our shoes hit the last step before the entrance.

"Your safety is never a problem. I was glad to come out." I glance around. Things are quiet. Although, it doesn't mean much if someone is hiding in the bushes. Hence all the floodlights. "Who's bugging you?"

Cece rubs her arms through her jacket. "It's Dusty.

He's a great guy." Her stance softens. "He gets in the way of the paying clientele." My sister was damn good at throwing our parents off her scent as a teenager, but I know she's keeping something hidden.

"You're not—" My jaw clenches. Carver may not give a damn if what the girls do on their time as long as it doesn't touch his property. But I'll be damned if my sister turns tricks to afford her tuition. The idea of her giving lap dances for extra tips makes me want to shudder.

"No!" Celine's palm touches my chest reassuringly.

"Then why are you so worried about Dusty being out here at night? He hasn't come on to you, has he?"

My sister gives a rather unconvincing shake of the head, glancing at the van. "Do you like her?"

My lips twist. "Great deflection."

Cece shoves my shoulder. "She's your type, minus the purple hair."

"Maybe she was, once. I have nothing to give a girl like her, and she knows it."

"That's not true. Carver and Trig have given you a second chance. No different than Jake and Carver helping me get through school, so I don't have to turn into what you accused me of a minute ago."

"I didn't accuse you—"

"I'm teasing, Morgan. Have faith in me, I won't do anything to ruin the good I've got. Things are looking up for you too. Maybe Aidy is part of that?"

"I live in Trig's attic and work under the table for Kimber to pay off my debt." I remind Celine. "Aidy needs a friend right now. That's all we are."

My sister ticks points off on her fingers. "I'm not dumb. I see what goes on between the club and inside these walls. I know to keep my mouth shut and not question the stuff that makes no sense to me. You'd have no place to stay or a job if these guys didn't trust you. Trig wouldn't let you around Aidy either. He and

Kimber are protective of her. I lived on the third floor with Kimber for years before finding out she had a daughter—and it was only from pictures at their house. It was nice to have the chance to meet her in person." I think Celine is finished until she rattles off, "And, dumbass, girls don't agree to go to anyplace like Sweet Caroline's with a guy if they aren't at least a little interested." She challenges me to say I don't want Aidy.

I do. I want Aidy in all the ways possible. Most of which, I worry about since I haven't been with a woman since before I was incarcerated.

"I went to prison." I remind Celine.

"You paid the price for something you did. not. do." Cece hates my decision to plead guilty. She argues free will and the guys who kept feeding Rob drinks were the ones culpable. "I won't tell you I'm glad you took responsibility. However, the fact remains you did. Have you ever stopped to ponder whether Aidy *is* the silver lining? She was who was waiting for you when you got out."

"I'm not tarnishing her reputation, Cece."

"Fuck that. You're a good person, Morgan." Her flat hand moves, tapping the middle of my chest. "Right now, you're doing what you have to do to get by since the future you'd planned got ripped away by a bunch of rich people and their fucking fleabag lawyers. It's all the more reason to take back what you deserve."

Chapter Fifteen

Aidy

I've tried not to make it seem like I'm spying, but the angle the parked van sits at makes it useless. Morgan hugs his sister and waits for Cece to use her key to get inside the old factory building. He even pulls on the door handle afterward to ensure it's locked behind her. I can't help smiling over how thoughtful he is. It's then that the night strikes me as funny. Like a schoolgirl, I've broken out in a fit of giggles by the time Morgan is jogging back across the street.

I hit the button to unlock the van. Morgan gets inside, looking at me like I'm a crazy person, wondering what he's missed.

My hands slap to my lap. It's me who failed to acknowledge the signs. I try to be pragmatic, but take things at face value because I've never considered anyone was out to deceive me. Unable to catch my breath, I recall how I've spent the past few hours at a strip club. The Aidy I thought I was wouldn't have sat around with two men, surrounded by a hoard more voyeurs, watching women take off their clothes. More to the point, I had fun tonight. How messed up is that given the circumstances?

"Oh my God!" I cackle. "You must think I'm such an idiot. My birth mother manages a strip club and the closest I'll ever get to having a hot boyfriend is a convicted felon who escorts an exotic dancer home each night."

Morgan blinks. "What did you say?"

"I'm an idiot?"

"After that."

"Ah, Kimber is your sister's boss?" I bite my nails, watching Morgan's curiosity pique. The sinful twitch of his brow shows me his concern isn't me missing Kimber is his boss too. "You're a felon?" I feel awful for blurting it out.

His finger twirls in the air. "In between those."

"You're the closest I'll get to a hot boyfriend?" It's said even lower than I'd brought up his conviction. Thank goodness the dome light has gone out and Morgan can't see how red my face is. I didn't mean to humiliate him and deserve to have my words thrown back at me.

"I'm not hot?" He's acting a little cockier than normal.

"That's what you picked up from me running my mouth off? Yes, you're hot." Has the man not seen himself in the mirror?

"Then how can I be the *closest* to hot?"

"No. You're the closest to a boyfriend. The hot part is proof of—I don't even know." I cover my face, muttering what a fool I am.

"Aidy." Morgan moves my hands. "I can't be your boyfriend."

"No kidding."

He places a finger over my lips. The simple touch has me warming all over.

"You gotta shut up for half a second, Sweet Pea."

My jaw drops as Morgan leans in. His breath is soft against my ear. "As I see it, we'd have to do more than you letting me hold your hand at the beach on occasion. Or me pretending to yawn in the hopes you're not offended when I try to tuck an arm around you. I haven't kissed you. And like hell is the first time I do it going to be in a utility truck. So maybe tomorrow, I pick you up, take you out, and—if you want me to when I drop you off—we'll take care of the formalities. That way you can have something close to a hot boyfriend."

"You wanna kiss me?"

"I do. But I'm not doing it unless it's what you want. What do you say, dinner tomorrow?"

I worry my lip. I haven't been on a so-called date since the night of the attack. Even then, I went to the party more to have a good time than entertain romantic notions. I'd mistakenly guessed I was going to get to know Brandon the way Morgan and I had at the beach.

For the first time, I see the sunny morning in an alternate light. It was a new beginning. I had the courage to dip my toes in the water and try again. The person who I sat on the beach with was tenfold the man whom I thought I was agreeing to spend time with. It's how he overshadows every negative.

"We don't have to," he concedes with disappointment when I don't say yes right away.

"I want to." My words rush out faster than the flub that got me the date of my dreams. And my first thought is how much I want to call my mom to tell her.

"Look at this one." Hangers scrape across the metal

rod. Mom holds up a dress in my size. It's blue with buttons down the front. "This is very you." She holds the garment close to me, the way she fitted my clothes when I was a child. "It will bring out your eyes, Aidy."

This shopping trip to the mall was to get a new tablecloth and a few festive decorations for Thanksgiving, which is in a few weeks. My mom was thrilled I'd agreed to come along. We haven't spent much time together recently. I'd waited until we were in the car to mention I had a date. My excitement and the fact it's the most information I've shared about anything in my life over the past two-and-a-half months became contagious. Once Mom spotted what she was after, she changed our target to finding me something to wear.

"I'm not sure." I tug at the hem. It's long enough to graze my knees and the dress's sleeves are rolled and tacked with buttons to three-quarter length. "I have a lot of dresses in my closet already," I hedge. I haven't worn a single one of my go-to favorite wardrobe pieces all semester.

Mom flips the tag over. "The price is right."

I worked last summer and have the cash. I shouldn't feel any guilt. I do, but not about spending. It's over keeping my secret from the one person I'd thought I'd be able to tell anything to. The more I talk with Sloan, the more I realize I shouldn't be ashamed of what happened to me. Some days that's easier said than done. Yet, as much as I refuse to believe my mom would be ashamed of me either, I don't want to relive the pain through her eyes. I don't want her to see me as anything more than who I was.

"The fabric is a little light. I may be cold."

"You buy the dress I'll pitch in for a sweater. You love dresses, Aidy, and you wear them so well. They're your style."

"Mom, I have a coat if I need it and a million other

dresses."

She concedes quicker than I expect. "Then let's stop at the salon while you're home and I'll pay for you to get your hair recolored."

"What's wrong with my hair?" I have it pulled up in a corkscrew pony today and touch a lock at the base of my neck the way Morgan had the night he asked me out.

"The red is so beautiful. I'm not sure why you had to go changing it. He might like it better—"

"I think Morgan might like it the way it is."

Mom frowns.

"What's more important is I like it the way it is. If Morgan wants to control my hair color, he can take a flying leap."

"Aidy," Mom scolds as if I've screamed to everyone in Marshall's I'm Sweet Caroline's newest headline dancer. Meanwhile, my tone has been conversational. I'm not sure what her issue is. "How are you going to get a job with purple hair?"

"Have you looked around, Mom? There are women your age here who look like this." I point to my ponytail.

"A professional job."

"I'm a sophomore. There's over two years before I have to worry."

"I want people to take you seriously, Sweetheart."

"Whatever." The word comes out smug, but my derisiveness isn't directed as much to my mom as it is to the idea that my red hair had made my attacker take me seriously.

Mom grabs me by the arm. "Aidy, what has gotten into you lately?"

"Nothing."

"You're overreacting. This isn't like you."

I sigh, rolling my eyes underneath closed eyelids, praying for the strength to keep my demons hidden and give my mother the respect she deserves. "Have you considered adulting is still new to me? I moved out for the school year. Came back home for the summer. Then, like boomerang, I'm back on campus again. Maybe all that change has made it harder to figure out who I am and dyeing my hair purple is part of growing up." *WOW! Where on earth did that self-actualized comment come from?*

I hang the dress on the rack. I love my mom so much. She's only ever done what's best for me and seeing how other friends didn't get the benefit of parents like mine, it makes me admire Mom all the more. She gave up her career for me, so I had every opportunity. I don't want Mom to believe turning me into a successful human being was all for naught. But I still deserve to take chances and learn from my mistakes without the decisions she doesn't approve of being thrown in my face.

"Listen, it means a lot we came into this shop to look around. I miss doing this with you. But I probably have something in my closet that'll suffice. Do you think we can go to the food court instead and talk?"

Mom's expression goes from downcast to cheery. She offers to buy us drinks.

"How about it's on me since I'm saving my pennies by not getting another dress? Baked Beans, the coffee shop Kimber raves about, opened a location new here. I haven't tried it yet, but hear it's great."

We get into line at the store and Mom asks about Owen as we wait for the barista to finish making our lattes. Once we're seated, she inquires about Morgan.

"He's a little older than me and he works for Trig's security company."

"Did he go to college?"

"Yes, for a few years anyhow. He makes good money and I get the impression he enjoys the people he works with."

We have plumbers in the family, so my mother is quick to ignore Morgan hasn't finished school. "If you were still home, you know Daddy would expect to meet him first."

"Mooom, I've been on first dates without Dad's approval before. Did you introduce Dad to your parents before going out with him?"

"I was away at school." I point at mom. She wraps her hand around it, folding it back to my palm. "Point taken, Aidy. We worry about you. You're all we've got."

I lean in and give my mom a hug.

"We do get to meet Morgan, though?"

"If I don't blow it! We hung out before he ever asked me out, so I hope this date won't ruin a good thing. Sometimes I think my nervousness around him shows."

"You like him."

"I do." I want my mom to like Morgan enough so, when she and my dad find out he has a record, it's something they can look past or at least take with a grain of salt. My dad is a bankruptcy lawyer with a big firm downtown. It's not like he hasn't represented people who've asked for second chances. "Oh!" I cross my fingers, squeezing my eyes shut. "Kimber and Trig are going away for New Year's with their friends. I told them I'd watch Owen for a few days. Maybe if things are going well over Christmas break I'll invite Morgan to come by?"

"That sounds lovely." Mom beams.

I blow out a breath because every so often it's nice to relax into the moment with someone who you love and appreciate things *are* going the right way. A tendril floats up. Mom catches it, sliding the hair behind my ear without another comment on the color.

Chapter Sixteen

Morgan

There are no installs today, so I'm biding my time at the mill doing odd jobs. One thing I can say for this place is it's never boring.

"Don't drop this on my toes." Skye grunts, blowing his blond hair out of his face as we lift the pool table in the oversized common area.

"Why is it going a foot to the left and twelve inches to the right?" I joke back.

"Because this is Sloan's house, and when your boss says you're moving multiple two-ton pieces of furniture for his woman because she thinks they'll be too close to the Christmas tree, you do it."

The old floors creek as we set the weight back down. This building is all that and a bag of chips. The bright living space opens to a party porch out back. There are large wooden tables for us to eat at near the doors to the kitchen. Its industrial-sized fridges are not only stocked with everything you could imagine—most of it fresh from the local farmer's market—but the kitchen itself looks like somebody awarded the lunch lady a million dollars to spruce up the place. That said, I hope when Carver was sparing no expense, it included a top-notch structural engineer. The pool table is weighty enough to fall through the floor. We have two more to move and Sloan wants the couches realigned to match the "aesthetics" of the room since this is where she entertains. Their apartment is off-limits, which I suppose makes sense if you work where you live and a lot of your employees have access to you in your bunny slippers on the way to the coffee pot before sunrise.

I snort inward. There's nothing warm and fuzzy about Carver except Sloan.

We shimmy the next one over and Skye sighs. "I'm bushed. After we're done rearranging, I'm out of here for the weekend." His plane landed a few hours ago and Skye had just walked up the stairs when Carver gave us instructions to play moving men. Skye threw his duffle on the floor and got to it. He's still wearing yesterday's rumpled traveling clothes and, with the corn-fed midwestern boy look about him, I'm glad he doesn't smell like a cow pasture.

I'm not sure why Skye was out of town and don't know where he disappears to. But over the past six months, I've noticed it's a pattern. Every few weeks Skye jets off, comes back, and then goes missing. There are so many people who live here, so many personalities, it's hard to keep up with everyone. I've also adopted the mentality that making it my business makes it my problem. If Skye wanted to share, he would. The guy is personable almost to a fault and a huge flirt with the girls. Yet, today dark circles and flyer fatigue have him exuding exhaustion.

"Got weekend plans?" he asks as we let go of the last set of edges and wipes his brow adding, "These table legs are as thick as Dusty's beast biceps."

"Not so much for the weekend, but I have a date tonight." We heft the first of the sofas.

"No shit? She hot?" Skye's shock doesn't surprise me. I haven't gone out with anyone since well before my incarceration. The guys tell me about their love lives, not in fucking girlie-detail, but Skye has kicked my leg a few times with a not-so-subtle thumbs-up to signify a woman will come along to give my hand a rest so I'm not stuck jerking off forever. He's got the impression I'm picky. Maybe I am now.

"Depends on what you think of Kimber."

"Fuuudge, man." There are hard footsteps on the stairs coming up from the lobby. Dusty ignores us on his way to fix something on the third floor while the girls are all out for the day. Skye waits until he's out of earshot to continue. "Stay the fuck away from Kimber. Like, move out of Trig's. Now."

"It's her daughter."

"No shit? That's a different story. Mini-Kimber, and no ass beating from an overprotective papa. I can get on board with those odds. So you like her or do you have a Ginger Spice kink you're working out?"

A throw pillow has fallen from the couch and I throw it at him. Skye laughs, catching it and stuffing it back on to the cushions.

"I'm kidding." He flops on the sofa. "And you answered my question."

I take a spot on the final couch we have yet to move, mirroring his slouch. I've had second thoughts since asking Aidy out last night.

"I don't have a ton to offer her. Seriously, she's in college. I got kicked out. Her adoptive parents are well off. I'm broke. I'm fucking picking her up in a windowless utility truck like a perv whenever we go anywhere." The night I'd rescued Aidy up from the party replays through my mind. I'm judging myself the way the campus cop disapproved of my ride. I scrub my scalp.

"Man, if Aidy agreed to go out with you, and deep

down she's anything like Kimber, that kind of crap don't matter."

"Nature versus nurture?"

Skye pshaws, waving his hand. "That's akin to saying Cece isn't a good person because of the parents you had. Give her some credit. You ever wonder how your sister got here? It was more than the way she was shimmying her hips and pulling in customers. She had initiative. Drive. Carver and Jake don't choose the girls from Sweet Caroline's who get rooms upstairs at random. They vet those women and they won't take anyone less than meets their standard. Cece was handpicked. They only want the best. Looks. Talent. Brains."

"That's fucking creepy. What if my sister was smart but butt ugly? Or a knock-out and dumb as a rock?" Not for the first time, I wonder what *else* goes on around here that I'm not supposed to be privy to.

"Don't be a putz where you don't know why Carver gives them a chance." Skye gets defensive.

"So enlighten me."

"Carver and Jake go way back. Their mothers danced together at Sweet Caroline's. I guess Carver's momma was a knock-out, but she didn't fare quite as well as Caroline did."

"Hold on, there's an actual Caroline?"

"There is. She's my aunt and a tough old broad. Although, I'll kick you in the nads if you say a damn thing against her. Jake you can talk shit all you want about. It's probably true anyhow."

I'm reeling that Skye and Jake are cousins. Their personalities are polar opposite. The unusual scolding tone Skye's using with me—the one Jake likes to take with everyone—is to get my head out of my ass.

"The ladies on the third floor don't get held back the way Carver's momma did. Whatever quality he finds in them gets fostered. You think Jake likes handing his best source of revenue over? Celine would be stripping a lot longer if she had to pay her rent and three squares a day."

"So what does he get in return? Jake's not the hearts and flowers type." More like kick a puppy. Well, maybe it's an exaggeration. He'd growl and bark back louder. Piss on its leg.

"A piece of the mill." Skye doesn't mean the actual building. He's alluding to what's going on in his office, Carver's frequent absences, the installs Trig has me do, and the surveillance happening when I'm not around.

I shake my head to clear my mind.

"Have you figured out why you're here, bootstrapper?"

"Huh?"

"Mull it over. Everyone says you're smart, but maybe Trig fucked up when he did your background check. Doubtful. But possible. Also—" Skye shifts his hand to his jeans pocket and tosses me a set of keys.

"Fuck, these aren't to the Maserati?"

"Hell, no. I've got my own set of wheels. Drop me off when we're done playing interior decorator and you can borrow it for the night. It's like a pumpkin, though I want it back before midnight.

On the way to drop Skye off, I learn a lot about him. Namely, he trusts me. In a place shrouded in secrecy, trust goes a long way.

Skye had come from the airport and since it's winter, he wasn't parking the motorcycle he rides most days in the garage there. It's why he drove this car and how I wound up finding out where he disappeared to.

He shrugs off his comment about the car having a curfew, but the way his palm slides over the ragtop convertible, it's obvious it means something to him. I hadn't thought he'd have more sentimental feelings for another machine than he has for his bike.

I check the time on my phone as I approach Aidy's dorm. I'm still getting the vehicle back at a reasonable hour, and I've been taking it easier on the slick streets than I ever do with the van. Standing under an overhang at her dorm, I text Aidy to let her know I've arrived. She's out of the entrance a few minutes later, looking amazing.

Her hair is up off her neck, but those few violet tendrils begging for me to touch them have fallen to her neck. She's got on a navy blue dress, lighter leggings and short leather boots, which match her jacket. I've never seen Aidy in a dress and my jaw is on the doorstep with how feminine she is out of her jeans, tees and bulky sweatshirts.

"You clean up nice," she compliments while I roll my tongue back into my mouth.

I flub trying to tell her how pretty she is. Why are we always so clumsy in these moments when other times were so at ease with the other?

Aidy's cheeks pinken to the same shade as her hair. I glance at my jeans and the button down I have rolled at the sleeves. Then I open up an umbrella for us to dodge the raindrops under. Aidy lets me guide her to the convertible, and I wait until she's settled inside before closing her in.

"Hungry?" I sit behind the wheel and shake off the wet weather.

She nods and smiles, biting her lip. I'd kiss Aidy now cause the anticipation is getting to me, but I want to show her a nice time first. Being rusty at this, I passed my plan by Skye. He told me I was overthinking since

Aidy and I are already having a good time together.

"The restaurant is a hole in the wall, but always packed. I go there all the time. I think you'll like it." I ramble. Rain is beating on the hood.

"Morgan, you have to start the car for us to go anywhere."

"Sorry, I—I haven't done this in a long time. Taken anyone out."

Aidy looks shyly at her lap. I catch a hint of her front tooth as she tries not to bite down again. "I'm nervous too." Her nose scrunches up. Still no freckles, Aidy's skin is porcelain white and luminescent in the street lamps. She covers her lips so she doesn't snicker. "I feel so stupid when I laugh, you know? Immature."

"I like it when you laugh. When you smile." I lick my lips right as Aidy glances up. "I like you, Aidy." Worry creases my brow. What if I never have enough to give someone as special as she is?

"We could put the whole thing to rest—Kiss and go back to, I don't know—whatever we've been doing."

"But if it doesn't work out, you've gotten dressed up for nothing and we'll both still be hungry. Can't let a meal go to waste." I give her a sly grin. The humid air in the car is heavy, weighing us down with hypotheticals.

"You don't have to kiss me. We can go dutch."

I touch the side of Aidy's face. "Yeah, I do. But I said not in the van and the same goes for the car. You're stuck with me for at least one more evening."

"Okay," she whispers.

The intimacy of the moment lingers. But, by the time we're on the road, Aidy's chattering about her day and a class she enjoys. Psychology of something-or-other that has to do with students. Aidy's an education major. I'd thought it was for elementary school, but come to find out she's studying secondary ed, and thinks maybe she'd like to coach high school softball.

Chapter Seventeen

"Color me impressed." Morgan holds the door to the Mongolian barbecue restaurant open. "The way you are with Owen, I figured you wanted to be a kindergarten teacher."

The scent of warm garlic, soy, and honey, and the sizzle of the large steel drum where the food cooks assault my sense. We stand waiting for the hostess. Diners pack the large room, leaving few open spots.

"I think we got here in the nick of time," I say as the hostess hands me the menu. I shrug off my jacket and Morgan puts my menu down.

"You don't need that. Come on." He snags me by the wrist so I'll stand. His fingers caress the underside at my pulse point. I only hesitate long enough to ask if it's okay to leave the coat behind.

"Yup, bring your purse, though."

We get to a long bar filled with vegetables and Morgan hands me a bowl. "Filler up, Sweet Pea. All you can eat." He uses a pair of tongs to place a single green pod in my bowl and begins heaping his full of zucchini, carrots, onions, and bean sprouts before heading on to a second bar with meat options. The final stop is the grill where the chef topples our bowls. At least ten other meals are cooking on the round skillet.

The knives they use to push the meat and veggies around on the skillet are swordlike and as long as my arms. The chef who took our meals notices me watching in awe and starts juggling them. I can't help but enjoy the show. I've never been to a place like this before. A second chef's knives are tap-tap-tapping and crack a raw egg, frying it for someone else's dinner.

"I want to add one of those next time." I lean up to say in Morgan's ear. He lays a gentle hand on my neck and while it doesn't linger long on my back, shivers run up my spine.

"I was hoping you'd like it here."

As each meal comes off, a chef grabs a huge scraper to clean the grill. The whole process is as interesting as it is entertaining.

Morgan waits until both our meals are finished grilling before we head back to our table.

"I love food!" Morgan moans, digging into the first bite.

I've noticed the man eats a salad faster than I do a piece of pizza. I'm a borderline junk-food junkie, and he's the one who talks me out of country-fried steak for a Mexican-style bean bowl. He's told me prison food was awful. The way he indulges makes my heart sing for him.

Morgan has been out of jail for longer than he was confined. I admire the way he still appreciates what he didn't have for those months.

I also love how similar and different our current dinners are. Morgan suggested the same house specialty marinade so the underlying spices are the same. Mine is full of beef, noodles and bell peppers while Morgan's is mostly veggies and chicken. We use chopsticks to pick off of one another's plates and try a bit of each.

"Tell me more about your courses," he inquires, eating up details of the psych class I'm taking along with the meal.

It's so good that we're finished before it seems possible.

"What do we do now?" I wipe my mouth and place the napkin down on my lap.

Morgan puts his on the empty plate at his spot across from me. "We couldn't find anything to watch last night so I figured maybe we'd try the movies? It's a little tamer than Sweet Caroline's."

"Not if we see *Moulin Rouge* or oh, what's the old Demi Moore movie?" I snap my fingers. "*Striptease!*"

"You're funny, Sweet Pea." He leans forward. "What did you think of Sweet Caroline's?"

"It was weird at first. Weirder Kimber works there. But after I got over the initial shock and we were hanging out with Jasper, I had a good time. I forgot we were anyplace I'd been told was unseemly."

"Are you okay that I work there?"

I shrug. "Do you gawk at the girls?"

"God, no. The first time I saw Cece" Morgan shivers. "Geez, Aidy. No. It's like my brain pops their heads off and puts my sister's on top." Morgan covers his eyes. "I used to do that to her dolls. It made Celine so mad. She said those toys would come back and stalk me like I was Sid strapping a bottle rocket to Buzz Lightyear. Don't laugh." His chortle is as loud as mine. "And don't speak a word of this. She can't know she was right in any way."

"Well, then it's settled. If you're worried I'm worried it's not like Kimber or Cece wouldn't narc on you, right?"

"Given Trig threatened to cut my balls off, I think everyone is Team Aidy."

"He did not! When?"

"The first night we took off to the beach. Listen, I keep my job at Sweet Caroline's to grab a few more bucks. If it's a huge deal, I can quit. But I have to draw the line at walking my sister home. Her safety is more important than anyone's hurt feelings or jealousy. We've only got each other. Cece calls and I'm there."

"I can respect your reasons, Morgan." In actuality, I appreciate he brought it up. "Do you mind if I tag along sometimes?"

"I was hoping you would. I'd like you to meet everyone. Be comfortable with the people I work with."

I snag my purse again after Morgan tosses enough cash on the table to settle our tab. "I'd like you to meet my friends too. Although since someone's been taking up a lot of my free time this semester, it's only my roommate, Hailey, who counts. She's around until the weekend."

Morgan pauses in the restaurant lobby. "Driving to Brighton isn't cutting into your study time? Bring your books, I'll cram with you. Maybe I'll learn something new or useful."

"You will?"

"I didn't *fail* out of college." He shrugs. "Are you still considering transferring to another school?"

Transferring to the university Morgan had gotten kicked out of was one of my many escape plans. The problem was, I'd have to wait months for an acceptance. Once the admissions office read this semester's transcript, I'd be doomed to stay anyhow. "No. Maybe my major."

I don't want Morgan to know going to Kimber's was the best way I'd found to get away from campus without explaining my actions to anyone. He faces his problems. I run from mine.

I also refuse to acknowledge rolling and shoving the mountain of blankets I sleep on in the closet while getting ready for our date. I'm biding my time at the dorm. I checked with housing months ago. There were no other spaces available. If I've managed in the room this long, with two breaks coming up, I can keep going. Maybe junior year I can get an off-campus apartment. I simply have to survive the next semester.

With my time split in Brighton, and the potential of going home more often after my parents meet Morgan, I can do this. The only stumbling block is my lackluster grades, and Morgan is offering to help me with that. On the drizzly drive to the cinema, I take him up on the offer. Considering how hard I've struggled with my classes, I'd be stupid not to.

We stand at the front kiosk trying to choose from what's playing in the next fifteen minutes.

"I haven't stood in line since I was a kid. We get our tickets online." The nostalgia excites me.

"I figured it was a slow night and didn't want to pick for you in case you needed subtitles instead of action-adventure. There's an animated princess movie?" Morgan's acrimonious tone tells me he'll sit through musical scenes, but only if he has to.

"How about superheroes? Something for both of us plus corny jokes."

"Something for both of us, huh?" Morgan snags my waist, tickling my side. "I'm afraid to ask who your favorite superhero is, and why."

I pat Morgan's chest when he's quick to let go.

He takes my hand, looking at my fingers as if under a spell.

The cashier interrupts whatever he's thinking with a loud, "Next!"

Morgan pays for our real paper stub tickets and we go inside, stopping for a bottle of water for me and an enormous Cheerwine for him. We're both way too full for popcorn.

Scurrying to our recliners, he offers me a sip but I decline, pushing the horrible feelings it brings to the surface back down the way I had when we were at Sweet Caroline's and he'd offered for me to try the drink from the bar. If Morgan had wanted to hurt me, he's had every opportunity to already. The knowledge bolsters my confidence.

Our drinks go in the cup holders between the seats as the lights dim. Morgan pushes the button, reclining his chair almost all the way back. I keep my feet closer to the floor. Somehow by the middle of the show we've hooked our fingers together.

I'm relaxed. The gracelessness in the car when Morgan picked me up has long since abated and I've stopped worrying he'll put his arm around my neck because he can't. But he did the next best thing by holding my hand.

It would be a lie to say by the time we get back to my dorm I've forgotten Morgan's promise. He rides the elevator up to my floor, checking out the building I'm supposed to live in.

I don't live here. I survive. Living is what I do outside the walls that trap me. He walks me to my door and, when I invite him inside, I'm struck by the sight of my bed. My worlds collide and I'm not sure Morgan can be here. The same way Morgan didn't want our first kiss to be in a utility truck, I don't want him to kiss me here.

My feet won't venture over the threshold. He moves between the doorframe, walling off the entire room. It's like an emotional gasp of air. All I see in front of me is Morgan. He blocks my past, the way it is when we're far from here, in Brighton, or at the beach where he's taken me so many weekends.

"Hey, Sweet Pea."

"Hey." I duck my eyes to the soft collar of his shirt. My cheeks are hot and pink when I look back up.

"Did you have a good time?"

"Yeah. Did you?"

He nods. "Are we going to do this again?"

It's my turn to nod. I press my lips together.

"There's one last thing; is it okay to kiss you? Cause if it is, you need to know I'm all-in."

I blow out a breath with a little squeak as I say, "Yes."

"One close-to-hot boyfriend coming up."

I laugh out loud as Morgan's lips descend on mine. His palm reaches back as if his fingertips have itched to touch my hair. They massage the base of my neck in soft swirling circles. His lips are as tender. His tongue doesn't force its way inside my mouth, but his teeth rake my lower lip before his forehead comes to rest against mine.

Someone clears their throat behind me.

"I hate to be *that* person." Hailey's fists ball at her sides. She's shaking because she feels awful for interrupting. "I'm sorry, I only want to get in the room? But I can get my books and leave if you need some privacy?"

"It's okay," I reassure her. "We're not kicking you out." For as much as my body tingles from the kiss, I'm by no means ready for anything else tonight. "Hay, this is Morgan. Morgan, Hailey. Oh, she works at the movie theatre we went to!"

Hailey's eyes go wide. Her eyes track Morgan from his head to the soles of his shoes. A burst of red flames up from her collar when she realizes what she's done.

"That's a coincidence." Morgan noticed too and, from the look of it, Hailey's attention has made him uncomfortable.

We let Hailey pass and we duck into the hall where she can still see us.

Morgan's knuckles brush my cheek. "I'm going to go. I'll see you this weekend?"

"Definitely." Our time between now and Thanksgiving break is limited.

"Bring your books, Sweet Pea." Morgan leaves a soft imprint on my lips with his and a rabble of butterflies take hold of my spine, lifting me onto my toes so the sensation lingers.

He squeezes my fingers, leaning to the side. Looking into my room, he waves as he says, "Have a great night, Hailey," by way of goodbye.

Morgan

I'm bouncing Owen on my hip while Kimber finishes packing the diaper bag. Aidy's sitting with her back to us at the kitchen table. Her books are spread over the surface, and the more Owen giggles and squeals, the more she looks over her shoulder at us with doe eyes. I turn my back, trying not to give in to temptation. I love watching her with her brother.

Seeing how happy the little guy makes her makes me wonder about the people who raised Aidy. If she needs the same kind of future to be content. I'm not ready to settle down, but I keep returning to the feeling I had a few years ago; when I did, it would be with someone like her.

I'm not sure if that future is out of my grasp. I'm also not about to drag Aidy down when she's still got a ton of potential.

Hence why, as much as I want to put this baby in her arms, I'm being more of a hardass than usual. Aidy hadn't told me how far behind she was in her classes until the weekend after our first date. Seeing as the one plausible explanation is she's been coming here so we're able to hang out, I've put her on a study system we'd used when I was playing collegiate sports. There's a timer set to ring in fifteen minutes so she'll get a break. I'll quiz her on some notecards she's got wrapped in a rubber band before she dives back in. I've built an hour in between, so we spend some time together.

When Kimber's ready I concede, bringing the baby over for him to leave a wet sloppy kiss on Aidy's cheek.

Aidy baby babbles with Owen about having a good time and he jumps like a kangaroo in my arms. I hand her brother off to his mom and tell Kimber to drive safe. She's meeting Sloan at the mill so they can discuss details of the upcoming trip. Afterward, everyone is going out to dinner. Aidy and I were invited, but I declined. I'm not ready for what everyone entails. It's been three weeks with her as my girlfriend and, with the uptick in studying, I want Aidy to myself a little longer.

Aidy's staring out a window when I walk back into the kitchen to make us a snack. My fingertips graze the back of her neck. Her shoulders reach her ears and she tells me it tickles.

"Eyes on the prize, Sweet Pea. You've got eight minutes left."

I can only laugh as she groans.

The timer goes off right as I'm setting a plate of nachos on top of her open book.

"Ah, sustenance." She drops her pen and picks it up, devouring a loaded chip greedily as if I haven't been placating her with food every few hours. Chewing and taking a gulp from her water bottle, she smiles and leans over to peck my cheek. "Have I expressed how thankful I am for your help?"

"At least a dozen times, but if you're going to keep kissing me when you do, I'm not complaining. What else do you have to accomplish for the week?" I ask, stuffing my face.

"I have this one paper due, then another in ten days. That's what I'm working on tomorrow. I'll get up early to do research so we can do something before I go back?"

"Wanna start it tonight? I can put on a movie to watch by myself. You being here is good enough."

"No." She shakes her head. "I'd have to pull an A on this particular paper to get an overall B. It's not as if I won't work my hardest, but I'm doubtful it will be enough to scrape by."

"I don't get it Aidy. How did this happen?"

"It was just a bad start to the semester. Everyone's entitled," she repeats the same answer she's given me on numerous occasions.

I lean forward and clasp her hand. "I'm not saying you aren't. But I wish you'd told me sooner. You have to know, where I didn't get to finish college, the last thing I want to be is someone who interferes with you being able to graduate."

"This has nothing to do with you, Morgan." Her words are unconvincing. Aidy stretches and her back pops.

"Break time. Get your sweatshirt. I'm walking you around the block before we start on the flashcards."

While we stroll the neighborhood, I tell Aidy about the house Celine and I grew up in, leaving out my parents. She chatters on about her mom and dad and asks if I'm okay meeting them over her holiday break. Winning them over won't be easy, but whatever this is we're doing? It's special.

I don't doubt had I graduated, which I long since would have by now, I'd have met someone like Aidy. As it stands, we're mismatched. We're from polar opposite backgrounds. She's got a bright future ahead and I'll probably work for Trig the rest of my life. I shouldn't have attracted someone like her, and I don't quite get why the things I feel for her are at my core. But they are, and I'm damn lucky for it.

Back inside, we pop on the TV. I don't have to fake it pretending not to put my arm around her anymore. Aidy snuggles in. She tucks her head to my chest and her hand over my heart. I touch my lips to her forehead and she looks up under her long, light lashes.

I put down the remote, tilting her chin and kissing her. It's the sweetest sensation when my tongue slides over her berry-flavored lip and she opens for me, deepening the kiss.

We haven't done much fooling around. Aidy's let me kiss her like this when she leaves, though. It's like a promise she's coming back and I'm not stuck surviving too long without her. Honestly, I'm not sure how I had sustained myself. But maybe Cece was right and Aidy is the silver lining to my dark clouds.

I reach up under Aidy's shirt. My thumbs inch toward the underside of her breasts. A tiny moan escapes her, bolstering my nerve to explore a little further. The skin on her belly is so soft. Almost as silky as the satin of her bra.

With one hand I pull the elastic from her ponytail so I can feel her hair between my fingers as I fuse our mouths together. The other cups her breast. Her nipples are hard points under the fabric. We're both breathing heavy. I tug her up onto my lap. Her legs straddle my waist. She's got a firm grasp on my biceps while I nibble up her neck, giving her tit the attention it deserves.

Aidy's clothes have become more feminine since our date. She hasn't put on another dress, but I've noticed her curves show a lot more and she's less likely to cover herself the way someone hunkers down with the flu would. I'd like to think she's making herself pretty for me. However, Cece has reassured me I'm a dumbass and girls chose what they wear to make themselves feel better. The confidence boost makes them more attractive.

Since she seems to like what I'm doing, I run my hand over Aidy's covered ass. Dragging her closer to the throbbing erection trapped by my jeans, I'm hoping a little friction might be what we both need.

I'm blocking out the mistakes I've made and reasons I don't deserve the woman sitting on my lap. If we have an expiration date—if Aidy's only mine for a few weeks or a few years before she moves on to someone better—then making each moment count is my priority. I want to get her off, see her head thrown back as she reaches the tipping point. Someday run my fingers through those waves of violet cascading across my pillow, across my skin.

I flick the clasp on the back of her bra and slide my palm underneath. She writhes and my name slips past her lips, cracking between syllables. I use the hand that undid the clasp to hold Aidy steady and flip her onto her back, lifting her shirt to get my first peek at her soft pink-tipped nipples.

As I'm about to latch on, all hell breaks loose. Aidy's hitting my chest with her palms, shoving me away and scrambling to get out from under me. She's so distraught she can't even stand as she clamors off the couch. Caught up in the moment, the fear on her face doesn't register until she flops down on her ass, ineffective at covering herself, and starts crying. She looks up at me and I see through her devastation. The dead blue stare is back.

"It's not you." She tries apologizing while righting her clothes.

Something about her bra is driving her nuts. Aidy doesn't seem to care that I'm even in the room. She flashes me while ripping the thing out from the arms of her tee and pulling the shirt over her torso.

Aidy has nothing to be sorry for. I know it's not me. Whatever someone did to her is the exact reason why I haven't pushed for Aidy to come upstairs to my room. Although, I regret my actions a few minutes ago. I was so caught up in how she felt against me, how much I want her in my bed, I'd forced those demons to the periphery of my mind. I don't want them here with us.

I sit up and forward, scrubbing my face. Then I slide to my knees onto the carpet to face Aidy.

"I've done stuff before." She wipes a fat tear toward her ear, staring at the design on the wing chair as I settle crisscross before her.

I've had my heart broken. My future ripped out from under me. My self-esteem annihilated. My self-worth stolen. Yet, nothing prepared me for the uselessness, the utter incompetence, and the desolation that obliviates my soul watching her reactions.

Aidy can't meet my gaze.

"Tell me what happened, Sweet Pea." I run a knuckle over her pants. She doesn't flinch the way I expect her to. I hook our fingers together like a lifeline.

Her eyes brim as she struggles with the words she doesn't want to speak and I don't want to hear. Tears slide down her cheeks.

"You didn't do anything wrong." The hurt in her voice is clear and powerful. "I know you won't hurt me, Morgan."

"But someone did," I whisper.

Aidy's whole lower lip disappears beneath her upper one. She tosses her head from side to side as if shaking away a horrible memory. It's then when everything she's been trying to hold back and protect herself from comes crashing down.

"He drugged me. I can't piece it all back together. I don't know if I want to, and I wish I could make it all go away."

"Fuck."

She flinches at my phrase. Her shoulders hunch and she cowers the way I had with my back pressed giant the cement block wall of my cell.

I do something I'm almost certain I shouldn't. I touch Aidy. I tip her chin, making her eyes meet mine.

"When, Aidy?" I ask, not so much gathering her up as wrapping my body around hers as a shield.

"The first weekend back on campus this fall."

She sobs and I press her head close to my chest, my heart wildly punches in my rib cage, trying to get out, and ready to pummel the person who did this to her.

Perhaps my gut reaction is vengeance because I'll never get retribution. However, that has to wait.

While traveling my own trail back from despair and falling in love, I hadn't realized the one thing capable of bringing me back to the breaking point was the crushing reality it has happened to her too.

Chapter Nineteen

Morgan

A part of me is glad Aidy can't see my tears as they fall, dampening and matting her purple locks as I rock her and cry. When she begins shaking, I worry whatever I did to trigger her has sent Aidy into shock. I wrap one of Owen's blankets over her shoulders, brushing my nose against the soft cotton and inhaling his innocent scent.

"I feel stupid for thinking it was worth waiting, Morgan. For believing anyone saw it as a gift. That it was special at all."

There is never a justification for rape, and somehow Aidy admitting she was a virgin beforehand brings her assault to a whole new level of human disregard.

"Since high school, I spent years listening to my girlfriends tell me about their first times. All the dirty deeds they've done. And whether or not they loved those boys, I thought I would. I was naive to believe the person I was with would be the one I'd spend the rest of my life with. That we'd be married. Or, at least, get married. That they'd be my first, last, and only.

I want to be her last. I want Aidy to be my only. I want to not have a complete understanding of what she's telling me, and for her to not to have to tell me at all because she never went through it.

"He took. Like it was nothing. Like my choice to wait was insignificant. He didn't care if we could have been something... I don't know, bigger. That it might have been the gift I gave him, instead of the one thing I had to give—more important than anything else—he stole.

"I don't even know why I'm telling you this. I must sound insane. Immature. Men don't even have to think about this. About being used and tossed aside like yesterday's trash."

It's what I am; The garbage my parents, the university, and society didn't want to bother with. Yesterday's news. The kid who could have gone somewhere, but went to prison. Surrounded by others who felt as disposable. And if you're nothing, you treat others as if they are worthless.

What are they going to do, lock you up? How is that punishment if you are already there?

My fingers itch, and I fold the corners of the blanket, making crisp edges in the fabric. While Aidy's still shivering, my temperature has gone thermonuclear. I'm clinging to her, afraid to let go of the one thing I've staked everything going right on. But there is also a scorching burn on my skin. My flight or response conflicts with the need to comfort Aidy. I have to let go of her and I try not to make her think I'm scrambling away when I bring the blanket to her chin before getting to my feet.

The atmosphere shifts as quickly as it had when Aidy shoved me off of her. It's paralleled by my concern that she thinks the reason I can't touch her is out of disgust.

It is, though, isn't it? There is an air of repugnance in Aidy's revelation since the only way of ensuring she doesn't take my need for space as revulsion is confessing this piece of her existence mirrors mine. I could have gone my entire life without revealing the truth to anyone.

But if I have any chance with this woman—where she felt safe enough to tell me what happened—I owe it to her to do the same. She needs to understand I'm not willing to keep our relationship alive while she wonders if I view her differently. And I wouldn't take this step for any other person but Aidy.

Aidy

I'm in the middle of not grasping my reality. At first, we were kissing. I felt like I could enjoy the way Morgan touched me forever. There were endless possibilities for the night.

Admittedly, none of them included sleeping in Morgan's bed. But I wasn't lying when I said I'd gone farther than second base.

It wasn't Morgan laying me back, which was a problem. It was the satin against my armpits; the way my bra bunched up over my breast and under my shirt freaked me out. The sensation overrode all else. The next thing I knew, I was punching him in the chest to get him off, landing like a fool on the floor.

I never expected his arms around me, the heat of his body protection from the icy humiliation.

What was I supposed to say? How did I make Morgan understand I wanted him too, but my brain short-circuited?

Right as I was moving forward, forgetting about Brandon, his actions drench me like a cold bucket of water.

If I hadn't told Morgan, would I have lost my chance with him? Have I anyway by revealing the reason I wasn't offended by what he did, as much as repulsed by what someone else had done? Will my revelation lead Morgan to view me the way I worry others will?

For as comforting as his arms were, he was quick to get up and stride across the room, stopping at the kitchen table with his back to me.

Heat, rage, radiates off of Morgan and I'm fearful of his next words.

Morgan shifts to the side. He looks at his shoes before glancing up at me.

"Not all guys use people, Aidy. But some of them, you're right, a hole is a hole." I can see his pulse beating in his neck and the way his jaw ticks. Something dark flashes in his eyes. "For some, it isn't even sex. It's about power. Putting someone in their place and letting them know the pecking order."

His face softens for a moment and he looks away. It's not that Morgan can't stand the sight of me. It seems as if he wants to crawl into a hole deeper than the one I've dug. I've seen the same reaction from the other woman in my counseling sessions.

My fingers press to my lips and I blink back tears. Not for me, but for Morgan. I finally understand the space he gives me. How he never pressures me to do things I'm not ready for. Why he backed away the times he did. They had little to do with my assault, but what he endured.

Again I feel an enormous sense of naiveté. Morgan hates talking about his time in prison and, because of this, I don't press him. There's so much about those months he's kept to himself.

Revealing this?

If my heart could ache more than it does over my rape, it does for him.

The DA put Morgan away on a what-if scenario. Yet, no one ever considered the other what-ifs; what if Rob hadn't had a chance? What if sending Morgan to prison meant more than him taking responsibility? What if it meant accepting the terror people don't speak about?

And suddenly, I understand what Morgan means when he's mentioned people have said worse things to him. Undoubtedly, someone wished this on him as retribution. And someone else extracted it. Likely telling him he was worthless while they attempted to prove it.

I pad across the floor and reach out to touch his shirt sleeve. He's turned, studying out the window, yet still aware of my presence. I pause because I don't know if my touch will comfort him and I don't want to invade his space. But Morgan held onto me like a buoy when I needed a path back to the surface.

My fingers tug at the fabric of his shirt. Morgan's gentle hand moves to the back of my neck. He pulls me close. His lips press against my forehead.

"What happened to you is why you don't sleep. This is why you're struggling in school, and why you're always here in Brighton."

Open my mouth to argue, wanting to remove my assault from the conversation and focus on everything Morgan's endured. The stern look on his face shows me he won't let me in any further. He draws his line and I'm left to imagine the horrors he endured. Yet, the way he holds me lets me know at this second he needs me as much as I need him.

"I sleep on the carpet."

His chin grazes my scalp. "It happened in your room? How can you stay there?"

"It's not as if I have a choice." I leave out how I've

over-pondered the women attacked in the homes, who can't break a lease, can't sell, can't get away even to stay somewhere for a few nights to a place like this.

"Hailey must've—"

"Hailey doesn't know, Morgan. I don't want her to. If I never had to tell anyone I'd be fine with it. The one other person besides you who knows has sworn they won't tell K—" I worry my lip before her name slips out.

Morgan tips my chin. "Who is it?"

"Sloan, she found out by accident. Swear you won't tell Kimber, Morgan. I can't come back here if she finds out."

"Aidy, we love you more than you grasp. But I won't tell her." Morgan sighs like he's beaten down.

My mind races with scary images of what it must have been like for him. They bounce off of the ones my imagination superimposes on my rape. Overwhelmed, I start to cry again. "I'm sorry," I say, using the backs of my hands to wipe away my tears.

"You don't have a damn thing to be sorry for."

"I pushed you off of me. I made you have to relive all these horrible things."

"I think about horrible things all the time. The worst one is you not coming back here. You're what makes it seem like enduring all the miserable stuff had a point. Tell me next time if it's too much. I'll stop. I'll do what it takes for everything to be right for you."

I whisper a little thank you.

"Last kiss of the night, Sweet Pea, then I'm putting you to bed. You need to sleep. We both need to decompress. I'll be here in the morning. Promise me you will too. Tonight is a bump in the road. We're getting through this," Morgan says with conviction.

I want to believe him, so I press my lips to his, letting Morgan lead me to the guest room where I'm certain he'll do exactly as he says.

It's a long night, separated by two flights of stairs and surrounded by our thoughts; good and bad. But when elusive sleep drags me under, I'm not wrong for staying over. The next morning Morgan's back by the sunny window, waiting to kiss me good morning. If we have enough dignity to stand by the other through this, we can manage anything.

Chapter Twenty

Morgan

I rub the back of my neck and yawn before digging my thumb and index finger into my eye sockets. I picked up a camping mattress pad for Aidy's dorm floor, but the nights I stay there to watch over her have me as bleary as Aidy was haggard earlier in the semester. There have been a few times I've sacked out in Hailey's Papasan and I get the appeal of it.

The first night I dropped her back at the dorm was torturous on us both. There might not be much I can do after the fact besides snuggle up next to Aidy, but being near her seems to be helping all-around.

So now Hailey's side of the room is sporting an unused top bunk. Since she's there when I am, it's a total hands above the covers situation. I wouldn't think of trying to love on Aidy in her dorm. From my point of view, it puts too much pressure on her and I don't want to do anything to trigger her again. Back in Brighton, it is a different story. We wait until the house is unoccupied. I'm also the fool who kept asking if what I was doing was okay until Aidy told me as much as she appreciated me being sweet, I had to stop ruining the moment. She'd let me know if I was taking things too far.

One downside is the tiredness. Making sure I'm in the right place at the right time for work and my nights at the dorm didn't go unnoticed by the guys. Skye, and especially Jasper, caught on in a flash. I'm burning the candle at both ends and frustrated as fuck on the days Aidy is in class and I'm hanging about the factory. I don't want to chance having Brandon anywhere near her.

"Whatcha got there?" Skye leans over, inspecting the search results.

We're in his cave: a first-floor backroom at the mill filled with servers and monitors. Considering what we're up to, and which ones Skye allows Jasper to touch and not me, I'm assuming most don't support Carver's legit business interests.

In another room down the hall, TV screens mounted to the wall are attached to more servers. Those belong to Trig. I'm not stupid enough, anymore, to believe when Trig locks the door to the room while he's in there with Jake or Carver, it has nothing to do with the fiber I've installed.

This may have started out as an industrial era manufacturing plant, but what it's producing nowadays isn't fluffy or lily-white. It had only taken one set of eyes over my shoulder for the other two younger guys to see right through what I wanted to know about Brandon, recognize why I needed to know it, and pull the blinders off of how easy the information could be to get.

Amongst other departments at Pinewood College none of us will admit to, Skye's shown me how to hack into the registrar's office. Apparently, when you have girl problems around here, they become more than your own business. It didn't take long for Skye's taunting over Trig not showing me all of the ropes turned into genuine concern for why I was digging for the information I'd been cryptic about.

"Junior. Pre-med." I scroll. "Decent grades. Ah, here we go! Academic probation."

"When? For what?" Skye asks.

"All it gives me is a reference code."

"Move over." Skye rubs his hands on his jeans, itching to get into my spot.

"Dude," I protest as he pushes me out of my seat.

"I have more experience. I'll get it faster."

I scrub my face, letting the master have at it. I can't believe we're doing this or how fast the windows open and flash on the screen as Skye digs deeper. He's Carver's numbers guy and, fortunate for us all, his skills started as a teenage hacker.

"We have hit the mother lode," he proclaims. His index finger clicks, making a few last keystrokes. The man hasn't reached for a mouse once, nor has he looked at his hands. It's crazy impressive. "Semester one; stalking. Two; aggravated assault. Oh look, the complaint was dropped. That doesn't look shady as fuck when this Brandon guy has a string of complaints against him almost every year he's been on campus."

"Does it say who filed the complaints?"

"Not here. They're cross-referenced to another department's server. But if it started out as stalking, I'm willing to put money on most of them being from women."

"How much?" Jasper leans back in a chair. His legs are crossed and his feet are up on the desk. Funky dress socks peek between his loafers and khaki-colored dress pants.

"You mean how many?"

"No, I meant how much money."

"It was a figure of speech. I'm not betting on someone else's misfortune. Karma's a bitch."

"Whatever helps you sleep." Jasper laughs.

"Sleeping is exactly why we're doing this. Hailey doesn't need me underfoot each morning." I raise an arched eyebrow. "Those girls shouldn't have to worry about some sleaze coming into their room in the middle of the night."

Jasper's gaze narrows and his lips pinch as he shuts the fuck up. He'd love to keep playing it off that he's helping because of what Aidy went through, but deep down he's worried about his girlfriend being away from home and his inability to safeguard her.

I swear the guy saw red while forcing me to explain Brandon raped Aidy in her dorm room. Ever since, both Skye and Jasper have had my back. The way they're standing up assuages the guilt I have over revealing Aidy's secret. I'm praying she never finds out, all the while understanding Aidy has every right to be livid with me. If she'd let anyone in on my past, I'd be rip shit. I keep convincing myself what the guys and I are doing is for the both of us. There's no reason to ruin an inmate's life when they've done a bang-up job of it themselves. But to get recompense for Aidy? That's two birds with one stone. I'll sleep soundly after that fucker Brandon's taken down a few notches and prove to myself on the outside I can protect what's mine, by whatever means necessary.

The younger guys have put the mill's resources at my fingertips. Jasper and Skye are also in their mid-twenties. Compared to them, I haven't been around long. However, I think they would have stepped up no matter who needed their assistance. Adding on that Aidy is Kimber's daughter, and me wanting payback for what he did to Aidy, their help became vengeance. The one other thing I've gleaned hanging out here is this group is tight knit. Hurting one is like hurting them all.

"Write these dates down," Skye instructs me, rattling off a range of months.

"Okay, now what?" I ask, feeling like a dumbass.

"It's your turn to work some magic, surveillance boy. Trig show you how to use those magic machines down the hall?"

"For the most part."

"Okay, so what you don't know we're about to teach. It's movie time. We're about to watch this scumbag implicate himself using the college's security feeds."

"Think they keep recordings that far back?"

"At least as far as we need to see for Aidy's sake, but if you're worried we're steamrollering the wrong guy, I'd check out the last date."

"It's a week ago," I say in disbelief.

"Yup," Skye pops the p. "He said it didn't happen. She said it happened close to campus." Skye reaches for a paper coming off the printer nearby. He hands me Brandon's mugshot and rap sheet. "The police booked our boy for sexual assault. And with the college's previous history of looking away, they're all about damage control right now. He's not supposed to be on campus."

"Sounds familiar." My sarcasm isn't lost on the guys. The university let the hazing go too far with the basketball team and ignoring it came back to bite them in the ass. "So what do I do with this?" I have an eerie pang of second thoughts. The assault charge could put Brandon away. If it sticks, and that seems like a lousy bet to take.

"You ask yourself what happens when Brandon gets off and does it again."

"Or what happens to this victim when his lawyer drags her reputation through the mud." Jasper pipes up.

"Then you make a decision and live with it."

I take the paper from Skye and crumple it into a ball. It lands in the wastebasket.

"Nothing but net," Skye quips. He's the worst player of the three of us, but gets a charge out of practicing and trying to surpass what his current skills are. The guy loves a challenge.

"Get over it, man." Jasper nudges his shoulder. "Morgan has yet to miss a shot…on the court. You sure on this?" he asks me and when I nod, Jasper walks toward the hall. "I'm going to talk to Mordecai's guy. See if he can take care of clean-up. Twenty-one after lunch?"

I let out an awkward chuckle. There's something odd about a buddy saying he's phoning a crook and following the comment up with an offer for a pickup basketball game in the rear parking lot.

Both Skye and I agree with Skye busting my balls about how good I am until we enter the security camera room. I run through hours of footage, fast-forwarding and rewinding. Watching Brandon swagger into Aidy's dorm to pick her up the night he attacked her. Seeing him hoist Aidy up while she was visibly intoxicated. Drugged. Then the same swagger out, vape pressed to his lips like…Well, I don't know what it was like. Aidy was so out of it. There's no way it was mutual. Consensual. Witnessing Aidy in the days after, her clothes rumpled. The bouncy red ponytail, which made her look so much like Kimber, flattened to her neck, and stray hairs clung to her face. I even see the day she dyes it purple because she wants to be someone different from the person he's made her. Fun-loving instead of broken.

Brandon's rap sheet is in the wastebasket already. I don't want to see anyone else hurt the way Aidy was, but I still haven't made my final choice.

Later in the afternoon, my nerves are on fire out on the makeshift court. I'm impatient the way I was in the days leading up to the day the State remanded me into custody. There's this feeling like I'm a racehorse penned in the starting gate and the gun is seconds from being shot. I miss shots I never miss. I stumble. I'm breathing heavy like this is the championship finals.

"Stop overthinking it." Jasper rests a hand on my shoulder. "Go take care of the girls. The rest'll fall into place."

"I'm not." I shrug him off, not wanting Jasper to think I'm a pussy. "I'm sore and bushed. It's throwing my game off."

"Yeah." He shoots the ball at my chest and I almost miss the catch. "Skye just scored on us both. When does that ever happen?"

"Hey!" Skye shouts. "I'm here to make you look good. Like at Sweet Caroline's you're there to make me look even better, wingman."

I toss the ball back at Jasper and he juggles it between his palms. "Go. Hay will let you into the dorms so you can wait for Aidy. You won't stop dwelling on it until you see her. And when you do, you'll know you're making the right choice."

When I get to the dorm entrance, Jasper is only half wrong. Brandon is the one holding the door open for me.

"Hey, how're you doing?" he asks in a friendly, nonchalant tone.

This is my in and I know what I have to do.

Chapter Twenty-one

Aidy

Given how the weeks dragged in September, it's hard to believe this one is closing in on the longest of my life. I've been on holiday break for six days. Being home with my parents has put a damper on spending time with Morgan. Morgan has had installs and worked late a few nights for Trig. We've talked on the phone, but it's not the same. Last weekend, I babysat for the family I had throughout high school while the parents shopped and then went to their office parties as a distraction.

There are still a few days until Christmas, and the anticipation of seeing him is what's kept me going. Not having Morgan close is driving me out of my mind. I miss him like crazy. And I may have the silly smile that Hailey got plastered across my face whenever he texts. He'll be here to meet my parents in a few minutes. I'm watching Owen tonight since everyone else is working. Tomorrow Carver is throwing a Christmas party at the mill. I'm beyond excited to go meet the rest of the people who live there and put faces to names. I'm also intimidated by it. Cece says Carver goes all out for the holidays.

Not quite a black-tie occasion, I have my dress for the party packed at the bottom of my bag sitting on the couch in the living room. It's one I haven't worn in a while and I hope Morgan likes it and I fit in with his friend's girlfriends.

I'm running amuck looking for all the stuff I'll need over the next few days. My belongings are spread between this house, my dorm room, and Kimber's. Trying to keep track of it all is nuts.

"What is she in a tizzy about?" Nancy, a neighbor who recently moved in across the street, is baking with my mother for a cookie exchange.

"She's babysitting over the next few days and is afraid she'll forget something," Mom replies.

I haven't made a big deal about the party when, for me, it's a bigger moment than Morgan's arrival here. I'm afraid I'll blow it. Embarrass him or Trig. Not be invited back. I want Morgan's family to like me even more than I want mine to like him. I think it's because we'll need their support once my parents find out about his jail time.

"I'm pretty sure I left my favorite hoodie at the dorm. The locked dorm. That I can't get into for the next three weeks!" I exclaim as if it's what has me flustered.

"Luckily, she's not driving all the way to Brighton. Her new boyfriend is picking her up and dropping her off." My parents think I'm watching Owen both nights. It's not untrue. I'm sure my baby brother will be on my hip at the party so his parents can enjoy themselves.

"Ah…" Nancy replies all-knowing. "How do this child's parents feel about your boyfriend?"

Considering he lives with them, I'd say, "They're okay with him being around."

"This is the first of two overnight stays during Aidy's break. The same family is heading out of town over New Year's and she's watching their son while they're gone." Mom doesn't admit our connection to Kimber. I take it to mean she's not close with the new neighbor.

"Well, it's nice that you might get a kiss next weekend when the clock strikes twelve, dear." Nancy's dressed swanky to bake and uses the parallel to tell my mother about a trip she's about to go on. Whatever she's saying slips right past my ears.

I'm too caught up in celebrating on the thirty-first. Morgan and I will be alone. I'm nervous as hell because I'm beginning to want what could happen to happen, and I'm petrified I'll turn into an over-emotional freak show in front of him if we do have sex. What if I slip back, trying to align those awful, fuzzy memories when we're intimate? I hate thinking about anyone other than Morgan when I'm *with* Morgan. He's patient with me and doesn't deserve the elephant in the room squashing any more of his hopes and dreams. Ugh, was that waxing poetic? I mean, do guys do more than fantasize about getting laid?

I'm guessing he's further along surviving than I am. He keeps details locked up. It makes me understand Sloan's advice even more. Morgan doesn't owe me an explanation and his gentleness when we fool around proves to me he'll never pressure me for more than I'm willing to tell. I don't like that both of us have gone through this, but feel like it helps us understand the other's needs on a different level.

"Mail call, Aidy." My dad slaps envelopes on the counter.

I dash back in the room, stuffing my cosmetics bag and toothbrush in the duffle. I've been stalking the mailman since break began and have told my parents my college portal login to access my grades online isn't working. Since it's winter break—and my parents are just figuring out how to download apps on their cell phones—they've bought my line that the tech department must be on vacation too and it's why I haven't been able to get anyone to assist me.

"Oh, your grades are here, Aidy! I'm opening them." Mom wants bragging rights so she can tell Nancy what a good head I have on my shoulders.

"No, mom, wait!"

I trip on the edge of the sofa, stumbling forward as she rips the adhesive. The smile on her face fades when she unfurls the letter.

"What is this?"

I can see gears working in Mom's head as she tries to come up with a plausible explanation for a D, two Cs and a B. The latter I'm proud of. With Morgan encouraging me to study and quizzing me, I pulled it out on my paper and got the much needed A. But the three close to failing marks overshadow how hard I studied at the end of term.

My dad takes the paper from mom, focusing hard on it like a legal briefing. My parents have never opened my mail, but this is why I was trying to get to it first. It would be awkward enough in front of company if my failure was as simple as partying instead of not attending classes. The underlying reason isn't something I'm willing to discuss with my parents. Ever. Not to mention, Don and Ghillie Fairley raised me with civility in a household where we didn't air our dirty laundry to anyone. Not even a soiled sock, or a failing grade. This is an embarrassment to them.

"We can talk about it when I get back. Morgan's truck is pulling in the driveway," I shove the grades in my back pocket, reminding them of how important this moment is, and zipping my bag. Making it to the door, I pull Morgan inside. The sight of him and his cautious smile relaxes me.

He doesn't kiss me, but cups my cheek. "Missed you."

I lean into his touch. "Me too."

My parents' file into the foyer with Nancy lurking in

the threshold.

Not aware of the recent uproar, my boyfriend is confident holding his hand out to my dad. "Sir, Morgan Wescott."

My dad's clasped his palm and is about to pretend he's pleased to meet Morgan when Nancy begins vehemently shouting. Time stands still and the four of us are in shock, trying to figure out what's happening.

"No. NO!" Nancy shrieks, pointing her finger at him. "Don't you have a shred of decency to leave a poor girl alone? There's your reason, Ghillie. Your daughter's grades have gone downhill because he's dragging her down to his level."

Morgan drops my dad's hand like it's on fire when his eyes lock onto Nancy's.

"You killed my son!" she spits.

"You're mistaken. It was an accident. A horrible accident." I come between the pair, trying to defend Morgan. He tries to tell me to stop, but I ignore the protests.

I know Morgan and what he's been through. There was no intended malice in what happened to Rob at all. Morgan took responsibility and did his time for his friend's death. We're facing our challenges together and finding ways to heal. However, this woman's grief cuts him to the quick.

"Oh, God, Morgan Wescott?" My mother's hand covers her face. "The boy you'd told me about, Nancy?"

Relief and confusion mar my parent's features. Nancy is crying. I don't blame her. She lost so much. All I can think of is Morgan describing how he'd expected Nancy's son to still be his friend today.

"You went to prison…" Dad trails off, looking like he's taken a punch to the gut when it's Morgan they're casting aspersions on.

"You can't judge what you don't know!" I demand.

They have Nancy's side of the story. I'm sure it's

awful. But is it more awful than Morgan's, mine? When it comes down to the basic facts, I'm clear. Pain is pain. No one will ever fully understand both sides, and sometimes you have to accept you're not entitled to it. Moreover, I haven't lived through Nancy's tragedy, so I'll never read the situation the way she is, and none of them have endured what Morgan and I did. They can't fathom the reason we're together is deeper than what's on the surface.

"I think maybe you should wait to go to Kimber's until we've talked this out." My dad has recovered and has his best lawyer voice on, trying to get me to take it down an octave.

"No," I reply, more in control of my emotions. "I made a commitment and won't back out because you don't have all the facts."

"I can't watch this. I can't believe you'd let your daughter lie to you like this and leave with a criminal." Nancy bolts out the door.

My heart sinks for her and I worry about the way she views my parents. Oddly, I'm not as concerned with what she thinks of me or Morgan.

"Aidy, it's obvious Morgan has something to do with the failing grades. He should go so we can sit down and get to the root of this." My dad is negotiating with me like I'm on trial.

"There is where you're wrong. Morgan has everything to do with me getting through this semester. But I'm an adult. I don't owe you any more of an explanation." I sling my bag over my shoulder. "We're going to be late." I'm determined to leave.

"If you need more time, I can come back with Owen later," Morgan offers.

"We can discuss this in a few days. When everyone has calmed down." I'm as blindsided by Nancy's connection to Morgan as my parents. We need to leave so I can figure out how to manage the fallout from this without it painting anyone in a poor light or revealing truths my mom and dad have no privilege to.

"Don't forget, I pay your tuition," my dad reminds me.

"What's that supposed to mean? One bad semester and suddenly I'm not good enough anymore?"

"You didn't even try." Dad digs in, badgering me to get to Morgan. Or rather, to get me away from Morgan.

"I tried more than you can imagine."

"Aidy, if you go, I'm not sure in good conscience we can pay for school next semester. Not with the grades you have. The effort you put forth. It's reasonable to believe the time you're spending with Morgan may not be what's best for you." My mom sidles up, taking her place next to Dad.

"You want me to leave Kimber in the lurch?"

"If you go, Morgan will stay with you, try to sway your sensibility." Mom initially thought it was sweet of Morgan to help with Owen. Now it's like his intentions are cruel and lascivious.

"He'll be there because Morgan *lives* with Kimber and Trig. They trust him while you condemn him! Kimber trusted *you*. Is she a poor judge of character?"

Morgan's hands cover my shoulders. "Aidy, I think we need space to cool off. Let's go get Owen and take him to the beach."

I sigh into his touch, leaning back, closing my eyes and imagining the sound of our voices drowned out by the gulls and waves. Then I take Morgan's hand and let him lead me to the door.

"I mean it, if you go…" Mom's words are as clear a threat to me as the tears about to fall from her eyes.

Their disappointment is obvious. This woman has given her whole life to raising me. Turning my back on Ghillie and Don is as if I'm betraying them. She thinks I've chosen Kimber over her. Mom doesn't see this as more than a youthful, impetuous decision. It's my fault for not telling her everything I went through last semester was profoundly adult. I kept my rape from her. I'd do it again because what I've shared with Morgan over the past few months has helped me to heal. And if my mom is this upset by the current situation, how would she react finding out I'd been drugged and sexually assaulted?

Sometimes you care for someone enough not to tell them the truth.

"T-This doesn't mean I don't love you," I say before closing the door behind me.

Chapter Twenty-two

Morgan

I've promised Aidy we can drop off her bag and go to the beach, but for the first time she doesn't want to. On the drive she's quiet, curled into herself. I've always known a smoldering fire can erupt into flames. However, it was shocking to see her stand up to her parents when it came to her feelings for me. Maybe because so few come to my defense. The fight exhausted her. Aidy looks like all she wants to do is pull the covers over her head and sleep.

Instead of bringing her stuff to the guest room, I lead her up the stairs to the attic and drop it on the floor by the door. I've never brought Aidy up to my space. The pressure seemed immense on both of us and I care about this woman more than anything. How she defended my jail time to her mom and dad isn't lost on me. Although, I'm wishing it hadn't gone down like that. I don't like the rift it caused or that she's got to go back in a few days and try to mend it.

Aidy walks the perimeter of my room, ducking her head where the ceiling vaults from the eaves and roofline. There are shades on the windows, but no curtains. It's rare I close them. The neighbors need a ladder to see inside, and the sunlight makes it feel more open. She picks up some origami animals resting on the sill because I have no other place to put them. There's a stack of used computer paper where a nightstand might go and next to it another pile I've been experimenting with so the folds are imperfect and the creases ruin the crisp paper at odd angles.

I lie on the bed and fold when I'm bored, tired, happy, sad, guilty my hand has strayed to my dick with images of her playing in my mind.

From the windowsill, she picks up a heart with a quarter set in the center. "I like this one." She turns to show me my art.

I'm glad because it's another one I've been trying to get right. I considered boxing up a bunch of them for her for Christmas with cash and the coins in the center like gems, but it doesn't feel like enough. I want whatever gift I gave Aidy to mean more.

Walking over to her, I replace the origami heart in its spot. Her eyes dart through the empty space.

"How can you have so little?"

I wrap an arm around Aidy and drag her toward me. "You're all I need." I've gained so much in this person and the idea I'm on the brink of losing it, her, has me as tied in knots as it does Aidy.

I lead her to the bed so she'll rest. We didn't stop at the front door to remove our shoes and neither of us takes them off. She rolls to her side and I snuggle up to her back, inhaling her shampoo, wondering if her scent will linger after she's gone. Aidy pulls my arm over her like a blanket, my elbow bends and it rests between her breasts. I place a gentle kiss on the back of her head.

"Nap, Sweet Pea." I have a shift at the club tonight and should be greedy about the limited time we're spending together. But all I want is one memory of waking with Aidy in my bed before it all goes to pot.

In her sleep, Aidy's rolled to face me. Her light touch through my shirt followed by her lips on my neck are the sign she's awake. She's traced my pecs the way she is now when we've made out down on the living room couch. I'm comforted it's her as I wake. My eyes are closed and I thread my fingers through her hair, pressing her lips closer, moaning her name. It's like a wet dream come true.

Her fingertips dip lower, playing at my waistband and the button on my jeans.

"Sweet Pea," I grumble low.

I need her to stop. I need her to guide me. For all the time's shirts have come off and hands have dipped below the beltline, stroking one another, pants have stayed on.

The bed shakes as she toes off her shoes and presses the top of her foot into my covered arches to get me to do the same.

My mouth has found hers. Pulling her toward me, I've trapped her hand between our bodies.

"I want this, Morgan."

"What do you want?" *Say me.* Remind me we're meant for each other and that we can forget our lousy morning and the rest of our troubles.

"To suck you."

My chest rumbles and she pushes against me.

"Do you want more?"

"I don't expect anything from you."

"I've done it before. You're not forcing me."

I'm not sure how I feel about her last statement. I don't want to think about her lips around anyone else's dick, so I pull us both up to a seated position and my hands tug at her shirt so I can get her bra off. We wind up on our knees, unbuttoning each other's pants. The awkwardness of shimmying them past our ankles has us both laughing.

My boxer briefs hang low on my hips, my erection strains the cotton. I'm kneeling on the mattress. Aidy's splayed before me in nothing but her lacy underwear. The strip of fabric between her legs is damp. It's not that I didn't think I turned Aidy on, but seeing it makes me conscious of it on a higher level.

Her nose grazes my stomach muscles as her gentle kisses descend lower, down my trunk. She pushes the elastic down my legs and she takes the tip of my cock in her mouth, swirling her tongue around it. Her palms rest under the v planes near my hips. I breathe in through my nose and move them.

This is my trigger. After Aidy fell on the floor that day, I had to think long and hard about what my own reactions would be. It's the sensation of rough hands right there. Hers are tender, but I'm not making Aidy worry the way I did. Instead, I plan to show her what I like.

She takes instruction easy, wrapping a hand around my stiff dick, pumping it with smooth steady strokes as she sucks me off. Her other hand cups my balls, rolling them through her delicate fingertips as if our skin is floating together.

I lean a little to kiss the top of her head, encouraging her sweet mouth to keep going. What she's doing is amazing. Cum is boiling in my balls and I'm having a hard time holding back. There's no fucking way she hasn't done this before. I hate it and love it. The only thing that could feel better is being inside Aidy. We're not there yet. But I know she deserves to feel what I'm feeling.

My hands have been resting on her knees, I glide one down her thigh. My knuckle teases her clit through her panties. I've been watching my dick slide in and out of her mouth and Aidy looks up at me with hollow cheeks.

"I've gotta touch you." My other hand cups her face as she nods, taking more of me down.

I slide her panties to the side and sink a finger inside. I swear her ass lifts off of the bed as her back arches. She's insatiable, seeking my finger to penetrate her deeper. Her lips leave my cock just long enough for the word "more" to slip out, and then she's back to licking my shaft as I use two fingers to fuck her.

The more noises Aidy makes, the more relentless I become in my attempt to get her off. It's too much for her as her pussy clamps down and she whines when she can't keep up her ministrations. As soon as she's come down from my distraction, she's back at it. Because I can't have Aidy touch me and I don't want to hurt her, I fist the base of my cock while she keeps pumping. Gathering her hair, I fuck her mouth, giving enough fair warning before I blow so she's not surprised when I jerk her face back and come all over her pretty tits.

Not caring about the mess we're making, I tip her back and cover my body with hers.

"So wrong." She's trying to catch her breath. "Feels so fucking right."

"Did you like that?"

"All of it, Morgan." She giggles. "How long before we can do it again? I'm not sleeping in the guest room anymore if this is what I've been missing out on."

Her honesty makes me laugh. I kiss her nose. "If you're lucky soon, but not today."

Aidy gets a puzzled expression.

"Sweet Pea, I want you, and I don't mind sharing my bed. But we're not ready for the rest of it. And the more this happens, the closer to not being able to stop becomes. No regrets for either of us." I tap her hip as she tries changing my mind by wrapping her legs around me and grinding up. "No."

"I'm supposed to be the one who says, 'no'."

"We both get a say." I give her a sharp look. "It has nothing to do with my past and everything to do with the future."

"You want me to stick around?" Her smile is shy.

"More than you know, but not if I can't give you the things you need."

"I need another orgasm."

"Oh, yeah? Prove it." I roll off of her, pulling my boxers up over my ass. "Touch yourself."

"Doing it myself isn't as fun, good, as the one you gave me." Her fingers trail down her soft belly, trying to entice me.

"Well, if you need it so badly, that's your option." My cock jumps, wanting to prove my intentions wrong. I get up off the bed and walk to the bathroom.

"Where are you going?" Concerned, Aidy rolls to her belly with her focus on my backside. She lifts her chest and her breasts hang free, glistening from the spunk I've shot across them. I may work at a strip club, but this is my kind of dirty. Sexy.

"I'm showering. Don't worry. After I've jerked off, there will still be enough warm water for you to wash up with. Have a good time, Sweet Pea. I'll be thinking of you."

I close the bathroom door and pound my forehead against it. Being a cocky jerk was all I could do to get my ass out of there before taking it to the next level. I meant what I said. We're ready for this, but not ready for sex. And if we can't get through the next few days, I won't have Aidy regretting giving herself to me. Not when she's already lost so much.

Chapter Twenty-three

Morgan

Once I'm finished showering, I tease Aidy a bit more. I can't help it. I want to see her smile. She laughs with the covers of my bed drawn around her to stay warm. The fabric of her tee has stiffened, matting against her skin. As much as I want to smell myself all over her, I tell Aidy to shower and leave the room so she has privacy.

Downstairs I pull out the bread and cold cuts and make us two ham and cheeses, wrapping Aidy's so she can eat when she's hungry. It's after lunchtime, I'm famished and can't wait any longer.

Like always, Owen's cups are on the countertops. Munching, I tip one to look at the design. This is what I thought the future held. The big house, the kid's stuff strewn over every inch. Making sandwiches when my wife walks into the kitchen with the baby on her hip, telling me I'm ruining everyone's dinner by feeding our children so close to mealtime. I imagine responding to Aidy that I'll make it up to her. We'll survive this one evening and I'll be in charge of our brood while she takes a break.

Trig walks into the room, an impassable expression on his face. He opens the refrigerator door, pops the top off of two beers, and pushes one into the opposite hand that holds Owen's cup.

He refutes the lame excuse I give him about not being much of a drinker, and I'm cognizant of how real the fantasy was and how close it is to imploding.

"Tough shit you've been through. I acknowledge why you stopped drinking, Morgan. But it wasn't a single drink that led to a tragedy. And, for this conversation at least, we both need one. Porch. Now."

I lay the plastic bottle down and shift the colder one into that hand, accepting it so Trig has one less weapon to use against me when he drains his beer dry. He leads me out the back door to a screened-in porch. We sit in silence until Trig's chugged half of his and he's assured I've at least taken a sip.

I expect the dark brew to sour when it hits my tongue. My cheeks pucker, but the bitter is oddly refreshing. I hadn't given up drinking because of the taste. I've missed it. The past few years, my life has lacked something as simple as shooting the shit on a porch and I'm flooded with the nostalgia of doing this when I was carefree and invincible.

The neck has no liquid and I'm considering taking the level down to the label when Trig starts talking to me. I'll need a hell of a lot more than liquid courage, though.

"Don called me. He's pissed as hell I'd let you around his daughter. She's this close from failing out." His thumb and forefinger pinch together. "Hasn't been to class for God knows what reason." He leans back in the seat and it creaks under his weight.

"It's not me."

"You're right, it isn't. Don also mentioned Aidy is moody and unlike herself. She's not like that here... She was for a while," he concedes, taking another swallow. "Even Kimber noticed how sullen she got. I told her it had to have been nothing, and she's not in a place to dig into Aidy's personal life when they're finally getting a chance to bond with one another. My wife knows when it's best to leave things alone. I hate lying to her even when they aren't my stories to tell." Trig rolls his tongue in his mouth. "I want to know what you know." His teeth bite into his lip and there isn't a doubt what we're discussing.

"As much as she's told me. Hacking into the college's surveillance confirmed a few things."

Trig nods. "When was it?"

"The beginning of the semester." I stare at the green fescue grass, unable to face Trig. Aidy may not be his daughter, but I feel a responsibility for her that extends past the moment we met. It's as if I failed her by not being a friend before then. Maybe if I'd held her in my arms over the summer. *Fuck,* those ideals are futile. I can't change the past. My refusal to let this go, to let Aidy struggle alone going forward, has more to do with me. I'm unable to stand tall with my heels in the shifting sand for the rest of my life. Vengeance seems like my only lasting tranquility. It's a new and usual feeling. And one I understand acting on will lead me down a dark alley that there may not be any coming back from. But I still find myself alone, asking my conscience if I can endure what I'm setting my life up for next in exchange for bringing Aidy peace.

"How do you know?" I dare to ask.

Trig makes his living learning other's secrets. He rarely shares them. I mean, he definitely shares shit our video feeds spy on with Carver, which because it lines their pockets—and, after what Jasper and Skye have shown me, I'm beginning to realize how deep those pockets really are—but the stuff that affects his friends and family personally? Nuh-uh. Nobody keeps anything under wraps better than Trig.

"Initially, somebody saw her at group, and you three morons are kidding yourselves if you don't think I have a pulse on what's happening with my own business."

"Sloan?" I ignore his hard glare for the moment. On both counts, Trigs is about to hand me my ass.

"Keep your nose out of it." He gives clear instructions. "I've known Carver for a long time. He will eat you alive when it comes to protecting Sloan."

I nod. "You've both done more for me than—"

"Yeah, we have. Don't fucking forget it. Skye teaching you all the shit I purposely hadn't gotten around to and Jasper calling in favors has a hell of a lot less to do with you and them being buddy-buddy and more to do with Kimber being mine and Aidy being hers. You're putting us in a position where we owe people and I. Don't. Like. That." He punctuates those last words. "Have you ever considered what happens when Jasper can't pay the price? Cuz' it certainly ain't you Mordecai's coming after for a favor when the time comes. Shit's going to flow up. Our activities fly under the radar. Keeping negative attention off of everyone is how we've survived. How we've fucking bootstrapped this into an organization that works. We all have each other's backs and the last thing Carver, Jake or I want to deal with is a friggin' MC, gangbangers or any other shitheads who want a cut of what's ours. Do we know them? Fuck, yeah. Scoping out the competition makes it less likely to get taken out by them.

"But you, kid, you've got a lot to learn. It's a damn good thing you only owe your fuckwit friends and that they consider Aidy one of us. They wouldn't go along with it for any other reason. And if anyone else ring mastered this kind of shit for a woman, using *my* resources—if it wasn't Aidy we're talking about—I'd be cutting you loose and I don't like loose strings."

Trig leans forward. His elbows hit his knees, and he

pegs me with a stone-faced stare. I'm left with a visual of him using the utility knife he splices electrical wires with across my neck and I start to sweat.

"Do you think I'd let a decent kid who got tangled in some bad shit near my family, Morgan?"

I stop to think about the way he's phrased the question.

"Yeah, yeah. I do."

Trig smirks, scoffing, "You're smarter than you look, dumbass. No wonder why Aidy hangs around. The pretty boy facade fades quick for her. It's gotta be biological since her mother is like that too."

"I have yet to figure out what she sees in me." I chuckle with humility.

"Herself." Trig's the one interested in the green grass now.

He won't expand on his meaning. We're aware of what's behind it. I'm thankful for the way he's showing his support, quietly acknowledging he'll never put me between a rock and hard place by asking about what happened to me. HIPPA laws be damned. He knows. He's seen my criminal record. My files. The blood tests to make sure I'm clean. He did his homework on me before letting me into his home, around his family. And I don't fucking blame him one bit. I'd have done the same. I'll do the same to keep anything from harming Aidy. Except there will always be something I can't stop her from hurting over. Things I didn't know until it was too late.

"Listen, Morgan, Cece's not naive. She had a good idea of what she was getting you involved in when she asked Carver for help. I kept you on the periphery all these months for your own good. You deserved to toe whichever line was best for you after getting the shit end of the stick. We've all been there in one way or another. It was your decision to take it further. Now? You're not standing on the high-dive waiting to jump.

You're six feet deep and I refuse to guarantee from now on what I ask of you won't chain you to the bottom.

"Most of the rest of the mill girls knew what they were signing on for before getting involved with any of us. Kimber made sure Aidy grew up with a silver spoon. It's not fair dragging her down if she's not aware of the way our life works. We may do all we can to keep our wives and women from worrying, but leading Aidy blind into tomorrow? It's not right. It is about to blow up in your face and you gotta figure that one out right quick if you think she'll make any effort to stand by you. Otherwise, it's all for naught."

I blow out a deep breath. "I didn't fucking know about *that* until Jasper told me."

"Periphery." Trig chuckles. "Take care of it before tomorrow. Don't fuck up Carver's Christmas party with petty drama."

"I'm going to lose her trust."

"Win it back."

"So what are you doing about Don?"

"Me? Fuck that. I told him I'm staying out of it. I may care about Aidy because she means so much to Kimber, but she's not my daughter. This is my house, though and Don doesn't get a say in what goes on here. No different than if I stomped into his place and dictated Aidy date somebody else. The Don shitstorm is for you to figure out. I'm only giving you the courtesy of letting you know you have one pissed off lawyer on your ass." Trig tips the bottle toward me, then drinks the last mouthful.

"There you are." Kimber steps onto the porch. "I want to make dinner soon. Aidy's the only person here tonight, so maybe something we can eat in shifts when we're hungry? I saw those sandwiches, Morgan." Kimber winks at me and beckons her husband to cook with an outstretched hand.

"I'll go clean up once I make a call," I apologize.

"Awesome. After do you think you can help Aidy with O?"

"Nothing I'd rather do," I respond because I mean it.

One of our favorite pastimes is hanging out in the living room playing with the baby. Kimber's begun teasing we like to play house and when they're around still be able to give Owen back when his diaper is dirty. I've changed my fair share while my mind's wandered to those far-off, futuristic places it shouldn't have.

I dial the phone and it starts ringing. "Hey, it's Morgan. Do you mind coming over?"

It's a funny thing when self-preservation aligns with reality. I'm about to get a huge slap in the face. If Aidy can't forgive me for this, she'll never be able to absolve me for what's about to rain down on Brandon.

Chapter Twenty-four

Aidy

Morgan's been on edge for the past few hours. Yet, whenever I've gotten him alone to ask what's wrong, he cups my cheek, saying he's fine, and we melt into one another, kissing and touching the way we had up in his room.

Sure the joking-to-all-seriousness has to do with what happened when he picked me up, I've tried to reassure him my parents will come around. Allowing my mom and dad to dictate what people I include in my life is juvenile. But what happens if Morgan decides I'm not worth the wait because their acceptance of him is tied to it? I can't let this fester, get to a breaking point where either of them tells me to cut off contact with the other. I'm realizing part of healing is having my choices respected. I need to figure out my limits and have the confidence to stand up for myself.

The doorbell chimes.

"I need to talk to you out back, My Love." Trig says a gruff voice. "Now."

Kimber drops what she's doing, dutifully following

Trig to the yard with her arms crossed. Morgan stays with Owen and I go answer the front door, surprised to find Hailey standing on the doorstep.

"What are you doing here?" I squeak, excited.

Hailey looks over her shoulder at a Maserati. It's only the second time I've seen one and weird it's been twice now. I guess they're getting popular?

"Can we talk? It's important." Hailey shakes my brain from the short tangent. Tension flows off of her in waves.

"Sure."

"Do you mind if we sit out here?"

Glancing back at Morgan, concern is written all over this face. He nods, indicating I should go. I trail Hailey to the front porch swing.

"Aidy, I wanna say first none of this was ever about hurting you. I wanted to get my way, and it sorta wound up that you were collateral damage."

"Hailey, this is the way one friend tells another she's slept with her boyfriend."

"Oh, God, NO! It's not that. It might be worse." Her voice fades. Hailey seems smaller, younger. "I don't have a job I go home for on the weekends. I don't have a mom or dad. What I have is an overprotective guardian by the name of Carver Galloway."

"What?" I grip the bench, trying to stop myself from standing.

"I only just turned eighteen. I'd finished high school online a year early out of boredom. I wasn't allowed to do any of the stuff other kids my age did. Carver basically locked up me in his stupid, ancient castle so I'd stay out of trouble."

"What kind of trouble were you getting into?"

"That's the point, I wasn't." She rolls her eyes. "My guardian's paranoid AF."

I let out an uneasy chuckle.

"Anyhow, last year Sloan convinced Carver it wasn't

fair for me not to attend college. Commuting sucks."

I want to agree and say, "tell me about it", but I haven't minded the drive back between campus and Brighton since Morgan's here.

"I know better than to snoop and listen in, really I do, Aidy. But Carver wasn't budging about me living on campus, and I—I wanted one glimpse of normal instead of being dropped off and picked up outside of a classroom like a preschooler by his butthead goons." She sighs. "By the way, my boyfriend is one of those butthead goons." Sarcasm drips down her chin when she tilts it toward a man leaning against the car, but the smile crossing her lips is the same one lit up by her phone in the darkness. I now recognize I've seen both before.

"Jasper is your boyfriend?"

"I'm supposedly all his to deal with now." She rolls her eyes.

"Anyhow, I heard your name, and it's so unusual. I'd put two and two together when we were in class together. I mean, I wanted to be your friend. It's not that I used you and didn't like you."

"Oddly, it doesn't make it any better."

"Nope. Still sitting here spilling my guts, hoping you won't hate me, or Morgan."

I blink twice. It dawns on me when I introduced them that they were already acquainted with one another. My boyfriend has kept this from me. But for what purpose?

"He had no clue we were roomies straight off the bat. That's not the way it works for us, Aidy. We get told what we need to know when the information is important. We're expected to keep whatever we do find out locked down. If you stay with Morgan, there's going to be stuff he won't ever be able to be truthful with you about. You'll have to learn to accept half the story—if you get any story at all. A lot of times you won't and he's not lying to you for any other reason than to protect you."

This makes zero sense. "But, Hailey, you're an adult now. Why don't you leave?"

"Ah, tuition?" She raises an eyebrow. "Really? This is the family I have. There's no one else out there and, all joking aside, I don't want to live my life alone. I've been left too many times before. When we talked about our parents, I wasn't making it up. I substituted 'dad' and 'mom' for 'Carver' and 'Sloan'. She's like the most epic mom without actually being one. More like this big sister you can tell anything to, you know?"

At least, having discussed my problems with Sloan, this is rational.

"She stuck up for me when I concocted the plan to be your roommate."

An anxious laugh escapes before turning indignant. "You're all aware of *everything* then," I accuse caustically.

"Everything?" Confusion crosses her brow. "Aidy, all I know is I'm sorry for my part. Carver agreed to me living in the dorms during the week because you were a good role model. I'm the one who took advantage, nobody else. And nobody figured you'd start dating Morgan, or show up at Sweet Caroline's."

My eyes widen.

"Kimber isn't aware. Like I said, we're only let in on stuff when we need to know it. Trig's gonna tell her."

"What if I beat him to it?" I sound childish.

"Aidy, Kimber and Trig have been together for a long time. There are bigger secrets Trig keeps hidden from her than I was your roomie." She scoffs, defeated.

"Was?"

"Carver's all done with my little independence experiment. He's making move my stuff back to the mill."

"Does he have a reason?"

"Yup. As far as Carver's concerned, it's none of my business—even if it does have to do with me." Hailey shrugs as if she's accustomed to being told what to do. Accepts it.

"I don't understand."

"Well, if you're staying with Morgan, it means you have to decide if you can find a way to. Today will happen again and again. Sometimes it's going to be little and, for all our sake's, I hope it's never huge. I like you, Aidy. I want you to stick around."

"Hay," I hedge. "Is the stuff they do, that Morgan does, illegal?"

Her blank expression answers my question before she opens her mouth. "They take care of us."

"Yet, the less you know, the more protection there is?"

Hailey nods, standing. She walks away as if she doesn't care if I accept her apology at all. However, halfway down the drive she turns back. "I really am sorry I lied to you, Aidy. I hope you'll still come to the Christmas party tomorrow."

I watch Carver's car drive away, not wondering anymore what he does. When I have the ambition to go back into the house, Morgan is leaning over with his head cupped in his palms. "Aidy, I'm—"

"Don't speak to me, Morgan." I hold up my hand. I'm not sure how to react. Whether it was a white lie or, like Hailey said, because he had to keep the information he had to himself, nothing changes the fact that Morgan lied to me.

I wasn't raised to cause a scene, and I'm trying my best not to scream at him while processing what I've been told. I make a bee-line for the guest room, cut off by Kimber as she storms into the kitchen from the backyard. The door swings hard in Trig's face. He catches it right as his fingers are about to get pinched between the wood and the doorjamb.

"Both of you assholes, get the fuck out of my house!"

"Kimber." Trig attempts to assuage her.

I'm standing stunned between the two rooms. My mom has never yelled at my dad with as much force or animosity propelling her emotions.

"Don't you 'Kimber' me! You waited to spring this on me? On Aidy? I accept putting up with a hell of a lot of shit loving you, Trig Avery. So you get the fuck out of here and don't even think of coming back until I tell you I want to see you again." She turns in my direction as I summon the courage to walk into the bedroom.

Owen starts crying on cue.

"And you better take our son with you and figure out a way to do whatever it is you're doing tonight while taking care of a baby. The priority right now is *my* daughter." I hear her screech as I close the door.

Fat tears tumble down my cheeks. The man I'm falling for couldn't tell me the truth. My parents and I aren't on speaking terms. It doesn't matter if Kimber kicked Trig out, this is still his home. But when Kimber was emphatic choosing me, I didn't feel quite as much like a man without a country.

"Dumplin'?" Kimber knocks on the guest room door. I say nothing and she slides in, without consideration to the cries of her baby on the other side. "I'm so sorry. These men." She shakes her head, sitting next to me on the bed.

"Who is he?"

"Trig or Morgan?" She looks confused.

I don't mean either of them. I want to be mad at them and Hailey, but I haven't processed that far yet. My mom's the type to calmly talk it out with my dad, and Kimber gave Trig a piece of her mind. I'm stuck ten paces back, not knowing who I am. How I'm supposed to react to any of this?

I hold Kimber's curious stare. She blinks a few times and the lingering anger she had on her brow toward

Trig washes away. There's a soft watery glimmer in her eyes. She presses her lips together, licking them, and smiling. She pushes a lock of my purple hair behind my ear, cupping my cheek.

"Your father was the most important person in my life when I was seventeen. The center of my universe. The way I loved him was a feeling I didn't think could get any bigger until I met you. I've been waiting for the day you were ready to ask about him."

"What happened to him?" I swallow, my arms are wobbly almost as if I'm in shock. Then I realize I am. My whole world is crashing down and I'm struggling to shore up the foundation of who I am and what I believe when a cornerstone was never set in place.

Kimber takes my hands in hers. "He was a boy, and where we came from there wasn't a lot to go around. It was too much for him, Dumplin'." She responds with grace.

"How can you forgive a man for leaving you?"

"It didn't happen overnight. I had to forgive myself first, Aidy. I made a lot of mistakes too when I was younger. The only right thing I did was giving you to Ghillie and Don."

"They hate me."

"No, your mom and dad are worried about you. They're reacting out of love. The same way those stupid men are." She throws a thumb over her shoulder. "Love makes you make a baby you're not ready for and has you holding onto the grief of losing her for years. Love is what allows a woman to let someone else raise the most beautiful soul into a whole person that you're so incredibly proud of. Love eventually opens your eyes to your faults, allowing you to forgive someone else's. Your father was not a bad man. The only person he hurt by not being around was himself."

"It hurt me!" I demand, taking out my frustration on the nearest target. "It hurt me that you weren't there."

Kimber looks at her lap.

"I-I shouldn't have said that," I stammer, wiping hot tears from my face.

"No, you're right. I shouldn't sugarcoat it. But I have you. You've always been my Dumplin' to cherish. In my book, more hurt comes from not understanding what you lost out because there's no way to ever fill the void in your heart. Doesn't matter if you don't know why it's empty. It still is."

Kimber tugs me into a hug and I break into sobs. She holds me the way my mom used to and because of the rift with my parents, I'm overwhelmed with guilt that another woman holds such a huge place in my heart.

Chapter Twenty-five

Morgan

It's the middle of the night when my shift at Sweet Caroline's is over. If it wasn't already a crap-ass day Kimber called into work, turning the night into a nightmare when Jake had to come in. I half expect she's driven Aidy back to her parents'. When I get home, I find Trig's legs hanging over the arm of the too-short sofa. He's wrapped in one of Owen's blankets and his arm is slung uncomfortably over his head, which rests on a stuffed dinosaur. He's not asleep by a long shot.

I'm exhausted, yet not talking to Aidy for the rest of the day has me unable to fathom heading to my room. There's no way she's up there waiting for me to return. I'd be surprised if she's in Brighton at all.

I look at the baby's empty playpen, then through the threshold to the kitchen, wondering what I'll find if I follow on toward the guest room.

"Left O at the mill with Hailey," Trig mutters, answering the first of my unspoken questions. "Door is shut, so I expect Aidy's still here." It's quickly followed up with, "Fuck this shit. This is my house." Trig throws the blanket off and storms up the stairs. I hear the door open and the arguing commences.

"Get OUT!"

"You don't want to stay on your own side, go sleep on the damn couch yourself!"

"Bite me!"

Kimber screams. I think Trig has actually bitten her.

I hear his pained bellow in return. "That fucking hurt!"

"Serves you right."

Their voices get quiet and the house settles into an eerie silence. The whole thing is odd because the only piece of advice Trig had when we were stuck sulking across town was to, under no circumstances, hit send on the text I'd been typing out Aidy trying to explain my actions.

"My first fight with my wife lasted three weeks. The more I pushed, the more she kept me at bay. Leave Aidy alone until she comes to you," he said.

I haven't gotten it out of my mind how Aidy would feel if I didn't at least try to contact her. A bed frame rhythmically squeaks above my head. I guess Trig didn't want to take the same risk much longer either.

I stumble toward where Aidy is and stand in front of the door with my knuckle raised to rap. Stopping myself, I worry if after all I've put her through today, she's finally resting. It's unfair to wake her. My palm flattens to the smooth white five-panel wood, jumping back as if I've been burned when light streams under the door onto the floor by my feet.

She's up. She's here. And if she's here, then maybe there's a chance we're still together. As I go to knock, the shadows change. She's approaching the door. I wait with bated breath, but it doesn't open.

For the first time, there's an ocean between us spanning good and evil, rich and poor, just and unjust. I'm not sure we can cross it. Yet, I remain rooted in place, unwilling to admit defeat. I deserve her anger and to lose her, but I'm not ready to concede what little hope life's begun offering me.

Deep down, I know she's on the opposite side of this door feeling the same way and I swallow hard.

"Sweet Pea." I choke on my words, clearing my throat. "Open up, please?"

The door's seam cracks. What little of her face I see is pale and blotchy. The sunk-in black circles under her eyes are back. But there's also a softness to her gaze and I inhale with relief that my callousness hasn't frozen all of her feelings toward me.

"I'm so sorry. I should have told you."

"And you didn't because of this *protection?* You've admitted things have happened to you that are far worse, but Hailey being Jasper's girlfriend had to stay secret? I'm not a relationship expert, Morgan, but that's not normal."

"You have every right to be angry."

"Yes, I do. You lied and, from what everyone is telling me, I have to accept you'll keep on lying."

"Not about the important things."

"Only about the illegal ones?" Aidy's arms cross over her chest in defiance. Her fire is smoldering. Her glare isn't icy. If she accepts me back, she will make me pay every time I'm forced to deceive her and I'll gladly grovel at her feet for forgiveness.

Trig is right. I'm six feet under with both mill business and the way I love this woman. I don't want any life but the one I'm leading because the people I'm surrounded by are decent at their core, and they're forcing me to be better.

It might make little sense to Aidy now, but it will. Each instance I stand up for what I believe in, even if it costs me. Every time I take responsibility for my actions.

"Aidy, if I'd known about where Hailey was before

our first date, I would have gotten the go-ahead to tell you. But I screwed it up by not asking because I'd become too focused on something more important."

"What the hell are you doing that's more important?" her voice raises, the flames of her anger lick at my soul.

"Brandon."

My one-word answer has Aidy covering her mouth. Tears brim in her eyes. "You're going after him?"

Tonight, Carver took me aside and told me, "We didn't set out to do what we do to hurt anyone. Now, we do what's best for us all to get ahead. A man can only take the high road for so long while another waits for him to stumble and refuses to hold out a helping hand." He went on to say that they'd all been in my shoes in some way or another and each of them had hit the point where the straw broke the camel's back and putting the people they loved came first, no matter the cost.

"Brandon needs to be taken down." I pull Aidy close to me as she begins shaking. Her chin rests at my shoulder and I press my lips to her hair. "There are things you don't know, Sweet Pea. I won't tell you because I can't bear to see your heart have to handle more than it has."

"You'll go back to jail," she cries.

"No. No, I won't if it goes according to plan." I cup her cheeks, looking into her blue eyes, promising myself I'll always tell Aidy everything I can up to the point she's no longer safeguarded from my actions.

"If it doesn't?"

"You won't ever have to worry."

"I'm worried now, Morgan. Don't you get it? My boyfriend, the friend I was closest to, Kimber, Trig, my brother, They're all wrapped up in this same world you live in. I can't go home, ignoring that I can't protect any of *you*. I can't even protect my parents if anyone else finds out why you went after Brandon."

"They won't find out. We're all in this together."

Aidy cocks her chin. An acute awareness flashes across her features. "This was what Hailey meant. I'm not supposed to ask questions."

"I'm being honest because you deserve to know that scum will get his due." But she can't ask me the day or time, or even what specific person acted.

I push past Aidy, grabbing the strap to her bag. Before lifting it, I look for her agreement. I won't force her into anything she's not ready for. "I swear I won't keep any information from you that you're entitled to. Please, Sweet Pea, come back upstairs?"

Aidy

Morgan loops my open bag over his shoulder as I nod. He holds out his hand. I clasp it, letting him lead me up the stairs to his room on the third floor. I won't say I'm not scared of what I'm committing to. But Kimber's words have replayed over in my head. I'm upset by what Hailey and Morgan did, but how much more hurt will come from the void not knowing if I ran away too soon.

I've wondered all day if I'd bolted before or if I hid from my troubles while I healed. If I did run, perhaps it was into the arms of a man who was as troubled and victimized as me. Whatever we have fills me up. With Morgan I'm not searching for happiness, I am happy. Together, our broken souls have stitched a life raft and

I'm not adrift in the ocean of my fears.

Morgan drops my things in the corner. My feet still in the center of the empty room. There's so much space to fill and even when I ask Morgan why he only has a bed, pushed against the wall, I know what he'll answer before he speaks: He needed the constant open space to embrace his freedom the way he used the blanket of sand that slips through our toes at the beach. He was seeking something on the horizon. Hope, love, opportunities, a way to resurrect the life he'd wanted to lead.

"I wasn't sure if I was staying. I didn't want to put anyone out," he says into my messy hair, wrapping his arms around me from behind.

There's a confidence I admire in his statement. Like me, Morgan's been rebuilding his faith in himself. Yet, it hadn't meant he'd given up on putting others first. He hadn't when he picked me up from the university in the middle of the night and took me to Wrightsville. Or when he put me on his old athletic study schedule to raise my grades. Every time he lends a hand to Trig and Kimber without being asked. And I have to be honest with myself that watching the way he cares for my brother, makes me realize there's a future within our grasp. I'd be stupid to give up a man who will make a wonderful father someday.

I worry he'll be taken from me too soon. That Morgan will go back to prison holding onto secrets he can't share for my own good. But what if he doesn't and I've given up all those years of happiness for naught?

Morgan guides me to the bed, pulling down the comforter so I can lie down. Face to face in the darkness, I see only him and the promise of forever growing in the distance the way day breaks over the dunes. He rolls on top of me, caging me in with his elbows, and brushing my hair back. There's no insinuation in his touch. He doesn't expect our first time together to be make-up sex or even blind forgiveness from me. When his lips touch mine all Morgan needs to know is in this moment his heart is safe in my hands and I'm willing to try to trust mine with him again.

I stare at this man. A man I hadn't thought would ever want me as I was, feeling cherished and offering him a small part of me I'd held back. "I found out about my father today. Who he was. Where I came from."

"How do you feel about knowing?"

"Like I've gathered all of the pieces to put me back together, stronger than I was."

We're young enough I won't fool myself into believing our feelings can't change. Morgan's associations beyond what he'll reveal have the capacity for destruction somewhere down the road. But every woman I know in this same situation has reached out and offered their support. Kimber, Sloan, Hailey, even Cece have become some of the closest friends I've ever had. We're so diverse, yet it's a sisterhood. Leaving now —leaving Morgan and accepting that emptiness is better for me—means leaving the others behind.

Falling in love is bigger than falling for a single person. It's accepting who they are and those they surround themselves with because every relationship, every experience, weaves together, making a person whole and unique and worth loving. If I can't accept Morgan's choices, then I can't in good faith accept the life Trig and Kimber lead. One on the surface seemingly so loving and normal that I hadn't judged it as less than the one my parents lead together. I've always known Trig puts Kimber on a pedestal. And because he isn't hiding his determination to go after Brandon, I believe Morgan will do anything for me. Am I the same kind of selfless person?

Morgan smiles and tips my chin to kiss me again. It's not sultry or seductive, but filled with pride the way he'd acted when I had shown him my final grades.

"There will always be 'what ifs' dangling on the precipice of my subconscious. What if my biological parents raised me? What if they loved me over those eighteen years, through thick and an awful lot of thin? Kimber was honest about their struggles and she alone understood my best chance was being rocked in my mom's arms. What if someone else was the fortunate infant adopted by Ghillie and Don Fairley and I didn't get the benefit of parents so desperate to have a baby of their own that they made her the center of their world?

"I want my mom and dad to see you the way I do, Morgan. It may be futile attempting to change their minds, but I have to try. I want you there, by my side, showing them there is more to you, more to us.

"My parents are two of the most important people in my life, yet I lie every day to keep my rape from affecting their lives. I do it to protect them and I'd have swiftly eased into hypocrisy, leaving Brighton without hearing your side the way they refused to hear me out. For as much I'd never trade my childhood, I don't want to make the mistake my biological father made when he left Kimber. I'm not ready to give up the person who reminds me all I have to do is look inside of myself to find I have the strength to keep going."

"Is that me?" His brow raises with the cocky quirk he had when I'd told him he was the closest to a hot boyfriend I'd ever get.

"Yeah," I let out a feminine giggle and his cheeks broaden. "I didn't know that when everything was lost, I'd wind up finding you."

"You're what makes everything I gave up worthwhile, Sweet Pea." Morgan's nose brushes mine and our forehead rests together as our lips connect, wordlessly exploring parts of ourselves we haven't yet shown one another.

My father was Kimber's first love and my heart is

certain Morgan is mine. Someday soon, I'll be ready to give all of myself to this man. And because of our pasts, he'll accept that gift with a keen understanding of its value.

Chapter Twenty-six

Morgan

In college I slept with girls in my bed, but waking with the woman you love is wholly different. The past few years have given me an appreciation for why Aidy and I take things slower. The number of times I've gotten blue balls aside, I savor each time I touch her and that all the moments aren't jam-packed into one big three-ringed circus of drunken sex acts. I don't want Aidy just to fuck her. Although I definitely want to fuck her with the reckless abandon, knowing she's sharing her body with no one but me.

She's mine. She's my person. My silver lining. The reason I'm still walking this earth is to give her every damn thing she deserves; support, love, justice, hopefully a baby on her hip someday after she's had the opportunity to graduate and focus on her own dreams. And while I'm doing all of this, I'm proving to myself there's still reasons to have goals. To want more for me so I can provide a little hope to someone else the way Cece and I had wanted to when we were kids.

I play with Aidy's lavender locks splayed out over my

pillow until I can't stand not hearing the sound of her voice and the lilt in her laugh any longer. Then I drag clothes up over every inch of her body I'd kissed last night and bring Aidy down the stairs to where the clock on the microwave oven reads well past noon.

Since it's Christmas Eve, there are no installs lined up. Trig is the only one dressed. He's already left to get Owen. We're expected back there in a few hours. Carver throws a lot of parties, but this one is what he calls "family only".

Aidy's never set foot in the old factory. It's been apparent the lot of them will do anything for her because of her closeness to Kimber. Yet, her place in my life doesn't seem tied to or overshadowed by that, almost the way Aidy's explains Kimber and Ghillie don't compete for her affections. I'm anxious to introduce her to the rest of the gang for the first time as my girlfriend.

She sits at the table with her palms worshipping a freshly brewed cup, chatting with her bio-mom who is on her second pot of the day. From their matched appearances, Kimber hasn't been out of bed much longer than we have.

Trig leans next to me against the kitchen counter, a mug in his hand, and snorts.

"I didn't get until I met her that women aren't supposed to be that beautiful. We're both hopeless and ungrateful motherfuckers."

It's a cool, cloudless day outside. The bright light streams in the back window making both of them look ethereal.

My chin lifts and I chuckle, agreeing with Trig's turn of phrase. Well, all except the last part. I'm grateful the girl with her messy purple bun and long flannel pajama pants has given me all the hope I need.

Trig and I listen to the girls' animated conversation until we all have to go get ready to leave.

I take a quick cat-bath and shave, letting Aidy have the bathroom for most of the time. She ducks in there with a sunny yellow dress I can't wait to see on her and walks out later, twisting her hair out of the way, exposing her skin.

"Button me up?"

It could have come as a command. I'll do anything for her.

There are a half dozen loops to secure the top tight to her neck, which she hasn't been able to reach on her own. Interesting how demure the back is considering the front of this dress has a huge cut-out piece. From this vantage point, I can see past the delicate lace trim straight down between her cleavage. The color contrasts with her purple locks. Highlights bounce off of it, creating shades of lavender and lilac. Underneath it's darker. I want to eat her up like a juicy plum.

When I'm finished, I pull Aidy to my chest. My hand slides up the skirt, searching for her panties.

She ducks her head as my other hand reaches up toward her breasts.

"I was so concerned I had the right bra, I forgot my underwear in my bag," she says a little embarrassed. Her breath hitches the way it does right before I kiss her, letting me know she's a lot turned on.

"Forgot intentionally, Sweet Pea?"

"No," she squeaks as my hand keeps exploring under her dress. The tips of her ears pinken, a dead giveaway she's bending the truth. They get redder when she's exhausted.

"Forgot and then saw the benefit of forgetting?" I whisper, kissing the soft spot behind her ear. She hasn't told me to stop and I can feel the dampness between her legs. "You're wet. When you realized you didn't have your panties, it started you thinking about what we did last night, didn't you?"

Aidy lets out a whimper, acknowledging she had.

"I've thought about it too. I think about being with you, Aidy. But now isn't the time to spread you out, make you understand how much making love to you means to me, and do it right."

Her body relaxes at my words to the point I'm holding her up. "Your trust means everything to me." I lean her forward, snaking a hand between the fabric of her top and her soft skin. She gives me an approving moan as I knead her breast and caress her ass.

"Take off those heels."

"You said—"

"There may not be enough time for some things, but there's more than enough to make you feel good."

The shoes come off with less protest than her mouth is making. There's no way she'll be able to keep her balance with them on. Not without practice anyway.

Two fingers from my other hand slide between her legs with ease. She's so hot and ready and I'm hard as a rock knowing she is. There's no fear. No trepidation. Aidy knew what she wanted when she entered the bedroom. She was setting this up. I don't think she had any idea what I'd do to her, but I'm sure she wanted to see where using a ploy to gain my attention led.

Her back arches with each stroke of her pussy. I'm slow and steady. Her body doesn't like it when my fingers come too far out, or maybe she does because she leans to my touch, searching out the next.

"Mmm…Morgan." A little flutter follows her words, dampening her thighs more.

I may be rusty, but I can do better than this.

I've never encountered a woman so into this. So willing to let me do what I want to their body with the faith I won't let them down. Maybe it's Aidy's limited experience. Whatever it is, I'll make sure she gets no less than what she deserves.

I ease up on her breast and guide Aidy so she's bent over the bed. Her heart-shaped ass is in the air and, if she likes this position now, I'm doubtless it will be one of her favorites later. I stand behind her and move my tit-grabbing hand to her clit. Two fingers spread her lips and I glide them forward and back, opposite the timing of my other hand.

Aidy's chest is to the sheets. Her hair spills over her face and she's writhing, saying the fucking dirtiest things I've ever heard spill from her sweet lips.

"You like this, Sweet Pea." It's obvious, but I want her to voice it so she'll keep telling me what she wants. I'll give Aidy as much of the world as I can afford.

"God, yes." Her hands strain against the bed and she pushes her hips up.

"You want more?"

The garbled sound she makes chasing her release puts a smile on my face. I add a third finger to the two inside of her. Realizing she likes the stretch, I use all three fingers to slick my thumb and trail it up, pressing into that rosebud.

"You can do this." I tack my nickname for her onto the end of the sentence when Aidy whimpers. It gets a little nod from her and I know she's okay. We're still in the moment together.

Aidy

I'm not sure what has possessed me. This is dirtier than when I sucked Morgan's dick or having his mouth all over my pussy last night. I'm letting him put his hands up my skirt anyplace he wants. I'm not ready to admit I like *everything* he's doing, but my body is betraying me in the most magnificent way.

I swear the rush of wetness from the first orgasm has me damp to my knees. I'm still letting him finger fuck me, drawing the next one out. Thank god he made me take off my heels. I wasn't prepared for this at all. It's not at all what I expected and nothing short of amazing.

We have to be out of here soon. I thought maybe Morgan would laugh and swat my ass for forgetting my underwear. It was an honest mistake. I was distracted watching Morgan getting ready and left my underwear in the bag. Although, it's not as if there's much to those panties. That I did plan, hoping maybe after admiring me dressed up, Morgan might like to undress me. I was trying to be pretty underneath my clothes for him for later. What he's doing to me now wasn't part of the fantasy.

I can't believe I want more. I can't believe I'm begging for it while using dirty words to entice Morgan to keep going. Trying to keep quiet has become a losing battle. Hopefully, noises don't drift down the stairs. It's more than our voices. The bed is squeaking, and the wet sounds prove I'm putty in Morgan's hands.

Months ago, I wouldn't have allowed anyone to touch me like this. Now, I don't want him to ever stop. Each sensation overrides the other. Tight and loose. Wet. Hard. Pain and pleasure mix. My pussy clenches.

"That's right, Aidy. Take what you want," Morgan encourages.

I bury my face into the sheets, screaming as I come. His fingers move until he's drawn every bit of the orgasm out. He leaves two behind when he lowers his front to my back.

"Where are those panties?" The coy smile in his voice is louder than the noises we made.

"In—In the bag." I'm breathless and having second thoughts about going to the party. I'd rather stay in bed. I want Morgan to fuck me. Probably because I know he'll put a stop to it.

"Are you planning to put them on or tease me like this all afternoon?"

My eyes widen at the idea. It has merit, but "What if a breeze blows my skirt up?"

Morgan kisses my neck, humming in agreement. "You're right. Better safe than sorry. I'm not sharing this with anyone."

I shiver floats down my back as Morgan's weight shifts. He gets off the bed and goes to rummage through my things on the floor. Ducking his head in the knapsack, he holds up the scrap the lingerie shop assured me is underwear, swinging the elastic around his finger. "All I found was this."

"That's them!"

The G-String shoots across the room. Somehow I catch it and slide it up my bare legs.

"Damn, Sweet Pea. You're killing me." Morgan watches it disappear underneath my skirt. "This is going to be a long evening." He strides across the room, knotting my hair behind my neck and pulling my lips to his for a punishing kiss. His erection strains against the fly of his pants. I realize what I've done. I deserve the way he's treating me. And that not only do I like it, it's also got my imagination playing out scenarios of what Morgan and I might do once the party is over.

"I'm not. You do it. I don't have a fucking clue what they're doing in there." I hear Trig whisper yelling from the staircase.

"Just knock," Kimber replies.

"No. No way in hell. If they're doing what I think they're doing, I wouldn't want someone interrupting."

"You said you didn't have a *fucking* clue what they were up to."

My cheeks flame at Kimber's response. Morgan tips his forehead to mine. The more embarrassed I get, the more his chest vibrates.

We listen to Kimber and Trig bicker on the stairs. I guess voices do carry. We must have been loud. Er, at least, I must have been. Trig insists on taking one for the team and goes to buckle Owen into his car seat to get out of disturbing us.

There's a faint rapping at Morgan's bedroom door. "Hey, guys? We're leaving in a few. You almost ready?"

Morgan purses his lips and I have to answer. *Men.*

Aidy

I clench Morgan's hand, stepping into the imposing historic building for the first time. A hall extends in both directions with heavy closed doors at either end. Morgan tells me they lead to the business offices and where he and Trig work on days they aren't off site for an install. The rich wood tones and exposed antique red masonry in the lobby are like nothing I'd assumed. It's hospitable yet industrial with clean architectural lines no matter which way I look. Try to take it all in, but there's not enough time to gawk. Trig and Kimber have already begun disappearing up a massive wooden staircase to the second story. As we take the first creaky stair, I note another flight down leading to a basement.

At the top, the tight, richly historic space opens up with blinding white walls and my eyes have to readjust. All the way to the left there's a threshold leading to a darkened hallway and two additional doors on the right. The first swings open and I'm hit with heavenly smells as Holly, a bartender at Sweet Caroline's, brings out a tray of food and places it on a table decorated with festive garland and green wreaths. When a second woman follows her out with the same, I surmise it must be the kitchen.

The main space has ceilings two stories high and a wall of windows and more doors showing off a huge porch. Light streams in, something I find interesting since, from the outside, you can't see anything going on in here. The glass reflects the outside to maintain privacy.

In front of the porch are pool tables and someone is playing darts near a bar rivaling a restaurant's. There are even hanging glasses of every shape and size to choose from. Underneath the swaths of garland, the details are exquisite. This room must be beautiful and inviting, even when it's not decked out for the holidays.

Kimber is making herself comfortable on a couch as if she belongs. And then—as Cece descends another staircase sharing the same wall as the dark hallway, a portion of which is hidden by the bar—I remember my bio mom used to live here.

Morgan brushes his thumb over my lower lip. My jaw is agape.

The door past the kitchen opens a crack and Sloan slides out. I can't see into the room. She's full of sass, mouthing off to someone. It has to be her mister because when she turns to us, closing the door, her wide smile broadens.

"You made it!" Her arms reach for me and Sloan, who looks stunning in a tight red number, compliments me on my dress.

The fabric is thin for this time of year, but I'm glad I feel like I can wear it again. Dresses were my thing. Since my first date with Morgan, I feel pretty. It has little to do with a man telling me I looked good. I'm getting dressed up more often now because I've regained my confidence and I want Morgan—and everyone else—to see me the way I view myself.

Sloan glances at Morgan as we hug. Like the other men in the room, he's edible in slacks and a button-down.

"You picked a good one to get your sea legs back with," she whispers so he can't hear.

The wink that follows, directed at Morgan, has red rising from his collar.

"You're going to get my ass kicked, Sloan," he remarks, uneasy.

"Don't be afraid of Carver." She pats his chest. "His bark is far worse than his bite."

Sloan points my attention to a tall blonde man who has Kimber's ear. He seems cordial enough. However, Sloan warns, "Do be wary of Jake. The club is open tonight. He's trying to persuade Kimber to work when he gave her the night off months ago. She won't say yes and risk missing Christmas morning with you and Owen, but nothing will stop Jake from putting the screws to her unless Trig cuts him off at the knees. I hate to get involved, but I should distract him, so he'll move on for a bit." Sloan shudders and I get the impression Jake's not her favorite person to deal with. "Enjoy. Eat! We have tons of food. Mister Bossy will be out soon. He's wrapping up some last-minute, uh, *gifts*." She waves, crossing to the couches.

Her friendly demeanor fades as she flat out instructs Jake he's not harassing Kimber in her home. Kimber goofily pokes his shoulder and Jake's expression darkens. The man is no wounded animal. I get the impression there are few who stand up to him, and though Sloan holds her ground, he's allowing it because it is her ground she's standing on.

Morgan's knuckles glide down my arm. "Want a drink?" I start replying with my normal, but Morgan cuts me off. "Bottled water. Cap on."

"How about whatever you're having, cap on?" It's likely a soda. I hadn't once seen him imbibe until tossing a brown bottle in the recycle bin yesterday. I miss a good beer, but love how neither of us needs alcohol to have a good time. It takes so much of the pressure off.

He kisses my temple. "Coming right up."

I find an empty place to sit and wait, nudged again as Hailey slides in next to me.

"Are we okay?" She mumbles, babbling on, "I'll leave you alone if we aren't. I just don't want to do the glance back-and-forth all night thing where I'm on pins and needles thinking you hate me. I mean, it's fine. You can hate me. I just need to know if you do."

Hay's appearance doesn't match her self-doubt. She's as put together as any of us. You couldn't tell a stripper from a Pinewood College student tonight. Though, seeing how Celine is both, there have to be a few more mill girls who fall either side of the aisle.

I don't want to not be her friend. And no different from the underlying connection I have with Morgan, I believe the reason our friendship has worked was because I needed her as much as she needed me. We get that you don't have to be privy to every detail about the other's life to be there for the other person.

"We're good, Hay." I rub her knee while focusing on Morgan, Jasper, and Skye at the bar.

"Listen, ever since Morgan started sharing our dorm room I've been thinking we should all hang out for New Year's. Come. Bring Owen. He's a sweetheart."

"You're his other sitter?" I turn to face her. Boy, am I slow to connect the dots.

"You're his *big sister*. Now that I can share, there's a bunch of stuff he's done that I've been wanting to let you know reminds me of you." Hailey knocks my shoulder with hers.

"Would you mind coming to the house instead?"

"Oh God, no. I'll take any opportunity to get out of this place."

"You really don't like it here?"

She eyes Jasper across the room. "Ah, it has its perks, like wake-up sex."

"Carver lets you sleep in the same room? My parents would never allow that."

"He expects Jasper to take care of me. I don't know if fucking was included in the negotiations, but you won't hear me complaining." Hailey worries her lip. "I heard your mom and dad found out about Morgan. I wasn't listening in. Everyone was out here talking yesterday while us girls were finishing trimming the tree. It's sort of common knowledge. Did they disown you?"

"Not quite, or not yet. I'm going back in the morning." I sigh, sweeping away the arguments on replay in my head that I've pretended to have with my mom. I want to enjoy Christmas Eve.

The tree is gorgeous, decked out in shiny metallic tinsel and huge round ornaments the size of the shimmering balls found on the one the city lights in downtown Raleigh. It's the biggest one I've seen indoors, outside of the shopping mall's.

"Oooh Merry Christmas, huh?" Hayley's nose scrunches, sensing my sadness.

"I fully anticipate a squabble and to spend most of the day in my room. The best gift they could give me is hearing me out, even if we have to go to separate corners until dinnertime."

I catch the door Sloan came out of opening again. From the tips of his perfectly coiffed dark hair down to the toes of his designer wingtips, the man who emerges makes the rest of us look scrubby. He ignores our stares, seeking Trig like a missile.

They exchange an envelope. Trig peers inside and hands it back, expressionless. He beckons Morgan over and his glance at me with a square-jawed tilt of his chin is a command to join them.

"Ever get the feeling you're in over your head?" I ask

rhetorically.

"Basically every waking minute. Though, I have a hard time with the notion anybody who lives outside these four walls feels any different."

I have to agree with Hailey. I didn't feel as if I was drowning any less in August. Now, with this circle of people, there is a feeling like the Captain will go down with the ship and he expects nothing less of his crew. I'm proven right in the next few minutes.

After the most intimidating introduction of my life, Carver gives Morgan the envelope.

"What's this?" The total on the check inside shocks my boyfriend. Me too.

"Your Christmas bonus, what else?" Carver replies. I understand every one of Sloan's nicknames for him in an instant. Yet, Carver is unaware that his mere presence is intimidating. He's tucked his hands in his pockets and his casual stance proves he is unaffected by how much money he's handed Morgan.

"I don't see anyone else getting a bonus." Morgan looks around, bewildered.

"I don't see the government forcing me to garnish anyone else's wages."

"I'm not sure if I can accept this, or what I'm supposed to do with it.

"Get yourself some fucking furniture," Trig suggests.

"Hell, with this much I can move out."

"Nobody's asking you to leave. Either way: get yourself some fucking furniture." Trig repeats, mussing Morgan's hair. My bio mom's husband looks at me with nothing but affection. I've never thought of him as my dad, but maybe he's thought of himself as Morgan's, and maybe it's not as weird as I once feared it was.

This might not be the world I was born into, but the way these men look out for one another when no one else will is what my parents me taught was important. Love your family despite their flaws. Stand up for one another. Admit your mistakes and move on. All of those lessons are there in their own twisted way. How many people actually follow society's rules of behavior, and how many of them pretend to while praying they won't get caught?

Morgan is still slack-jawed by their generosity when Skye walks by, plucking the check from his grasp. "Hey!"

"You have no investment strategy," Skye calls over his shoulder. "You've got to learn to make this wad-o-cash work for you."

"And you've got no hoops game." Morgan hollers back.

"Give him back enough for a dresser, not a cheap one either. Morgan's done storing his shit in a cardboard box." Trig instructs Skye before he bounds too far off.

"Got it." Skye finishes his convo with Trig, volleying back to Morgan, "I've got it on the court too." He sticks up two shooter fingers. "Meet you outside once I find a nice shell game for your treasure chest."

"Thank you." A dumbfounded Morgan shakes Carver's hand, and the two older men go find their better halves.

I give Morgan a congratulatory kiss.

"Sweet Pea," He pauses, wanting to maintain a sense of truthfulness between us. "You know what this means, right? What the check signifies?"

"I have no clue?" I return a quizzical look, feigning innocence, but a giggle breaks forth when Morgan's stance slumps, crestfallen.

Tipping his chin up, I run my palms over the broadcloth covering his biceps, and let my fingers dance through his dark hair. "I do know you'd never do anything intentional to hurt me and that you'll be honest whenever you can."

Morgan wraps his arms around my waist. "How can you be so certain?"

I shrug my chin toward my shoulder to where Kimber, Sloan, Hailey, and Cece stand behind me gossiping about how cute we are. "They are. And we're all in this together."

Morgan chuckles and kisses me so that the other ladies whoop and clap.

Morgan

It's Christmas morning and Aidy's sitting between my legs on the floor with her back to my chest. All four of us are bleary-eyed from staying late at the party. Owen's wide awake, beating on a big empty box like a drum. He's discarded the actual drum that was inside in a pile along with a few other opened presents. He bounces, dancing as his chubby fingers slap the cardboard, as amused with himself as we are with him.

The adults have opened their gifts for one another. Aidy got me reams of high quality solid and patterned origami paper and some advanced folding technique books. She added a gift card for the craft store so I could get more paper when I ran out—something which happens frequently—apologizing that what she'd gotten me wasn't anything crazy expensive. Thanking her, I kissed those fears away. The value wasn't in the price tag. It was her knowing the exact thing I needed.

My gift to her was along the same lines. As much as I hadn't wanted to rely on anything monetary, Kimber had clued me in that the purple color I love so much that Aidy dyes on her own. I filled a box with a flock of paper cranes and other sea animals made from various denominations so she can go to a salon and get a little pampered.

Aidy also has my cell, and we're searching the local furniture galleries' selection of bedroom sets. It's becoming apparent while she scrolls that we have the same style and we've found a few to bookmark and check the availability on.

Owen's holiday spirit tops out in the next ten minutes, ready for his morning nap early. He rubs his eyes the way we had before the coffee pot had finished perking. It's good timing because Aidy's expected home before ten o'clock and I still have to get her there.

Trig's about to bring O up to his crib when Kimber holds both of her kids tight. Aidy's hugging her bio-mom when Kimber pronounces it the best Christmas ever. Despite the uncertainty with Aidy's adoptive parents, I agree with her before realizing this is the first December twenty-fifth Kimber has spent with Aidy. Sharing today is special for my girlfriend in more ways than it is for me. I hope we have more than this one together, and none of the rest of them have any problems looming in the shadows.

I tickle Aidy up the stairs so she can shower and get changed. There's a bit of dread on both our parts she has to go, but my ass is she going to show up at five past and make the conversation with Mr. and Mrs. Fairley harder.

On the other side of the curtain, under the spray, she jokes with me as I shave that they may disown her. I doubt this and tell her so. She's coming up with contingency plans to get through the next semester.

I pull the wet liner to the side to peek at her nakedness and pull her head out of the clouds. "We need to get through the next week, Sweet Pea. You have almost all of January to figure out your next steps."

Aidy's piled her hair high on her head. She's been using my body wash to scrub herself and the water sluices off her curves. She drops her arms to her sides, jutting her hip when she notices me watching.

"Like what you see, Morgan?"

"You're so fucking beautiful."

Aidy smiles, placing a delicate kiss on my lips. Leaning in, the spray douses my face. Not that I give a damn when wiping the towel over my chin and handing it into the stall for her as Aidy shuts off the stream. I'd have my head buried between her legs if we didn't need to get a move on. I leave the steamy cube to pull a pair of jeans off the top rack in the closet.

"Maybe Jake will give me a job at Sweet Caroline's?" Aidy's seductive hips swing. She approaches where I'm sitting on the bed, shoving my feet into the denim. She's got on one of those sexy matching sets where the panties and bra go together.

My jaw tightens and the wood I've been sporting deflates as I scowl.

"What's wrong? You don't think I'll be any good at it, do you? Kimber danced. Cece could teach me." She reminds me I'm surrounded by strippers and former ones.

"No." I stand, hitching my index finger into the loops on my waistband and pulling my pants up. I'm not normally demanding, but pull Aidy to straddle my lap. She needs to understand my vehement opposition to this. "It's bad enough my friends watch my sister take her clothes off. Nobody looks at what you have underneath but me." My low voice reverberates against the walls like a Neanderthal.

"What about when you take me to the beach?" She tips up my chin and rocks against my groin. "I wear a bikini when it's warm."

"I'm buying you a modest one piece and a parka to go over it this summer. The kind with a big fuzzy hood."

Aidy giggles. Her happy is the best sound ever. Our lips linger together. I tug at the lower one with my teeth. She sighs and I hesitate telling Aidy I love her. It seems like a lot of pressure right before taking her home. However, something in her blue eyes gives me a "me too" vibe.

"You aren't talking to Jake—or Kimber," I warn. "She'll tell you what I'm about to say anyhow. Sweet Pea, you're sexy as hell and it wouldn't be fair to the other dancers. They'd lose all their tips."

"You're such a horrible liar." She swats my chest and I grab her hands, moving them to my mouth to kiss her fingertips.

"Really, Aidy, you're where half of those women would kill to be. You're past needing to work in a place like that."

"*You* work in a place like that."

"Again, because you tower above me. I am only good enough to worship at your feet."

She wrinkles her nose and raises a brow. "Nobody's better than anyone."

I know what she's thinking. It's hard to keep it off my mind too.

"Make up with your parents, Sweet Pea." The Fairley's are an older couple. I'd guess their ages are closer to sixty. Aidy's been their world for the past nineteen years. They're not going to give her up. Having parents who gave up on me, I don't want them to either.

"No, not if it means losing you, Morgan. I'll figure it out."

"Why do you think you're going at this alone? I don't need you to defend me."

If anyone needs sticking up for it's her, and when Trig raps on the door I'm proven right. "Let's go, kids. I'm warming up the car."

"Aidy's finishing getting dressed. Hold on, I thought

you said the pissed off lawyer was mine to deal with?"

"I changed my mind. I'm not the most objective, but it's clear Don isn't either. I'm not letting either of you get railroaded. There's too many people telling Aidy what to do and not enough of us listening to her."

Is that what I've just done? I'll never be okay with Aidy working at Sweet Caroline's while she's been respectful of the reasons behind why I'm keeping my shifts there after getting the mammoth bonus last night. If push came to shove, I'm sure we could brainstorm a better job. But what if that's the one she wants and Aidy sees the growing circle of friendship with Cece and Kimber as an appeal? I have to admit I like Sweet Caroline's because of the vibe I get from the guys and other employees being there—minus when Jake's on and as long as I'm not looking at the stage. But how is it different from working anywhere else?

I have to be honest with myself; given the rest of my surrogate family is on-site, the placement of video feeds Skye has shown me inside, and security cameras outside, the club is one of the safest places Aidy can be.

My internal caveman is still growling his discontent as we pull into the Fairley's driveway. I'll go along with what Aidy wants, but not unless she's got all the options laid at her feet. Knowing her, that's what she was trying to explore anyhow when she brought it up.

Aidy's mom greets us at the door. Neither she nor Don hides the surprise over Trig accompanying us, but they're shocked when Aidy hugs them both. I'd expect no less of her. Aidy has a lot of respect for her mom and dad and it shows. She's only asking for them to return the favor and treat her like an adult. It's harder for me to understand how tight the Fairleys are holding on since my parents were glad to get rid of us at eighteen and only ever proud of our accomplishments if they reflected on my mom and dad in a positive light.

I don't want to lose Aidy, and I don't want to come

between my girlfriend and her parents. If Trig hadn't taken a seat in the Fairley's living room, I'd probably turn tail and run. Attempt for a third time to rebuild my meaningless existence because Aidy's shown I'm not wholly worthless, and she deserves the perfection all these people have tried to encircle her with.

While our connections aren't comparable, somehow I feel a small kinship with Kimber, recognizing I love Aidy enough to let her go. And doing what's right for Aidy these past few months has made me strong enough to accept that.

The silence in the room is thick. Trig's about to cut through it when Aidy speaks.

"First things first, I'm considering changing my major."

"That makes no sense Aidy—"

"It does Mom, the class I did well in last semester was about behavioral health in educational environments."

"You've worked too hard to change your mind."

"I've been in college for a year and a half. You gave up your career when I was born."

"But teaching, being in the classroom—it's been your goal since you were six."

"Because I came from a supportive background, I never needed those other services. I hadn't realized there were more ways to help students. Guidance counseling is something I could be passionate about."

"Changing high schoolers' schedules is beneath you." Her dad rejects the idea offhand.

"And changing diapers wasn't?" Aidy remarks in as judgmental a tone. Mrs. Fairley isn't hearing, and Mr. Fairley has on his lawyer hat.

"That's different. More goes into motherhood than you can imagine."

"More goes into being a good counselor. And I want to explore psychology, Dad, work one-on-one with teenagers, not fill their days with prescribed coursework. But, you know what, now that you've brought up guidance counseling, I can see the even broader scope of how those two positions work together. And I won't diminish anyone's career to prove my superiority." She tacks on, stunning me that she'd have the courage to say it to her practical, yet solidly upper-middle-class parents. I doubt they have a clue how much income a tradesman like Trig draws in before Skye *invests* it.

"I don't know if I'll wind up in a school or want to join or open a practice of my own. All I do know is over this last semester my eyes have opened and shutting them isn't a possibility anymore."

"That's marginally better," he concedes, but digs back in. "However, I'm not spending money on room and board if you're never there or off partying. I'm not financing another dalliance while you find yourself, Aidy." He uses those stupid air quotes.

Damn. I want to like this guy, but his tone is the same familiar one another attorney used in a courtroom against me a couple of years back. Aidy's dad knows how to argue a point. Unfortunately for him, so does his daughter.

Chapter Twenty-nine

Aidy

"I'm not interested in living on campus anymore."

"Do you expect us to pay rent on an apartment? For heaven's sake, move home."

"No!" I recognize where they're headed with this. If I'm home, they can control me.

"We can get a place together." Morgan laces his fingers in mine.

It's not as if the suggestion hadn't come up between us when we were looking at bedroom sets this morning. Although, it was more like a "where do you see us eventually living" idea.

Trig's head has lobbed back and forth listening to my parents and I duke it out. He sees my dad's disapproval grow into a simmering rage and he holds up his palms. "Aidy can stay with us for now." He's pointed in the declaration. "If you guys work something out later on for her to go back to the dorms, that's cool. But she's not going to be homeless, and she's been under enough stress. I don't want her to have anything else to worry about."

My mom sputters about the appropriateness and my dad's eyes are laser-boring a whole into Morgan's forehead as if he's trying to explode it.

Oh, my God. They're worried I'm sleeping with him. That our affection and connection stems from lust and I've let a man take advantage of me. Except it's the wrong man they are directing their fears at.

"Don," Trig offers. "I'm trying to help your family. I already know Aidy's roommate isn't returning to campus. Aidy doesn't want to be there and, other than to celebrate today, she doesn't seem to want to be at your house. Don't look a gift horse in the mouth."

"But Morgan lives under your roof." Mom's stuck on Nancy's outburst and pleads for me to give him up.

I won't. I can't. I love him enough to linger in his life the way my biological mother had. Kimber wanted better for me and I want better for Morgan. He may have Cece, Trig, Kimber, everyone at the mill, but I get to be part of his support system too. He wouldn't have let me in on the most awful parts of his existence if he hadn't needed me.

I wish my parents had gotten a glimpse of who Morgan is before grief and despair clouded their judgment.

Trig levels them with a none-too-subtle glare. "I'm reminding you of two things. First, it's my goddamned house to make the rules for. Second, when Morgan needed help, I lent a hand. He's not my kid. But my wife gave birth to yours. So if you think that alone doesn't make Aidy special enough for me to look out for, we can end this malarkey. I think if you saw Aidy the way Kimber and I do, you'd realize what amazing parents you are to her. Catch my word there: *ARE*. Aidy and I have discussed the role Kimber and I play in her life. None of what's transpired has had a damn thing to do with her wanting Kimber as her mother. It's been all about falling for her first love and them creating something better. If you think Aidy hasn't worried Morgan living at my house wouldn't make it seem to you she doesn't have respect for your role, then you underestimate her. I'll be honest, you toss your daughter away, and I'm standing in line behind this young man for a chance to make it right.

"There's no doubt in my mind the grades have anything to do with Morgan in a negative sense. I saw Morgan take my son from Aidy so she'd study more often. He's not looking to tie her down, trip up her dreams. I think he's hoping to make a few they both have in common come true when the timing is right.

"She's been sitting here trying to remind you she's a grown-ass woman capable of making her own decisions. And the only reason I'm flapping my gums is because of your unwillingness to accept her side of the story. It's a shame you think a man needs to come to her rescue and a sham that you can't see Aidy's the one helping Morgan salvage his goals."

My mom's lip wobbles and looks at her folded hands.

I reach across to snag one. "I need you to trust me. I had a bad semester. If there's another one, I won't hide it. I hadn't wanted you to worry. I didn't want you to be ashamed of me."

"Why would we ever be ashamed?" Mom's concern is genuine.

I hold the line. It's drawn in the imaginary sand lying on the table between us. And I won't cross it because I get to own my story. It's my choice who I reveal it to, how I heal, and when I use what I've been through to help others. I don't owe anyone.

Instead of answering for myself, I defend Morgan's injustice. "You're ashamed of my relationship with Morgan."

"We want the best for you," Dad says, rubbing his nose.

I hate Trig's verbal sucker-punch, but the clarity in

their eyes is evident.

"Get to know Morgan. You might find he isn't the same person who went to prison. Isn't that the point? To come out better. Reformed. I'll be honest, I doubt it happens much. Bad people keep doing bad things and there are plenty, who you think are good, who are as vile at the core. But every so often, maybe there is a Morgan. Someone who took the blame placed on his shoulders with humility and now wants to go on with their life and try to rebuild it."

Morgan swallows. "Don't, Sweet Pea. Your mom and dad don't have to get to know me or like me."

He doesn't like me defending him.

"I won't let you concede again without knowing someone's been there fighting for you and won't leave when the fight is over." Cece had tried, but Morgan was bound and determined to protect his sister and did what was right to keep her from any more pain. He'd been looking for a way to get back to her faster.

"They need to understand you won't ever hurt me and that you never intended to hurt Rob or his family." I turn to my mom and dad. "Ask him about it."

"I don't think now is the time, Aidy. Subjects like these are better suited for another day."

"I beg to differ, Mom. Christmas is about family and forgiveness and coming together."

There's another long silence while what I've said hangs in the air.

"Would you like to stay, Morgan, so we can all talk some more?" Dad offers an olive branch.

"I'll go wait in the car." Trig's stands. His shoulders relax and he yawns. I laugh. Even though I hadn't met Trig until right before Kimber and he got married, I used to watch him sleep in a car outside our windows on my birthday. All the while I wondered who he was and what it was like having a handsome man waiting in a carriage to swoop me away from a party the way he'd done with Kimber… And now I know because there was this guy who picked me up in a utility truck.

"No need." Dad rises to shake Trig's hand. "I'll drive Morgan back to Brighton after dinner." His lips flatten to a line when he glances at me. I can see the war he's having letting me go and I have the feeling I'll see my dad's same resigned expression on the day he walks me down the aisle. But my gut says these will be the only two days my father looks at me like he's lost me. The willingness to hear me out means there will be more happier moments than sad ones.

I hug Trig tight before he leaves and my mom does too, so I know they're okay. He's assuaged any worry she's had over the past two days that Kimber's replacing her.

I'm glad for it. My mom is my mom. At the risk of getting ahead of myself, it's her face I need to see when I try on wedding gowns because she was the one who took me to try on prom dresses. Those memories belong between us.

As if nothing is a miss, my parents ask Morgan about himself and we get to talking about the party last night and how he'd shot hoops outside in the cold with Jasper and Skye while I stayed toasty enjoying Cece's company.

The guys Morgan hangs around with have the "I take care of my woman" vibe. However, my mom and dad are old-school in their beliefs that the prince rescues the princess. They like hearing Morgan's sister is attending Pinewood too and how he wants to help her pay some of her student loans. I play off Brighton Hailey and Pinewood College Hailey are one and the same, but mention she was there as Jasper's date. There will be plenty of time to explain later, when I figure out how, and what, Hay wants my parents to know. I get that some things are nobody else's business.

The subject changes with a natural flow to all the

points Morgan put on the board with the university squad. By the time we circle around to the morning Rob died, he's scored with my mom and dad too. They see him closer to the man I know, who took responsibility when there was no clean-cut guilt or innocence. He's a young person who made the same poor choices so many others do, and the consequences haunt him.

Morgan refusing to imply Rob's death wasn't his fault truly gets to my mother. She cries as if it were me who'd been abandoned. Wiping her tears, she asks him to accept her apology for the way she acted when they met.

"You too, Aidy. I'm sorry," she says as we set the dinner table. Dad's about to carve the turkey and Morgan's got a side dish in either hand.

"You were only trying to protect me, Mom. As much as it hurts that you weren't willing to hear, there's something to be said for the fact that everyone involved was doing what they were out of love."

"It never crossed your mind that we didn't hate Morgan?" she asks in private on our next pass through the room.

"Honestly, I knew his jail time would be hard to accept. But, no, I never thought you'd ever dislike him."

Mom stops in her tracks.

"What?"

"You're so different. The girl who left for school in August isn't the woman talking to me today."

I raise a finger to my lip. "Shh... Don't tell anyone. Adulting is hard." I wink. "Morgan gave me a box filled with bills folded into origami sea life animals and birds. It's so I can go get my hair done. I'm not sure If I want to spend it now or wait a while and go back to being redhead this summer. I've heard sun and chlorine can strip the purple away."

"You do what's best for you. When you're ready. If it means moving to Brighton—"

Teary and thankful, I don't let my mom finish her sentence. I toss my arms around her again, nearly splatting a platter of stuffing against our clothing.

Morgan

"Hey, man, how're you doing?" I slap Brandon's palm and take a seat next to him at the bar.

Skye is walking in along with Jasper. We acknowledge their presence as they approach us. I don't let on to Brandon that we've all been across the street tying up loose ends.

Jasper set us up with burner phones. It's easy to presume anyone else Brandon had associated with is steering clear. He makes constant contact and was overeager to hang out when it's New Year's Eve.

"Never better." He lifts a squat glass to his lips and tips the remaining liquid back.

I wiggle my fingers, encouraging Holly to bring him another round.

Many of the late nights I've led Aidy to believe I was at work have had more to do with settling this score. It hadn't taken much over the past few weeks for the three of us to ingratiate ourselves into Brandon's pathetic existence. He's out on bond and the college evicted him from the dorm he lived in. He's not registered for any upcoming classes, and I switched off the news when the local channel flashed his mug shot. I already know way more than the reporter ever will thanks to Skye, and Jasper's connections.

I'd like to have more remorse that his life is crumbling around him. I've been there. The difference is I didn't rape anyone once, let alone sexually assault numerous people on as many occasions. I also know if this gets tied back to me—which it won't—I'd confess. Leaving everyone else out of it, of course. I mean, other than dying, what's going to happen to me that hasn't? And Aidy knows whether she'd choose to stay or go, I did this for both of us. I can't get my guy, so hers will have to do.

I shake my head, watching Brandon take in Holly's short shorts and long legs.

Thank god Aidy and Hailey are back at Trig's, safe and none the wiser. We told them we were making a champagne run after finishing up a few things at the office. The bottle Jasper picked out is chilling. I doubt it'll have time to warm before this is over.

"You ever been here before?" Brandon's obvious while adjusting the dick in his pants like the dick that he is.

"A few times." I haven't mentioned I work here. Using the club as a ruse to get Brandon on our turf was brilliant. His ridiculous interest in strippers was a fucking cliché.

"I *come* here all the time." Skye undresses Holly with his eyes. He turns, leaning his back against the wood and pointing to Celine who is working the floor. She moves closer to the bar, flirts and winks at Brandon while whispering to Holly. "That chick gives an out of this world lap dance." He tacks on lewdly, "With her mouth."

"Fuck, ya?" Brandon's lip curls up. Amped up by the tiniest advance, he's down with paying a stripper to go down on him and doesn't notice my jaw clench at Skye's comment.

"What are you having, boys? I've got other customers." Holly taps her manicured fingertips on the counter.

Skye one-eighties to see across the bar. "A little of you."

Holly chuckles, pretending she's flattered by the attention Skye gives her. "Sweetheart, we've been over this one too many times. You may come here a lot, but I'm not going home with you tonight. What do you want to drink?"

The rest of us make the man-child low "ooh" burn sound as Holly spurns Skye. We give her our order—the specialty drinks Kimber concocts for the staff to order while they're on the clock—none of which have alcohol in them.

"Dude, you can't say Cece's slobbering on your balls while Holly's in earshot." I punch him hard in the arm. Lie or not, Celine's my sister.

"Sure I can. It's not like Holly doesn't know the dancers will suck a tip if it means a bigger one in cash. This is a strip club, for Christ's sake. And it's not like I've screwed them both at the same time. *Hmm...* That sets your mind reeling, doesn't it Brandon?" He waggles his brows and grins.

"There's a mental image I didn't need." Jasper shivers. "And fat chance. I've heard a rumor Cece is tight with her pussy." He leans back as if he's challenging Skye.

"What do you mean?" Brandon takes the bait.

"It means she'll only go so far. She draws the line at having actual sex with the clientele." Jasper cautions.

"A lot of strippers are like that," Skye interjects.

"Not all of them, though," Brandon says, almost as if it's a question.

Jasper bats his hand in the air. "Nah, I suppose most

are in a position where they can be persuaded to do just about anything. I mean, how desperate do you have to be to take off your clothes for money?"

I grind my teeth, thinking of my sister. I'm glad Brandon's hanging on Jasper's words instead of paying attention to me. Jasper knows the girls who work here better than I do. The disrespect he's showing isn't normal for any of us. I'm stuck going along with everything he and Skye spew because they're doing this for me.

"My girl? She's sweet."

"The bring-home-to-your-momma-girl-next-door type," Skye proclaims.

"I don't know about those types." I goad Jasper about Aidy's former roomie.

"Are you kidding me, Morgan? Those women have the tightest cunts and they're wild in bed." I know Skye's acting a part.

Holly and Cece are in on it to a degree too.

It hasn't been for lack of trying that Skye's never fucked Holly. She's an attractive woman, but puts a full-stop to his constant advances, saying Skye is too young for her. I'm unsure whether or not he's been with Celine and I'm not about to ask because *she's my fucking sister* and my mind won't be able to unknow that. I'm glad both ladies are on our side.

I shrug my shoulders, looking at Jasper for confirmation. Aidy and I still haven't. The fooling around we do aside, it's been long enough for me I qualify for born-again status.

"She ain't ever been anybody else's so I can't compare," he replies with a hint of remorse. Jasper keeps his relationship with Hailey under lock and key. He also keeps her on a tight leash, saying it's for her own protection because she is so young and sheltered.

"I had a girl like that one time." I've noticed Brandon enjoys sharing time. He's like a kindergartener raising his hand for the teacher to pick him next to show off a shiny bauble. "Nice chick and all. But, after a few weeks of being led around by my balls, they were blue."

I choke on my beer. A few weeks? I'm not sure Aidy knew Brandon for a full week. Skye slaps my back a few times. I shrug him off and call him the name I'd rather spew at Brandon.

He smiles good-naturedly. It takes a lot to piss Skye off, and half of the shit he's saying isn't even true. He wants to see how far he can push Brandon. I need to cut him some slack. Skye's in my corner.

"Thought it would take more to get her to put out, but she didn't put up much of a fight." Brandon brags.

"You're talking about high school girls. They'll believe whatever you tell them to get in their pants. There's no challenge there," Skye pshaws.

"She was a Pinewood College girl." Brandon stops for a second, pondering. I can almost see him replaying events in his mind. "If I'd known she was a virgin…" he cocks his head. "I might have stuck around for round two. I figured she was toying with me and I'm too damned young for the girly-love-relationship crap."

"So what? You take her to dinner, home, blow your load, and leave?" Jasper yawns, stretching as if the conversation is boring him.

"Got her loaded at a party and carried her back to her place."

"Do that a lot?" I ask.

"Same story, different lay." Brandon is nonchalant, joking he's taken advantage of more than one woman.

Holly's had her back to us at the bar mixing drinks. "Special delivery from my friend over there." She places a cocktail in front of Brandon. He turns and Cece is wiggling her fingers in his direction. Brandon grins like the fool he is, taking a sip, and toasting a thank you to my sister.

"Any good?" Skye asks about the drink.

Considering the buzz Brandon's already got a head start on, I doubt he's even tasted it. He shrugs and hands Skye the glass to try. It gets passed around, so that even on camera it'll be hard to figure out which of the four of us laces his drink.

A few minutes later Brandon's blinking his eyes, trying to stay focused on Cece while his lids droop. She strides up, gripping his shirt front. He trails after her to one of the private curtain rooms like a cartoon dog on a leash with his tongue dragging on the ground. The guys and I pretend to laugh at his luck, but it's really watching his drunk ass stumble as he disappears.

It doesn't take long for Cece to signal us Brandon is out cold. We all walk toward the tiny space as if they're asking us to join in.

Gross.

We're crowded shoulder-to-shoulder and Cece sits at the far end of a bench, rolling her eyes. "I'm not even going to ask where you found this one or what you're up to. He's the worst of the worst." She's skevved by his presence. A tiny tremor runs up her spine.

"Did he hurt you?"

"No. But not for lack of trying. Holy shit, I'm used to being groped by drunk guys, but I've never felt like I needed a shower to delouse myself more than in the ninety seconds before he conked out."

I pull Celine up and hug her. "Where's the bag I gave you?"

"I stuffed it between the wall and the cushion. Do not get yourself in over your head, Morgan," she warns, glaring at Brandon like he's the root of all evil.

My sister is too damned smart and I know she's onto me when I tell her, "I won't." Because I am. Trig said if go through with this, there's no turning back. After seeing the way the system works, all I have to say is all is fair in love and war.

"Tell Aidy I'm wishing her a Happy New Year." Cece

kisses my cheek before leaving. "You too."

"I will. Hope you don't mind Dusty's getting you home safe tonight, sis."

The shake of her head is imperceptible as Cece draws the curtain close behind her. A beat later, the music on stage becomes deafening.

I'd like to say we stood there and did something as innocuous as pissing on Brandon. However, he's bragged that he's applying to med school to become a surgeon and to make that happen he'll need years of physical therapy on his hands.

His upper limbs are a mess when Skye pulls the gigantic duffle out from between the wall and couch. Although no blood's been shed, the worst is yet to befall Brandon.

Jasper puts his cell to his ear after we've crammed buddy-boy in a fetal position into the bag. "Feeds are good?"

Skye checks his own phone. "The bug I planted is active and will override tonight's surveillance and copy last night's over it with a fresh timestamp. Mordecai's guys have ten to get in and out."

"And they have the decoy in case another issue arises with a camera on the block we don't control." I mention.

"Can you make it in the next five minutes?" Jasper asks whoever is on the line. The response is an instant knock on the emergency exit this room has.

With an oomph, a guy double our size shoves an identical bag at Jasper, which seems as full.

"Don't forget. He'll collect." The guy states before hoisting our bag over his shoulder.

Skye ducks out to tell Holly he thinks the emergency exit in the room has a problem and he wants a no admittance sign, so no one takes a client back here.

Jasper lifts the bench cushion and puts the large bag inside to hide it.

"I owe you," I say to him.

"I knew what I was signing on for when Carver recruited me."

"This is different. We both know that."

"Forget about it. I already have." He grips my shoulder. "Happy Fucking New Year."

Morgan

I take a few minutes alone behind the steering wheel to collect my thoughts. As easy as it played out, I don't think Jasper or Skye have orchestrated anything like what we did to Brandon before. There's something about physical violence that doesn't mesh with the way I see Carver's business run. Right there is the major difference with white collar crime: We had to call in someone, whereas an MC would have zero guilt dumping an actual dead body. My friends and I retreat to separate corners under the pretense that nothing that's happened in the last half house troubles us.

In the rear view mirror, I watch Jasper come out of Sweet Caroline's alone.

"Where's Skye?" I ask.

"Flirting with Holly. He said we should send Aidy and Hailey his regrets."

A noise that sounds like agreement comes from my throat and I pull into traffic.

After settling things between Aidy's parents and me, I'd wanted January to be a fresh start all around. I can't lie to myself and say I'm unaffected by what we did to Brandon. It's far worse than the negligence I went to prison for. The only thing keeping my guilt at bay is, given the opportunity months ago, I'd likely have beaten Brandon within an inch of his life on my own for what he did to Aidy. All we did was give him a dose of his own medicine and change the trajectory of his life by taking away something he valued. If he gets off on the charges against him, he'll have a tough time getting back into college or a medical school accepting him, let alone have the dexterity to write a prescription. There's poetic justice in it because if the guy was this big a deviant now, what would it take for him to drug a patient later on?

I don't know what will happen to Brandon from here on out. I'm not even sure I care to keep up with his trial or the outcome. I've gotten what I needed to settle the score. When the emergency door closed, he was alive. Jasper's vague instructions to his contact were to get rid of Brandon. They weren't asked to kill him, simply make sure none of us are linked. If Brandon isn't found, I want to believe I won't have that on my conscience.

Our girlfriends meet us with the television playing the ball drop festivities on low in the background. Takeout from the Mongolian barbecue fills the counter. They'd gotten the food. We'd snagged the booze. I have one beer with Jasper and he winds up downing the others in the six-pack. Next New Year's Trig and Kimber should be around. As the countdown begins, I'm already making plans to take Aidy to do something special then. Maybe get dressed up and go out on the town.

"Five. Four. Three. Two. One!" Aidy and Hailey chant in unison.

The champagne cork pops and they both squeal, jumping out of the way of the frothy foam spurting from the bottle's neck and laughing.

I wrap my arm around her middle and draw her close to me for a kiss. She's still smiling and giggling when Owen starts crying in his nursery.

"Oops. We were a little loud." Aidy darts up the steps and brings him back down. Unwilling to reveal the underlying reason she doesn't want the drink Hailey has poured her anymore, she uses babysitting her brother as an excuse.

Hailey gives him a paper top hat to play with, pronouncing him Baby New Year. We let him toot the noisemakers like kazoos. An hour later, the time catches up with us. Since Jasper's been drinking, he and Hailey sack out in the guest room for the night. Hailey and Aidy have already decided we're going to a diner with Wolfpacker omelets when everyone wakes up.

Up in the attic, Aidy snags one of Owen's blankets off the dresser that's gotten left up here while we're taking care of him. The furniture company delivered everything a few days after Christmas, except the Papasan chair Aidy's settling into as she wraps Owen up to get him to sleep. Don—I'm still getting used to calling Aidy's dad by his first name—helped me pick up the chair from another store and carry it up here. He and Ghillie had wanted to see where Aidy was living.

They've agreed Aidy will pick up a few courses at Brighton Community College, but she still has one or two she'll take at Pinewood's campus. It's a fair trade. Aidy can still dive into psychology while pulling her GPA up.

Most of Aidy's stuff is down in the guest room. She's even brought some silver-framed pictures she loves, but I don't think anyone's fooled we're not living together and that includes her parents. I'm sure the only reason they're loosening the apron strings is because of what Trig said on Christmas Day.

I lie in bed with my nightstand drawer open. A piece of paper from the stack I keep tucked inside slides through my hands. My nails form creases, folding the way a carver sculpts rock. It's taking a little longer than normal for Owen to settle. So far I've made three cranes, a frog, and two butterflies. The actions are so natural my hands move without comprehending what the next angle will be.

With the baby in her arms, Aidy comes over to the bed. She takes the half-folded paper from me, lying O on my chest.

"Kimber hates it when Trig does this." I wrap my arm over Owen, repeating one of the first things I ever said to Aidy.

She leans against the pillow and her fingertip traces the bumps of my knuckles. It's only then I notice they're bruised with tiny scratches.

"Was it tonight?" Her expression is unreadable.

I lick my lips, unsure of how to respond, but I promised Aidy I'd be upfront. "He abused women. *You weren't the first.* You weren't the only one he assaulted."

"I know. I've seen the news." She rubs Owen's back as his eyes flutter shut. "I was so caught up in what he did to me, considering he'd done it before or would again took too much energy. I lacked the strength. Part of me wishes I could have stopped it without anyone else getting hurt... Her, my parents, you."

"Self-preservation isn't selfish. What was Sloan's advice: It doesn't matter what other people think, you heal doing what's best for you? You don't owe anyone your story, Sweet Pea. You owe it to yourself to understand not everyone fights the same way.

"No one is one hundred percent in control of their own life. You can work your ass off to make yourself a better person, and someone else will exploit your weakness and use it to tear you down. At the lowest point, you have three choices; be your own hero, ask for help or wallow in the power held over you. In my book, only the last one is defeatist. If you want to come forward now, I'll stand by your side."

"And if I don't?"

"I'll stand by your side."

"What if I did, and it comes out that you'd planned all along to hurt Brandon?" She waffles.

"Even then, the decision is up to you."

Aidy inhales a calming breath. "I know it won't change the past, but I feel like there's a way for me to fight the battle, be more of a silent warrior."

We watch Owen sleep for a few minutes and I get the impression Aidy has known all evening. She's been quietly supporting me and her intent on making me hold her baby brother was a reminder of all that is good and innocent in this world.

"You want kids, Aidy?" I sit up, cradling him like a newborn, even though Owen's too big now to do the thing where he curls himself into a ball.

"Someday." She runs her palm over his soft red hair.

I want to ask her if she wants to have my kids, but it's a little too presumptuous and even sharing a bed, we're not there yet.

"When I do, I want them to sleep like this. Certain everyone around them wants nothing but the best for them."

I get it. I want that too and always have.

I carry him back to his nursery so Aidy can get ready for bed and snag a spare monitor from the charging station on the way back to the third floor. She's between the sheets and the lights are dimmed when I get back to our room. I take off my pants, lying on my back to work out the knots in my spine. Her leg curls over mine and I slide my hand up over her hip, aware of her nakedness.

Aidy straddles my waist, taking down her messy top knot. Lilac waves fall to her shoulders. I move one that's caressing her creamy white breast so I can do it instead.

"I want you, Morgan." She leans forward, kissing me.

"Are you sure about this, Sweet Pea?" I don't want her to regret this.

Her pebbled nipples graze against my chest. Aidy's teeth scrape my lip as she pulls away. She pushes up to her knees and pushes down my boxers, freeing my dick. She fists it, stroking me. Although, I'm not sure I could be harder or more ready for the girl who wants to give all of herself to me.

It's important she's in charge, makes her own choices, and has the ability to tell me if she's changed her mind.

"I don't have any condoms." I hadn't wanted Aidy to find them when we were moving her in and have it put any pressure on her.

"We'd have to get special ones anyway. My tests have all come back clean. I'm on the pill."

I nod and swallow. I've seen the pill pack in her cosmetic bag but figured her reasons for being on it weren't any of my business.

She bites her lip, hesitating as she lines me up. I lift my hand, cupping her cheek.

"Only if you want to, Aidy. It can be tomorrow. A week from now. A year even. I'll wait."

Once she decides I'm the one for her, I'm not letting her go. She's dooming me to forever. Her life can go on without me, but if she ever leaves me, mine won't. I'll pine for eternity for the woman who healed her wounds and mine, reminded me of what I could have had. I won't be able to put myself back together a third time.

My fingers pinch into her thigh, stopping any further movement. About to plunge into her sweet heat, my dick has never hated me more. But I have to tell her the words she needs to hear. And not because I'm an ass who desperately wants Aidy. My feelings are genuine. "I love you."

She closes her eyes, licking her lower lip, and sinks

down. My impatient cock thrusts up twice, filling her before stilling so she can adjust.

Aidy's lips part. "Oh, God, Morgan." She pants, planting her hands on my chest.

I'm about to tell her we don't have to go any further when her hips begin a slow rock. I let her rise and fall, figuring out what feels best, before pulling her closer. We're chest to chest. With two hands, I hold her hips steady as she grinds her clit against the base of my dick.

Aidy lets out a strangled sound as she comes. Her body quickens, tightening against my cock the way she has around my fingers, and I'm in ecstasy.

"Let go. No one can hear you. Take from me, Aidy." *Take all of me and don't ever leave.*

Her whimpers get louder and her pussy has me in a vice. It takes every ounce of self-control fighting off the urge to chase her orgasm with mine. She lifts so her forehead rests between my pecs. Our bodies have stilled. She plants breathy kisses at my sternum before sitting back up. I watch her hands trail up her body, squeezing her breast before tangling in her hair. Aidy's head lolls back with a moan. I feel each tremor at my tip and want to explore all the ways to bring her pleasure.

This woman is better suited to a life other than the one I lead and am asking her to compromise for. But I'll give her the wide sky if only one day she'll tell me I mean anything to her.

"You ready for more?" I ask.

Chapter Thirty-two

There's more?

Logically, I know this. I've gotten Morgan off after he's taken care of me. I know he's not done. But my brain is so slow on the uptake after an orgasm I felt in my toes. The idea of a second one isn't part of my reality. It's a fallacy the way some of my chattier girlfriends had said they got off multiple times and others bitched a guy got their rocks off, leaving them unfulfilled.

In my mind, those events evened out. I'd get one and Morgan would. Slap your hands together, sex and orgasms were done.

I've been so fucking naive about what I'd like in bed. It shouldn't be a surprise when Morgan offers to take care of me again. Yet, I'm dumbfounded.

"Aidy, you wanna be done?"

I blink a few times as Morgan's knuckle slides down my bare stomach. He has a loose grip on my waist.

"No," I say as it sinks in he'd let me get *my* rocks off and leave him hanging.

"What do you want?"

"I want to feel you come inside me." I blurt out.

His dick twitches and Morgan shifts in me. The new and unusual sensations aren't foreign. They feel natural and it's odd. I'm wondering why I was ever intrepid about sex back before. I push those beliefs away, but have second thoughts as to why being with Morgan makes it so easy to forget. Do I make Morgan forget the awful things done to him too?

He sits up, bringing my body along with his, and tilts my chin so we're looking into each other's eyes.

"It's just us. We're safe. I am. You are. This is our moment."

There's pain behind the mask of protection Morgan wears. He stays strong for me. He makes me stronger. I won't let him regret laying his heart on the line.

"I love you." I do. I love this man and how considerate he is of me when the world has taught him that few will be as mindful of his needs. I love his inner strength and that he allowed himself to bare his secret to me. I'm grateful to be the one with him, experiencing this right now.

The ugliness of our pasts fades to the background, while we indulge in touching one another. I stay on top, meeting Morgan's fluid strokes until they become short thrusts and his hands tighten on my hips. The agony on his face is beautiful as he tries to restrain himself. I slink my fingers between the sheets and his skin, grabbing his ass and pulling him deeper.

The action was meant for Morgan, but my body quivers. The way Morgan pushes inside of me builds an insane pleasure as he thickens. I let out a scream of filthy words, pleading for him to keep fucking me when he holds me to him. I feel his release in my core as he empties himself inside of me. The unexpected power of his release allows my inexperience to seep back in.

I curl against Morgan's warm chest. Dampness seeps

from inside of me and I turn my head as tears trail down my cheeks. I'm more confused than worried I'll get pregnant. Making love didn't feel the way I thought it would. Sex is supposed to be painful. I should feel a sting, a burn. Not a horror story, but I expected some discomfort. Your first time is awkward, right?

It's not my first time.

"Tell me I didn't hurt you, Aidy."

"It should have been you." My heart shatters into a thousand pieces and all I can do is cry. The way Morgan touched me was so tender. There is no doubt in my mind he'd never hurt me. Morgan loves me the way I needed to be loved when this finally happened.

"It was me." It's said with conviction. "In every way that matters, Aidy, it was me. I don't deserve this, but I'll cherish it because this was the way you wanted it to be. The way I wanted it to be for you. And the way it always will be whenever we're together. I love you. All I want to do is show you I'm a decent man and protect you in any and every way possible. I don't deserve having you sleep in my bed, but I want it so badly."

Morgan rolls me onto my side, brushing my hair away from my face. My lip wobbles and I smile through tears at his admission.

"There are times I'll fail you, Sweet Pea. But let me try to make amends." His voice is washed with remorse. My hand cups the cuts on his knuckles, cradling his palm to my cheek.

Morgan will do anything to prove he loves me. Repair the damage someone else inflicted. But it's also apparent feelings about his own worth are woven into his actions.

"I'll always want to fix any problems we have," he says in the same quiet manner that he's used with me for months.

I nod because so much of it he already has. Morgan pulls me close. His soft lips touch my forehead and the monsters in the dark disappear.

We wake to Hailey's voice in the crackling over the baby monitor.

The sun is up. I go to move out from under the blankets and find my clothes. Morgan drags me back, caressing my bare skin the way he had during those lingering touches before we fell asleep. When Hay says something about finding Owen his bottle and not disturbing the rest of the house, Morgan takes this as an invitation to keep me close to him longer.

He slides his body over mine, nipping my bottom lip and trailing kisses down my chest. I tent one knee and it's just enough access for his hardness to ease against my core, reminding me of what we'd done in the wee hours of the morning.

The corner of Morgan's mouth twitches when I writhe underneath him. A cocky look for sure, but he's not so sure of my answer that he doesn't ask permission before we make love again.

I almost feel guilty for leaving Hailey with the baby. Then my toes curl and I realize the next time Morgan and I will be alone together, Hailey will be back at the mill and we'll be solely responsible.

I start giggling.

"Love your laugh, but not the reaction I was going for, Sweet Pea." Morgan's scruff brushes my neck.

"I was just thinking Hay is making up for not telling me who she was."

"Should I be making up for that?" he pushes inside of me.

"*Ohh,* I think you are." I dig my nails into his ass.

Morgan groans, "We fit so damn perfect."

I want to make fun of him for the cheesy line, but all I can do is agree. Waking up like this is perfect.

Morgan eventually lets go of me long enough that I can use the bathroom and make myself presentable.

Jasper and Hailey are in the living room, dressed, and ready to go. Luckily, so is Owen, since Hay knows where all of his stuff is.

Famished, we take off for a retro diner and stuff our faces with amazing greasy-spoon specialties. O flirts with the waitresses. After the third one stops by to refill our coffee, intending to tell us how adorable he is, I stop explaining he's my brother. It doesn't matter anyway, and Owen still squeals "Aiy" when he wants my attention. He has a mom and I'm certain over the next few years, Morgan and I will be as active raising him as we are now. I know I'm getting ahead of myself, but it's good practice for when we're ready.

Morgan gives me a wipe to clean Owen's chin as he asks Jasper if they want to join us for a road trip to the beach.

"You're kidding, right?" Jasper wraps his arm around Hay as she mock-shivers. "On January first?"

"Why the hell not?"

"Cuz it's cold!"

"The sun's out."

"Hard pass." Hailey pounds the proverbial gavel, rendering a decision, while tickling O's cheek. "I'm bushed anyhow."

We let the subject drop before saying our goodbyes in the parking lot and buckling Owen into his car seat in the back of my car.

"I'm hoping his big breakfast keeps him satisfied on the drive," I say.

"Most of it wound up on the floor, but he'll probably conk out on the way there. You should too."

"What about you?"

"I'm fine, Sweet Pea. I need the drive and to be there with you today. I'll snag a soda when I fill up at the gas station and nap when we get home." He interlaces our fingers, pressing a kiss to the back of my hand.

I'm not surprised when we get there that we have the beach to ourselves. We stay farther away from the water and I scatter sand toys for Owen to play with next to our blanket.

He sees Morgan take his shoes off and makes me take his off too. Morgan buries and reburies O's toes, and Owen giggles so hard each time he pulls them out of the sand that he nearly topples over. Morgan shoots a broad grin, looking between my brother and I.

"What?" I ask when I can breathe.

"Nothing I'm ready to tell you yet." He winks. "All you have to remember is I've got everything I need right here."

I brush sand out of my brother's red hair. "Can I ask you a question, Morgan? Did you mean it when you said last night that that if I changed my mind, and wanted to contact the police about Brandon, you'd stand by me?"

"Why, Sweet Pea? Is that what you want to do?"

"I don't know. I don't think so."

I have to admit there's a small part of me that's wanted Brandon to get his due outside of a courtroom. I'd be a liar if I said I hadn't thought of the worst scenarios while enduring my grief. In my anger, I'd wanted to be the type of person who could plow him down with a car and not have a single regret. But I'm not and won't ever be.

What Morgan did last tonight—or maybe still is planning to do—compromises the principles of the Morgan had who plead guilty. He's changed. Reformed. Although, I'm certain it's not the definition of the term or what the law intended when they placed him in a penitentiary. Despite this, I think I've fallen for a better man than the one he'd have become had he never endured these past few years.

Retribution comes in many forms, and perhaps Brandon's first handshake with Karma was months ago when he and I were introduced. Maybe this was his fate all along? And what I wouldn't give to be a fly on the wall when Morgan exacts that punishment. Because instinct tells me imagining what goes down will always be far worse than what happens, and that plays into my fears.

Fears this man wants to set at ease. We understand one another on a deeper level, keeping our secrets from the most important people in our lives so they don't have to endure our pain.

"Then what made you think of it now?"

"You mentioned I had three choices. I might be greedy and take all of them."

"How so?"

"The way I figure, the first day we came to the beach, I'd decided not to wallow. I've acknowledged and found help with Sloan and going to group. And you want to be my hero, which I understand, but that doesn't mean I can't be heroic myself."

"You don't think you have been all this time? What we've been through isn't easy."

"I know." I huff and smile, looking out over the water as the waves break. Like a boat on the ocean, there's something else out there. Something I'm not seeing yet. A way for me to make a difference while protecting our privacy.

"I love you," I whisper, hoping to prove to myself this ordeal has somehow created a better version of me too.

Epilogue

Aidy

I'm lingering in bed later than usual for a weekend morning. My eyes are closed and I'm listening to cars drive down the street. Morgan's left the windows open so we get some fresh spring air. The neighborhood is louder than normal yet, it's still tranquil.

I wiggle my toes under the covers, thinking about calling in sick and taking a road trip to the beach. I have a shift this afternoon at the Baked Beans village location in downtown Brighton, where I began working a few evenings a week after the spring semester started last year. It kept me busy while Morgan stayed on at Sweet Caroline's and I didn't feel as dependent on anyone for cash. He's not taking shifts anymore unless Kimber is short-handed. Cece graduated and, true to his word, Morgan kept his job at the club for as long as she needed him.

This morning is the first time I've considered calling in sick, and I have a *somewhat* valid excuse. I'll be on my feet most of the day. Although it's slow after five o'clock unless a customer gets a hankering for something sugary, and even then, they tend to pick it up from the bakery counter to have boxed and brought home.

Hailey uses my job as an excuse to escape her confines, so I see her a lot even when we're not hanging out as couples. I'm glad. Had we gone our separate ways after moving out of the dorm, I would have missed her. Since I'm scheduled to go in today, she's decided all of the ladies are showing up during my downtime when I'm wiping tables clean and restocking cups.

Little feet stomp up the steps to the third floor. The door creaks open. I hear a loud roar as Owen runs toward me, scrambles up on the bed, and throws his body onto mine, attacking me with gusto.

I pretend I'm asleep until he yells, "Happee birday, Aiy!"

I sit up to lean against the wall of pillows with my brother on my belly. "What's this?" I show as much excitement as Owen exudes. I can't believe how much he's grown.

O shoves a package wrapped in pink with an organdy bow from Sterling's in my face with toddler exuberance. Kimber has gotten me the same gift every year; a silver frame with my age engraved and a photograph already placed inside.

This year, Morgan's gift was having Dusty help him install pipe shelving in our room to display them all. Our space is homey and comfortable with dashes of Morgan and I everywhere, plus quite a few of Owen's things he leaves during his *visits*. We won't live here forever, but we are building a life together.

"Open." My brother grows impatient.

Teasing, I'm slow to untie the bow and he takes over, pushing aside the tissue paper and putting his fingerprints all over the shiny heart-shaped frame.

"You and meeee!" he sing-songs.

"Thank you. It's beautiful!"

Owen hugs me with a growl and points to the shelving. I get up with him still attached to me, carrying my brother and the snapshot of us while I was teaching him to hit a baseball in the backyard over to the rest of the collection. He decides where it's going and his chubby hands pick up another frame Kimber keeps a duplicate of downstairs of him in a newborn stocking cap.

"Das me." He rattles off the names of the people in it. "Das my mommy. Das you mommy." His finger slides over the glass identifying everyone in the image from the year he was born. I nod and smile. "Show me. Show me!" He bounces in my arms. Reaching for a picture of Kimber when she was eighteen and pregnant with me. "Das you, Aiy, in my mommy belly!" He pats his own proudly, and I can't help giggling.

We arrange the frames and I pad back toward the bed, plopping Owen down.

"Where's Moron?" His palms spread wide to the ceiling.

"Mor-gan." I correct him, unable to contain a snort.

I think Owen's attempt to say my boyfriend's name is hysterical. And if Morgan is being a moron, I call him that in jest. Like any couple, we've had our fair share of disagreements. It's not easy being a couple, living in the same space, juggling my course load with his job and the mill stress he can't always share. But somehow we manage because deep down I think we both realized early on that the other was the person we were meant to trust with our heart.

"I'm not sure. Where is Morgan?" His side of the bed was cool.

I amble toward the closet to find a dress to slip into. Everyone at home has let me sleep since it's my twenty-first birthday, but if I don't get ready for the day now, I'll run short on time later. I want to make the most of enjoying everyone's company.

"He make piza pancakes." Owen balls his fists, shaking and baring his teeth, eager for a snack. I've never seen anyone indulge in pepperoni the way he does.

Hidden by the partially closed closet door, I sniff the air. "I don't smell pizza bagels, O. Maybe cinnamon buns?"

"Piza pancakes fowa me only!" Owen jumps on the bed.

"Hey, you." I walk over while pulling my red-again-with-a-few-stripes-of-violet hair into a ponytail. "What's the rule?"

"BEEEE SAAAFFFFE!" His legs fly out from under him, falling back and letting the messy covers catch him.

I tickle where his belly hangs out from under his shirt and hold out my hand. Owen uses me as leverage to leap onto the floor and insists on walking down the stairs.

He's all boy, and one of my favorite things is watching Morgan interact with Owen. It always has been. Sometimes my boyfriend and I talk late into the night about having kids of our own. When Morgan makes love to me, it's a promise that will happen.

"Ji-leeeeee," Owen booms in a dinosaur voice, forgetting about the last few steps and launching himself at my mom. His arms wrap in a stranglehold around her neck. "Look, Dahn!" He's as quick to wiggle from my mother's hold and run to the kitchen to see my dad. "Aiy's awake!"

I have zero expectation that I'll see Dad soon. My brother eats up any attention he can get from the males in the house. Today there are a good number of them here that I hadn't expected. It sort of looks like a middle school dance with Trig, Morgan and my dad surrounded by Jasper, Skye, Dusty, and Carver in the kitchen and all my girlfriends in the living room.

I focus on speaking to my mom, though while my eyes land on the streamers. "What are you all doing here?"

"It's your birthday!" She embraces me tight with slightly less force than Owen, but as much delight. "Since you have to work later, Kimber and I decided to throw you a surprise brunch. We all wanted to celebrate with you."

"Oh my goodness, thank you!" My eyes water. "Hold on, was all the noise on the street everyone coming in?"

"Ding-ding-ding," Hailey sounds as she taps her champagne flute with a utensil. "You got it right. Give the woman a prize!"

Skye jokingly jogs across the carpet and hands me a gift he lifts off of the coffee table. I tug Hailey around the neck when she gets up to hug me.

"Cece and I are still coming to visit you at work."

My boyfriend's sister gives me a conspiratorial wink.

"Any excuse to get out of there?" I whisper in her ear.

"Duh, yeah," She mutters back with a fake smile for everyone else in the room. "However, this is the best reason. Happy Twenty-first Birthday."

Mom hands me a glass filled with frothy orange bubbles. It still takes me a minute before I can sip the mimosa to remember this is my mother. She's not out to hurt me. The sweet deliciousness hits my satisfied tongue. I smile and look across to where my boyfriend is standing with a smug look on his face.

"You knew!" I yell, laughing until my cheeks hurt. A strange sense of embarrassment laced with happiness waves through me.

Morgan pushes off of the wall he's holding up and comes over to wrap his arms around me. "Some secrets are worth keeping from you, so I get a glimpse of how happy you can be."

"I'm always happy when I'm with you."

"Hence, why you let your brother call me 'moron'." Morgan pulls me tighter, holding me up as I belly laugh.

"Only when you deserve it!"

He pulls back and gives me the kind of kiss that he really shouldn't in front of a crowd, but I don't care. I love him so much.

"Enjoy your party, Sweet Pea. Your mom and Kimber worked hard to pull it off. The only thing I had to do was keep you in bed longer." There's a humorous yet, oh-so-devious glint in Morgan's brown eyes.

I'm glad talking to Hailey distracts Mom because my cheeks flame remembering Morgan's persistence last night. He had intentionally kept me up well past midnight with some persuasive and exhausting "distraction techniques". Now I understand why.

I make the rounds, thanking everyone for coming on my way toward the kitchen. There's more breakfast food than we'll ever eat spread over Kimber's counters; scrambled egg casseroles and fruit, fluffy waffles with real whipping cream, and enough bacon that no one should feel any guilt swiping more than their fair share.

My plate is loaded high when Morgan pops an ooey-gooey cinnamon bun between my lips. Drooling, I resemble a pig on a spit with an apple in its mouth. "I'm trusting you'll eat this the right way," he barbs.

Owen toddles by, munching the pizza bagel in a circle. Morgan microwaved it for him as a reward for getting me downstairs and placed the snack like a ring around his index finger. My chest shakes and I try not to drop my treat on the floor.

I settle between Mom and Kimber on the couch, placing a full plate on my lap, and digging in.

I've had birthdays of all shapes and sizes. The year Owen was born, I'd wanted nothing more than just the six of us around the table with a no-fuss cake. This year is better than all of those combined. My mothers are amazing, but what else should I have expected? They've been a team in their own way for over two decades. How lucky am I?

Bonus Chapter

Aidy

"I'd like to thank our panel for coming to share with us today and," I swing my attention toward the crowd of student-athletes "say thank you to all of you for attending. I know that these are serious, sometimes uncomfortable discussions. When you signed up for the season, you had no idea that this training was required. Over the past hour, you've blown me away with your questions, and the maturity displayed while your peers have asked them. Guys, Ladies, my door is always open if you need a safe place.

"After lunch your coaches will have the roster and instructions on your next session and activities. Enjoy the break." I congratulate, aware that many need to decompress over the break hour while they eat.

The school year starts in a week and this session is the part of a new fall training camp they have to attend to play this fall. It's one thing for us to ask athletes to sign contracts saying they won't drink or do drugs, it's another to show them the reality of how those choices affect their lives.

The crowd of teenagers claps and a low murmur echoes off the gymnasium walls. It's the most noise a normally rowdy and pumped up group of kids has made. As a whole, they were quiet during the presentation and got a unique perspective on parallels between sexual assault and underage drinking that many kids don't see until it's too late.

Some teens stand up and stretch from sitting on the hard bleachers, but none look as if they're about to run for the hills. As a matter of fact, their rapt attention to the presenters took the entire faculty by surprise.

We had an emergency room physician here to describe what happens when you lose consciousness after drinking to excess and what it's like to have your stomach pumped. His descriptions led into a powerful testimonial by Parker, one of Morgan's university teammates, who went to this high school. He came back to talk to the students, so they had a real-life look at how easily one them could be held responsible for the death of a friend, and how fast it changed the course of your life.

Parker's part of the talk was like hearing a new perspective on what Morgan had gone through with his roommate, Rob. It was hard not to get over-emotional. My heart went out to Nancy and the son she lost.

It also made me wonder how different life would have been for Parker, Morgan, and Rob if they participated in a frank discussion like this before entering college. Parker told me he was glad to come, but that he wasn't sure if he could get through it with Morgan here. It's been over ten years, and they still have a profound sense of loss. Rob really was their friend and they wish they could go back and change what happened so they'd all be sending those funny memes to one-another and texting witty comebacks.

A group of basketball players swarm Parker before the coaches can hustle the kids off to lunch. I sigh with relief that Parker's invitation hasn't left him a pariah. The boys' genuine interest in him amazes me.

We also had a lawyer present to answer more detailed legal questions about roofies, date rape, and prison terms for both sexual assault and manslaughter. The kids were so specific in their questions I think all of them came out with a better understanding that these things happen to real-life friends and have real-life consequences. It was a lot to absorb and I'm not sure if these two hours were enough, but if the time stopped one of these students from making a poor choice or encouraged another to take responsibility for a friend, then it was worth it.

I see a few of the girls tentative in their approach to a woman who opened up to share details of her own date rape. To give them privacy, Dr. Nash gathers her things and approaches me. "I think that went well." She smiles and waits for the okay to hug me.

It's strange since I feel as if I've known her forever now. Yet, today I appreciate her respect for boundaries.

When Brandon's trial started, I got overwhelmed. I'd kept going to group sessions, but had never seen a therapist to deal with the aftermath of my rape. I needed someone to confide in. So did Morgan. We approached Dr. Nash to see if she'd counsel both of us together. I hadn't known until I saw the bandages from surgeries Brandon had to have to repair his crippled hands what had happened to him. Whether Dr. Nash surmised Morgan had any involvement never came up. Although I'd confessed that he was my attacker, and it was the news stations' coverage of the story that triggered me. She treated us with respect, and I'm grateful to her.

"This forum was better than well. Well is an understatement. I think it was a huge success. Thank you so much for being here." This turned out better than I'd ever hoped.

"Coach Fairley," The county athletic director motions for my attention, indicating I should walk over to him with Dr. Nash. "The other varsity coaches and I were talking. We want to open this up to other schools in the district next year. Dr. Nash, would it be too much to ask you to come back?"

"Not at all." Her response is immediate. "When you're passionate about advocacy, you always make the time." As someone who works with sexual assault survivors on a daily basis, she's a warrior.

But today—without highlighting my own experiences—my armor shines, and the culmination of my efforts leaves me speechless. The only response I can form for the athletic director is, "Thank you. Thank you so much!"

The idea for a high school panel discussion came to me when I was still a senior at Pinewood working towards my psychology degree. For most of these kids about to enter adulthood, the world is their oyster. They think they have a grasp on reality, but it changes quickly. If their eyes weren't already open, I wanted them to know as simple as a social drink with friends can change into something they hadn't imagined could happen to them.

It took a year of effort and discussions with this high school's administration to bring the program in for our senior varsity players. It was a concession I had to agree with to get this off the ground, despite the entire faculty being aware teenagers drink and have sex. I jumped through hoops, double-checking to ensure every one of them had signed consent from their guardians to be here. Only one of two hundred senior athletes missed out, and it was because her mother was uncomfortable with the topic. She's a star-pitcher on the softball team I coach. I plan to reach out to the student once classes start and try to create an open dialogue. My goal isn't to go against her parents' wishes. Had my high school asked students to participate in this years ago, I think my mom would've had similar reservations. However, I want my players to have someone they trust to come to if there's ever an issue.

It's this achievement that makes me proud of my survivorship because in my own little way I am advocating for change. I needed to heal on my terms. To this day, neither of my mothers knows what I went through and how Morgan played one of the most important roles in my journey. While it's rare outside of our sessions with Dr. Nash that my boyfriend and I speak of his own assault in prison, like Sloan is for me, I'm Morgan's safe person. Because we've both been there, the way our relationship works makes sense.

At the end of the day, I walk back to my office in the high school's guidance department beaming. On my desk are a bunch of little paper animals Morgan's created for me. I also have a stack of thin colored paper and instructions posted on the wall to make most of them.

When I recognized Morgan used folding to calm his brain and heal, I added it to the repertoire of things my students could do while we talked. They've filled the shelves across the room with their handiwork in a rainbow of colors. Some are truly impressive works of art. But what's more, those teens can identify which ones are theirs. When I see them smile, holding up an origami frog they created, I know the fact I keep them makes those kids feel valued.

About to rest my clipboard on the desk, I stop right before squishing a paper box. Picking it up, I inspect each side. There's a top and bottom. I slide the two pieces apart. Inside is an intricately folded heart. I twist it around to see if there's a message attached to the back, noticing there is a pocket in the center of each side with a round gold band tucked inside. My brow furrows.

"Congratulations." Morgan is standing in the doorway with a bouquet. "I overheard the kids talking in the parking lot as I walked in. I'm not even sure you'll need to tell me what the grown-ups thought of the presentation. I've never been prouder of you."

He holds out the flowers. I take them, shaking my head in confusion at the heart from the box.

"Morgan, did you make this? It has rings in it."

"Oh, that." He removes the rings from the paper and shoves one in his front pocket. "This one is mine." He looks through the other at me, winking. "I thought maybe you'd want something close to a hot husband."

I cover my mouth as my face reddens.

"Nuh-uh, Sweet Pea." He moves my palm from my face. "Your laughter is the best sound on earth. I want to hear that sweet giggle every day for the rest of my life."

"Are you asking me to marry you?"

"Yeah, you wanna seal it with a kiss and become my hot wife?"

"Not here." I snort. "This place is about as romantic as the utility truck."

Morgan loops a finger into my waistband and tugs me close. "What do you say we take a drive to the beach for dinner? There's a Sterling's jewelry store near Wrightsville. You interested in helping me pick out a diamond for your right hand to match these bands?"

I squeal, wrapping my arms around his neck. I'd always thought that if Morgan gave me a ring, he would have picked it out himself. I like that he wants us to do it together because we've been healing that way.

The day has been a whirlwind by the time we leave Sterling's. The setting sun reminds me of the breaking dawn the first time we parked on Lumina.

As Morgan drops to one knee in the sand, I recognize that every moment of my life has built to this point.

There is nothing we can't get through because we've proven we're able to endure some of the worst curveballs life can throw at a person.

I have an inner strength I was never aware of. I'm whole. I'm loved... I'm a survivor.

*Thank you for reading **Shred of Decency!*** I hope you loved Aidy and Morgan's emotional journey as much as I do.

Enjoy this preview of **Sliver of Truth,** featuring Celine and Dusty. There's more than meets the eye to this injured hero, secret lover's romance!

SLIVER OF TRUTH

Celine

Water swirls down the drain of the old clawfoot tub as I wrap myself in a fluffy white bath sheet. I take a smaller one I've twisted around my head off, rubbing my scalp to wick as much of the moisture away so I'm not stuck blow drying my hair. The ends split on my long brown locks when I do. Year-round, the North Carolina heat does mighty fine on its own without my meddling. However, we're enduring a mid-December cold snap and wet hair makes me chilly. I'd used the hot bath to warm my bones and limber my muscles before work.

Other dancers at Sweet Caroline's swear by wigs. For me, they're a job hazard. I apply enough tape to keep my costume in place and prefer not stabbing my scalp with bobby pins. I've been stripping long enough to have watched hairpieces go flying across the stage, landing in patron's laps like the pelts of dead rodents.

A giggle escapes me, bouncing off the vaulted ceiling. Everyone should have memories that make them laugh.

I'm so darn relaxed it's easy to forget I'm about to spend the next few hours in sky-high fuck-me pumps parading around in less than my bathing suit covers as the evening's headline showgirl. This is my last night on stage. Within the week, I'm graduating from the physician's assistant program and will finally finish school. The past few days have been the most time I've had to myself in forever. Thank goodness clinicals are done and over with, and don't even get me started on how hard the prior year was. They ground us into the dirt, weeding out survivors with each exam. This month, I scored a nine-to-five in Dr. Randolph's clinic, a pediatrician who I'd shadowed. After tonight, dancing is my past and I have a whole new future.

The steam in the tiny washroom is like a sauna, and the linens I pulled from the shelf are the sort you'd expect at an expensive day spa. Thank heaven the ladies who live on the third floor at the mill have what we need, even if we hadn't known we needed anything this decadent.

None of us are footsteps away from slumming it at the no-tell-motel anymore. Each of us has a story, most of which is made up of the nastier stuff in fairytales; those low points of abandonment and loss swept under the carpet because what folks remember about bedtime stories are the parts where everyone lives happily ever after. For girls who grew up the way we did, getting to the point where, on our own, we didn't have to figure out where the next meal was coming from was half the battle. I'm fortunate I've never had to choose between selling my soul or affording my rent and tuition. But I came damn close to choosing if they were worth going hungry for before Jake hired me at Sweet Caroline's. A few months later, he set me up with Carver, the mill's owner.

Living at the old cotton factory is an enviable spot to be in. Carver foots the bill for our living expenses while each of us attends college. Although, given all that goes unsaid around this place, I figure it's pragmatic to understand Carver has a vested interest in what we become. I've yet to figure out his endgame for me. Nobody's that altruistic.

I run my razor over a spot I missed near my ankle while soaking. I'm between waxes and I swear those little patches sneak up when you're positive your skin is pristine. I understand the audience is none the wiser when I'm on stage—and it's not as if they'll lie down on the stale carpeting to inspect my Achilles Heel—but it matters to me. Maybe because the last time I saw my mother she had a whisker on her chin and a glower on her face.

Is it pathetic, while I was quick to get over feeling like a slut taking off my clothes on stage in front of all of those men, that I still worry over every nasty remark my mother would make if she knew I afforded my tuition by dancing? Defending my actions against her judgmental words are the ugly phrases on repeat in my head while getting to this point. Mom's transgressions never seem to bother her. Soon enough it won't make a difference. I'm proud of myself for achieving my dreams instead of succumbing to her nightmare.

Rubbing lemon and basil scented lotion over my arms, my mind wanders back to happier thoughts. Against the odds, my brother, Morgan, and I have stuck together like glue. He wasn't thrilled at my choice to become a stripper, though he picked up shifts at the club to monitor my safety which means everything to him. That right there reminds me I have someone to count on. My best friends—who started out up here as my floormates—are also with men willing to walk over broken glass for them. With the changes about to happen in my life, the last thing I have the energy for is a relationship. But a girl can hope the notion of the right guy coming along when you least expect it rings true.

I can't help the dismissive shrug of my shoulders. What's meant to be has a way of working out. One thing I've realized is luck's more likely to shine on those who are prepared, and I have a plan for the next few years.

A thump on the other side of the wall has me cracking open the door to the little room where the original to the factory building antique clawfoot is. I glance around the bigger bathroom area with its clean bright tiles and periwinkle blue, sage green, and light tan shabby chic beach house decor. A tap drips along the far wall where multiple sinks are set into an immense marble countertop. Gooseflesh appears on my skin while I wonder for a second if I hadn't turned the handle all the way off. Not seeing anything else out of the ordinary, I leave the frosted glass door ajar, stepping out to put my stuff away in the decorative locker-style cubbies. I appreciate not having to lug shampoo and bath bombs down the hall in a caddy.

When I started college, I'd have jumped in with both feet given the chance to live in Pinewood's dorms. They'd seemed like the epitome, a normal experience out of my grasp. Now, I'm glad I lost out on the opportunity. My friendships at the mill have meant so much more.

As I place my razor, lotion, and a bottle of bubbles on the shelf, a calloused knuckle grazes my bare upper arm.

"Cees."

His voice is a guttural growl I feel at the apex of my thighs.

My pulse speeds up and my breaths grow shallow. I want nothing more than to tell Dusty "No". This has gone on long enough. I should have stopped it before it started, but resisting proved futile.

His fingertips skim the hem of the towel, pushing the soft cotton up over my ass. He cups each globe. The rough fabric of his jeans scratches against my bare skin as he moves closer, caging me in.

I try to look over my shoulder.

Dusty's lips touch my neck, sending anxious chills down to my toes. "Door's locked. Nobody's around."

I swallow hard.

The standing rule is women only on this floor. Not all of the rooms are occupied anymore, but the ladies who live here have always worked at Sweet Caroline's. I'm sure Carver's edict is to stop us from bringing clients home. He's forthright, refusing to accept any of us turning tricks on his property. What we do at Sweet Caroline's and outside these four walls is our own nevermind. But Carver's insistent the rule also serves a greater purpose: to keep us safe. Aware of what kind of people are out there, it's difficult to argue with.

No man other than Dusty goes past the last step before the landing. He's allowed a free pass because he's the maintenance guy here and over at the club. Everyone trusts him. I trusted him more than I had myself, and should have said no to his advances on the night he took Morgan's place and walked me home. Ever since, I've lost count of the number of instances Dusty's left me with his cum dripping down my thighs.

The first dozen times I was sure we'd be found out. Then, recognizing I broke Carver's cardinal rule, shame made me more concerned with keeping this secret closely guarded.

"Don't make a sound," Dusty warns me the way he always does.

I bite my lip, hearing the metallic zip of his fly coming undone. He thrusts his impossibly huge cock inside of me and I whimper.

I hate that I love this. I love that I hate it too because the feeling keeps me sane.

"Shh… Take it all, Cees. You know you want it."

The warm rush between my legs proves him right. With Dusty, the condemnation of my choices is ever present. I let him do this to me and I don't tell a soul. Admitting we've been fucking for over a year will lead to questions I'm unable to answer.

He removes my palms from the polished lockers, placing them on the cold tiled walls. Dusty drills into me over and over. It's pure ecstasy and I can't stand how wet it gets me. How dirty I feel letting Dusty use me for sexual gratification whenever he damn well pleases, like I'm no more than a toy.

Dusty loosens the knot in my towel. It falls, pinned between his front and my arched back. My nipples are hard points instead of the tender rosy circles they had been when I got out of the water. They ache for attention. His large rough hands knead my breasts, squeezing them as he thrusts, almost as if he's using my tits for leverage to piston himself harder.

As the wave of pleasure builds, I choke down any sounds so they don't reverberate against the tile and walls. I want to scream out. Dusty moves one palm, covering my mouth to keep me quiet. I suck one of his fingers into my mouth, and he murmurs dirty words, urging me closer to the peak of my orgasm. A little mewl hums from me as my tongue swirls the digit and I crest over, my pussy contracting. His climax follows with hot streams of semen painting the inside of me.

I'm stupid for not making him wear a condom, but I've always considered birth control my responsibility and I'm clean. This happens so often I doubt Dusty has the stamina to fuck anyone else. I also lie to myself that even though the sight of this man can stop a woman dead in her tracks, he wouldn't have the opportunity. I'm easy. A sure thing compared to him having to try to get in anyone else's pants. I acknowledge this makes me a bitch. Because if it weren't for me relying on a flimsy excuse, I'd have to admit the gorgeous man inside of me could have any woman he wants.

Dusty's thick arms encircle me, stopping my weak knees from buckling. My head lolls back against his massive chest and his dark hair and beard brush my cheek. I let out a sigh. He turns my head to shush me, thrusting his tongue into my mouth. We groan together in sorrow. Round two for us is rare.

I know so little about him, and yet I'm keenly aware of the safety of his body afterward. The way his lips glide over my skin in reverence. His always-warm palms' lingering touch. We're strangers outside this act, but inside of it? The trust and familiarity are like nothing I've experienced.

He waits before pulling out and when he does it washes the awarenesses away. He's back to being the lumbering maintenance guy. I'm simply another one of the women who live on the third floor. Dusty doesn't sing praises for my pussy. Ask me if I'm okay. He doesn't need reassurance that I liked it. We're a means to an end for one another. He'll show up again tomorrow or the day after until I'm gone.

I won't confuse what we have as anything more than great sex. And I can't feel sorry if the next occupant of my room winds up pushed against the lockers with her legs spread.

Ready to read more?
Sliver of Truth is available now!
www.jodykaye.com/sliveroftruth

Author Notes

First off—If you've bounced here without reading Trig and Kimber's short story, Splinter of Hope, you might want to do that. Go ahead. I'll wait...

Good? Awesome!

I realized after each book I complete that I couldn't have written it if I hadn't done something else first. The Shattered Hearts of Carolina series is no different. I had to write Trig and Kimber a backstory and Aidy played huge part in it.

Kimber had done what she believed was right to give her daughter the perfect childhood, the perfect life. But life tends to be a bunch of flawed events that you learn from and sometimes manage to string into something better than what was handed to you. I mean, how many times have you been broken and still keep going? For me, the number is higher than I count anymore because I chose to focus on the better parts—like the fact that I made it through stronger.

Shred of Decency, and several of the Shattered Hearts of Carolina books, were unplanned—a flaw in my ideal timeline. Not necessarily a massive tangent from where this series is headed, more like a silver thread that helps weave them all together better than I'd planned.

I wanted to explore bonds that had less to do with blood, and I knew that all of the characters were going to have more baggage than those in my Kingsbrier books. That said, if you read this line wrong, "...my parents don't have the foggiest I'm not in Brighton because I'm trying to reconcile some fairytale relationship with the mother I wanted more." Go back and re-read it. Aidy's relationship with Kimber isn't a mother/daughter one. Ghillie is her mom and had I written it any other way, I think it would have been disrespectful to adoptive parents.

I also realize many of you needed Aidy stronger sooner, but you know what? It's okay for people to be to weak to fight. It's okay to not be 100% in control at all times (COVID anyone?) It's okay to need a hero before you become one. The point is, she moved past her situation and eventually found the strength within herself. That's life, it its twisted glory, y'all.

So much thanks for Shred of Decency still goes to my Quinters, who I rode out the spring of 2020 with online. You are incredible!

Behind the scenes, I couldn't have done it without the support of the utterly adorable A.K. MacBride, who brightens my day and nudges me to take chances and believe in myself.

Kristina Beck, if anyone had told me the spring of 2017 we'd become friends I'm not sure I would have believed them. Your side projects are a sanity saver when I need a break from everything in my head.

I worried a ton that this book wouldn't resonate with the readers who have been around the block with me— Thank you Jessie, for stepping up to beta read and assuaging those fears.

Jill, if this is the only time one of my books has a wow-factor for you that made it worth writing. Thanks for pushing me to better when points weren't right and for being patient when I left you without the end of the book for way too long!

MJA, you've been my best friend and husband for 20 years. Now, we're indefinite officemates. Here's to commuting a flight of stairs, sneaking out of the house when the kids aren't looking, working lunches, afternoon delights, and four o'clock bartending. And since you've had no option other than to invade my space, *I officially love you more in 2020.*

Add your voice and help readers discover
this love story by writing a review!

Also by Jody Kaye

Shattered Hearts of Carolina
Splinter of Hope
Shred of Decency
Sliver of Truth
Holding Onto Hope
Home Wrecker
Deep Gap
Bleeding Heart
Shattered Soul

The Kingsbrier Legacy
Love Thy Neighbor
Gray Sin
Going Down

The Kingsbrier Quintuplets
Eric
Brier
Daveigh
Miss Cavanaugh
Cavanaugh
Adam
Colette
Colton

The Canvas Duet
Canvas
Imprint

To view more great titles, sign up for Jody Kaye's newsletter, or find her on social media go to www.jodykaye.com or

Scan Now!

Jody's husband asked what she'd been doing all day. After five years she finally confessed, "When no one is around, I write."

Okay, it was more like a bunch of stammering and trying to get out of saying a thing. Jody's a writer. You want it pretty. Let's compromise.

"Just finish one," he said, challenging her to complete a story and share it. Little did he know that those words of encouragement meant they'd return from a family vacation with a wild and defiant set of quintuplets stumbling their way into adulthood. Wasn't raising their three sons enough?

A native of nowhere, Jody settled in New England for 17 years before agreeing to uproot her brood of boys and move to North Carolina. She's a part-time graphic designer and marketeer with over twenty years' experience, and full-time writer. If Jody ever gets lost, you'll find her reading, all the while hoping that her ravenous children haven't eaten all the ingredients before she's cooked dinner.